D0231491

NIGHT VISION

A Naomi Blake mystery

What had Neil Robinson been about to tell journalist Jamie Dale? Whatever it was, it got them both killed, and Alec and his DCI are called away to help with the investigation. Jamie was an old friend of Naomi's, and now she is being harassed by phone calls seemingly from the dead journalist. With Alec away, Naomi turns to another old friend, Harry Jones, for help. Then the violence strikes close to home, and Alec is forced to question which side of the law he is actually on.

Recent Titles by Jane A. Adams
from Severn House

The Naomi Blake Mysteries

MOURNING THE LITTLE DEAD
TOUCHING THE DARK
HEATWAVE
KILLING A STRANGER
LEGACY OF LIES
BLOOD TIES
NIGHT VISION

The Rina Martin Mysteries

A REASON TO KILL
FRAGILE LIVES
THE POWER OF ONE
RESOLUTIONS
THE DEAD OF WINTER

NIGHT VISION

A Naomi Blake Novel

Jane A. Adams

Severn House Large Print
London & New York

This first large print edition published 2014
in Great Britain and the USA by
SEVERN HOUSE PUBLISHERS LTD of
19 Cedar Road, Sutton, Surrey, England, SM2 5DA.
First world regular print edition published 2012 by
Severn House Publishers Ltd., London and New York.

British Library Cataloguing in Publication Data

Adams, Jane, 1960- author.
Night vision.
1. Blake, Naomi (Fictitious character)--Fiction.
2. Ex-police officers--Fiction. 3. Blind women--Fiction.
4. Detective and mystery stories. 5. Large type books.
I. Title
823.9'2-dc23

ISBN-13: 9780727897091

Severn House Publishers support the Forest Stewardship Council™ [FSC™], the leading international forest certification organisation. All our titles that are printed on FSC certified paper carry the FSC logo.

Printed and bound in Great Britain by
T J International, Padstow, Cornwall.

PROLOGUE

'Do it now, don't hesitate. If you don't then someone else will and they will not be so kind.'

'Kind?' He laughed. 'I could never be accused of that.' He sat back in his seat and looked at the old man lying on the bed. 'Christopher, we've known one another for a long time.'

'And now everything is changing, Gregory.'

Gregory. Christopher was the only person to use that name now. And then only when they were alone. Gregory was, what, three identities and many years ago.

'The old guard are almost gone.'

'And no bad thing. Except for you and I of course.'

Christopher smiled, and Gregory noticed how skeletal he had become. How thin and drawn. 'And our days are numbered,' he said. 'Gregory, I've done all I can for you and for them. We kept them both safe for as long as we were able, kept them from judgement.'

'She isn't a threat.'

'You may not think so, but there are others who do. Make it clean. Make it simple. Make it soon.'

But he hadn't, had he? Gregory, a man known for decisiveness, had hesitated, and it had ended badly. For all of them.

Neil Robinson should have been a happy man. Release date a week away, family that had stood by him, a home to go to and even the vague promise of a job, working with his brother-in-law – though he had mixed feelings about that. Neil and Paul had never really got along, and the idea of selling second-hand cars really wasn't Neil's idea of a proper job.

As it stood, though, happiness was a long way distant from how he felt. Scared was more like it.

The first postcard had arrived the week before, and he had presumed it had come from Freddie Gains, released the previous month and promising to keep in touch. The powers that be seemed to have reached the same conclusion; Neil had been handed it along with a birthday card from his sister. *Counting down the days*, she had said inside.

Too right, Neil had thought.

Wish you were here, the postcard told him. A photograph of some seaside pier or other on the picture side. It had been signed only with an F. 'F' for Freddie, he had assumed, though the rather neat print hadn't looked like Freddie's scrawl.

Then another card a couple of days after, bearing only the words *see you soon*. Also signed with an F. The picture this time looked familiar, and Neil looked for the little printed legend postcards normally bore which would tell him where this view of a marina was situated. He was puzzled to find that there was none.

He had gone back to look at the photograph of the pier; no clue there either, and it occurred to Neil, rather belatedly, that these might not be commercially produced, shop bought postcards after all, but something someone had printed off themselves. On a rather good printer and on some pretty fancy cardstock.

Definitely not the sort of thing Freddy Gains would have had the nous to do.

It got Neil Robinson to thinking, and that thinking finally coalesced into an answer that woke him in the night in a cold sweat.

He *did* know where the little marina was; in fact, he knew the owner of the boat tied up alongside the dock. And he could make a further guess as to the seaside resort that was home to that particular pier.

And then that morning a third postcard had turned up. *Not long now* was all it said, not even a signature of any sort this time. He turned it over and looked at the picture on the front. A woodland scene, with a family picnicking in the shade of summer trees. They had their backs to him, but Neil didn't need to see their faces to recognize his sister and her kids.

And Neil was suddenly sure he understood who the messages were from and what they meant.

ONE

Patrick had been fifteen when he and Naomi had first met. Son of a childhood friend, he had come into Naomi's life when she and Patrick's father, Harry, had renewed their acquaintance.

Patrick had then seemed young for his age; slow to grow, uncertain, and naturally sensitive and gentle. The past few years had conspired to turn sensitivity first into introspection and then into quiet confidence, and the young man, not quite eighteen, who sat in her kitchen discussing plans for university seemed unbelievably far removed from the shy boy she had first come to know.

He was telling her about the portfolio he had produced for his end of year show at college. His exam portfolio – more restrained and constrained by the brief he had been given – had been sent off, and he could do no more about it. His efforts now focused on this, the first public exposure of his work and the first real opportunity to show something of his personal interests.

'It's still sort of graphic heavy,' he said. 'But I've been playing around with all these Japanese influences – I mean, not just the manga stuff. I started looking at all these old Japanese prints. You can kind of see how Japanese artists got from those to the manga—'

'Really?'

'Yeah. Kind of, anyway. It's like both styles pare everything down so you can represent complex ideas with just simple outlines and a few colours and the minimum of shading. Did you know that in the nineteenth century Japanese prints were used as packing in crates? You know, like bubble wrap? That's how a lot of them made it over to Europe. I mean, what a waste.'

Naomi hadn't known that. 'So, you'll be learning to make woodcuts next?' she joked, was met with a beat of silence.

'I'd kind of like to give it a go,' Patrick admitted. 'I like the discipline of it. It's like the discipline in graphic novels. Nothing goes to waste. If it's there, it's there for a reason, and you have to notice it because you're going to need it later, if you know what I mean.'

Naomi nodded. 'I really wish I could see it,' she said wistfully. There were few occasions now when Naomi allowed herself to feel any kind of self-pity for her loss of sight, but there were definitely times when this regret was unexpectedly overwhelming.

'So do I,' Patrick told her. 'But I'm really glad you're coming to the exhibition. Dad listens to you, even if he doesn't get what I'm trying to achieve. If you say it's *OK*, then—'

Naomi reached across the table and fumbled

for Patrick's hand. 'He's trying really hard to "get it",' she said.

'Yes, I know.' Patrick laughed suddenly. 'I think the only way Dad would really appreciate my work is if I copied The Hay Wain or something.'

Naomi smiled. There was no bitterness in this statement, simply acknowledgement that Harry Jones was, well, Harry Jones.

The big black dog, lying beneath the table, beat his tail against Naomi's leg and then sat up and laid his muzzle in her lap. She stroked him absently. Napoleon had been her guide dog for just a few months longer than she had known Patrick, and she always saw them as being part of the same package, somehow. Good friends converging on her life in very close order.

'Sue is expecting again,' she said, changing the subject.

'Really? Think she'll have a girl this time?'

'I think she's hoping so, but I don't think they really mind either way. A baby is a baby to Sue. Some people are just born to be parents.'

'You think you ever will?' The question was slightly tentative. 'I mean, you and Alec would make great parents.'

'Alec would,' Naomi agreed. '*I'm* not so sure. I think you've really got to *want* children, and right now I'm happy sharing my sister's.' She paused, thinking of a conversation she and Alec had had some months before, but not reprised, when Alec had been keen to start a family. At the time he'd also been mad keen on moving to rural Somerset and starting a smallholding, or, alternatively, going back to university, none of which options he had pursued since.

'We have talked about it,' she said.

'You have?'

Naomi smiled, amused at how shocked Patrick sounded, as though he just couldn't imagine the reality of it: Alec and Naomi and babies. 'Yes, before Christmas, when we stayed in Somerset. Alec was really in the doldrums. It was a difficult time with the job, and for a while I really didn't think he'd want to go back to work.'

It had been a difficult time since too. Disciplinary hearings and major inquiries into cases Alec had been involved in the year before. Alec had been largely cleared of blame; he'd been reprimanded and suspended for a couple of weeks, then eased quietly back into work. The biggest changes had been at the top – a new Superintendent and DCI – but there was also the unspoken, general feeling that Alec was still under a cloud. Big investigations had come and gone, and Alec had largely been sidelined. He had said little about it, but Naomi knew it rankled.

The sound of the front door opening and a voice calling from the hallway brought Naomi out of her reverie. When Patrick came round after college, his father often dropped by to collect him on his way from work. Naomi always left the door unlocked so he could come straight in.

'In here,' Naomi called. The kitchen door opened, and the presence of Harry Jones seemed to fill the small space. The dog nuzzled Naomi's hand, as though asking her permission, then left her to go and greet Harry. Patrick got up to put the kettle on, and Harry bent to kiss Naomi on the cheek.

'You're soaking.'

'That's just running from the car. June rain. At least it isn't cold, I suppose. How are you? How did the hang go, Patrick?'

'Took ages. No one could decide where they wanted their work to go, so I just picked a wall in the end and put my pictures up. It looks *OK*, I think.'

'It will look more than *OK*,' Harry reassured him. He eased down into one of the wooden chairs with a sigh of relief.

'Long day?' Naomi asked.

'Oh, far too long. Too many figures.'

'Well, that's what you get for being an accountant.'

'It is indeed.'

Harry freelanced for half the week now, keeping his old job on part time. He seemed happier, Naomi thought, though the workload was sometimes much heavier. He was eight years older than Naomi, but Alec always reckoned he looked ten more than that, with his once sandy hair now faded grey and a face creased by too many wrinkles. A lived-in face, as Patrick always said. To Naomi, who had lost her sight before Harry had returned to Pinsent, he was still the older brother to her then best friend. A freckled teen, with a friendly smile, pale-blue eyes and a slight tendency to carry weight around his middle even then.

'Your mother phoned to finalize Florida,' Harry said to Patrick. 'We'll be flying out on the first of August.'

'Good, we'll be in time for Rick's birthday.'

'That was the idea.' Harry sounded a little uncertain about it. Not surprising, Naomi thought, as Harry and Patrick's mother had been divorced for several years now and it must feel a bit odd to be going along when Patrick went to visit. Rick was one of Patrick's stepbrothers. Patrick got on really well with both of them, as the need for both families to buy a Skype phone attested. He even liked his stepather now he didn't actually have to live with him, and relations between Harry and his ex and her new husband – once Harry's old boss – had thawed, largely because of the way both sets of children had clicked.

'It'll be fine, Dad,' Patrick told him. 'I want you to be there, and I'm really looking forward to New York.'

'Ah,' Harry said mischievously. 'Now we're getting to the crux of the matter. You want me along just so you can get to New York.'

'Parents have their uses you know.'

The sound of the front door opening again surprised them all. Harry looked at his watch. 'Early for Alec.'

The front door slammed.

'Not in a good mood,' Naomi said.

'You want us to leave?'

'No, of course not.' Too late by then, anyway. Alec had opened the kitchen door and stood in the threshold.

'I've got to go away,' he said, sounding utterly aggrieved. 'They've bloody seconded me.'

'Who has? Away where? And don't I get a kiss?'

'Oh, sorry.' He bent and kissed her. Harry had been more enthusiastic, Naomi thought, amused. She heard Alec pull out a chair and sit down and Patrick set a mug on the table in front of him and then Naomi.

'So tell,' she said. 'What's going on? Where are they sending you and when?'

'Tonight,' Alec told her, and she understood why he felt so put out. 'No notice, no time to even think about it. I've got to collect Travers in an hour and will be gone for God knows how long.'

Naomi, who had been a serving officer herself, was familiar with that problem. She'd once gone on what she'd been told was a three-day cover for an industrial dispute and ended up being away for a full month. 'So—'

'Fraud case,' Alec said.

'Fraud? But you're not—'

'It impacts on a case I was involved in a year or so ago. Apparently, there have been developments, so I've got to reprise the investigation from my point of view and bring the current team up to speed and then ... Well, then who knows?'

Naomi tried to work out what case it might have been. Had they been alone, he would have told her, but Alec was discreet, even with very close friends.

'We'll get off,' Harry said. 'Let you pack. You know we'll be around for Naomi while you're gone.'

'Thanks, I appreciate that. Naomi, any chance of a sandwich while I throw some clothes in a bag?'

Naomi saw Harry and Patrick out, settling on a time for Harry to collect her for Patrick's exhibition and assuring them that Alec would be fine when he'd got over his fit of pique.

'So,' she asked, when he came back down and settled to wolf his sandwich, 'what's going on?'

Alec swallowed and took another gulp of tea. 'You remember Neil Robinson and that insurance scam he had going?'

'Um, vaguely.'

'Well, whatever it is I'm being seconded to do is related to that. There, now you know as much as me. I'm not even sure where I'm going. Travers is coming with me, so we're taking his car. I dropped him and then drove it here. More reliable than our heap is at the moment. Look, if you get the time, can you ask Harry to take you car shopping? Three times this week the damn thing refused to start. I had to leave it at work this time.'

'It's probably just the battery.'

'I changed the battery.'

‘Two years ago. But yes, I’ll ask Harry. And you don’t know how long—?’

‘Don’t know a damned thing. I’m sorry, Naomi. We had plans for this weekend.’

‘Which will keep. Don’t worry about it. Patrick will be disappointed you’re missing his show, though; we’ll send pictures to your mobile.’

‘Do that. I’m sorry, too – this is a big thing for him, isn’t it?’

‘First of many, I hope. Seriously, though, how long do you think you’ll be gone?’

She felt him shake his head. ‘I’ve packed for three or four days. Hopefully, that will be it. And I’ll make a point of getting back as often as I can, you know that. Just now I’m not even sure *where* I’ll be going. Someone’s supposed to be sending a route through to Travers so he can program the satnav.’

‘It all sounds a bit mysterious.’

‘Doesn’t it, though. But that would fit. Apparently, Robinson was ripping off some big names, government bods, and there was a hint at foreign government deals.’

‘I thought it was just an insurance scam?’

‘Sort of. I mean, that was one part of it. That was what we actually got him on in the end, and on that basis he should have been out of jail any time now, but we knew he was something of a con artist – some kind of Ponzi scheme, you know, stock market stuff. I’d started to make inroads there, but it’d lost me and I handed over to the experts. We prepared a case based on what we knew about the insurance scam, got him to court and sent down for two years, and that's the last I heard. There was talk about filing other charges later.'

'So the prison sentence allowed them time to prepare another case against him.'

'That's about the size of it. Seems they did, and I was right: Robinson was part of something much bigger.'

'You said he should have been out of prison by now?'

'This month, yes. He'd served most of his sentence in a category C open prison down South. All seemed fine, so he got time off for good behaviour and because we can't keep anyone for too long, not with the waiting list we've got. Anyway. Last week Robinson was found dead in his cell. He'd been complaining of chest pains, and the medic had been called. By the time he got there it was too late. They did a *PM* and found someone had poisoned him.'

'Poisoned? No chance it was suicide?'

'Apparently not. He was about to be released, so the assumption is—'

'Someone on the outside didn't want him around?'

'Someone didn't want him talking. Turns out he, or someone on his behalf, had made three phone calls to Jamie Dale, in the past month.'

'*The* Jamie Dale? *Our* Jamie Dale? Wasn't she—?'

'Killed in a car crash just over a week ago.'

'So, what had he told her?'

'Or what was he about to tell her? And what was she about to write about it? Whatever it was, she can't tell us now, but we can't rule out the possibility it had something to do with him getting killed, so the pressure is well and truly on.'

When Alec had left, Naomi felt flat and very out of sorts. She had looked forward to an evening with Alec, probably not doing anything very much – a walk, maybe, down beside the river, a bit of television later on. And she hated sleeping alone.

When she had moved into her flat she had relished the idea of her own space and her own bed. Of being independent of anyone else's wishes. Since marrying Alec and moving here, into what had once been just Alec's house and, more particularly, since the events of the winter, when at one point Naomi had been certain she was going to die – and a meaningless, pointless death at that – she had grown more and more to dislike being on her own at night. Night-time was when the world and all its memories crowded in upon her and when bed was not a sanctuary unless that space was shared. Not even Napoleon's comforting presence could really sooth her.

She poured herself a glass of wine and took it, and the phone, outside into the garden and settled in the swing seat beside the pond. She heard Napoleon bend to lap the water and then dip a paw to splash at the fish. Birds sang out to mark their evening territory, and something rustled in the flower beds. Peace, she told herself. Quiet and calm and warm evening sun. All was fine.

She remained unconvinced.

Naomi sipped wine and listened to the night-time sounds gathering around her and breathed in the scents of jasmine and honeysuckle and the thornless rose – the name of which she could never remember – that Alec had planted next to the swing seat. And she tried to remember what, if anything else, she knew about the Robinson case that had now called Alec away or about the dead journalist, Jamie Dale. Professionally, she and Alec had run into Jamie Dale on a number of occasions. She'd started out working for one of the free newspapers, covering school fêtes and consumer issues, and Naomi and Alec had inevitably met with her when, as young, uniformed officers, they had been present at some of the same events. For a while, Jamie and Naomi and a group of other young women had met regularly for nights out. As, one by one, they had begun serious relationships or got more demanding jobs, those regular nights had become occasional and then diminished altogether.

Alec and Naomi had gained promotion, and Jamie had become a stringer for a couple of national papers. Apart from the odd Christmas card, and occasionally remarking upon her name when they happened to spot her by-line,

Naomi had largely lost touch with her. Naomi vaguely recalled that Jamie had moved away; she had turned to filmmaking as a way of reaching broader swathes of the public, and so far as Naomi could remember Jamie now lived in London or wherever it was they produced such things. Pinsent had certainly never been big enough to contain the likes of Jamie Dale, anyway.

Naomi closed her eyes as she still always did when trying to recall something more sharply and tried to remember Jamie the last time they had met. Small, slightly built, coffee-coloured skin and intense brown eyes. Hair that was always either braided or embellished or extended or dyed some unlikely hue; that last time it had been adorned with sky-blue streaks. But she had been young then. They had all been young then. A smart jacket or blazer worn with faded jeans; that had been Jamie's uniform. She had once told Naomi that she carried a coordinating skirt in her bag, just in case, along with a decent pair of shoes. Back then, Naomi recalled, it was a standing joke that it was always the same skirt and shoes; Jamie had once confided that her jackets were all bought in sales or were her sister's cast-offs and *The Skirt* went with any of them. She was, she had joked, mistress of the capsule wardrobe.

'I liked her,' Naomi told Napoleon, slightly surprised to remember how much. The dog came over and nuzzled at her hand, and she stroked the silky ears and smooth head.

And now she was dead. Accident? Coincidence? Or was there really a link to Neil Robinson – and if so, what?

Naomi sighed. It must be getting dark by now, she thought, wondering if Alec had arrived at wherever it was he was going. He'd promised to call, and she knew he would, when he got a minute, but Naomi knew from experience that might not be until much later – earlier, even; he'd let her know all was well, even if that meant a text at two in the morning. She picked up the phone and wine glass and, Napoleon pressed against her leg so she didn't slip into the pond, turned back towards the house, almost wishing herself back in her little flat again, an almost overwhelming sense of isolation crashing around her.

TWO

It had taken three attempts to program the satnav. They'd been given directions and an address, but no postcode, just a building name and road. Travers had no patience with technology.

Finally, Alec had taken over, assuring his boss that they could always phone when they were within striking distance, make certain they were heading for the right place. He sensed that Travers' impatience and bad mood had little to do with the mini computer suckered to the windscreen.

'Maureen isn't pleased at you being called away?' he ventured at last.

Travers grimaced. 'We had plans for this weekend,' he said tightly. 'I kept telling her I'd do my best to be back, but she kept reminding me that I'm Detective *Chief* Inspector now and that I'd promised her promotion would mean less time on the job and more time at home.'

Alec said nothing; there didn't seem much point in remarking that this was the first weekend Travers had come close to working in the past year. He'd become very apt at being elsewhere, out of reach, if a call came in. Alec could sympathize. He, like Travers, had endured a long career of interrupted plans, lost weekends off and unscheduled – often unpaid – overtime. Time off in lieu never really panned out.

'You're lucky,' Travers grumbled. 'Naomi understands these things.'

'Naomi gets impatient with it too,' Alec said mildly. 'After what happened last year, she's not so keen to be at home alone at night,' he added pointedly.

Travers was momentarily contrite. 'No, I don't suppose she is.' He paused. 'Likely, I'll come back to the decorators or some new three-piece suite Maureen's taken a fancy to. Credit cards are weapons in her hands.'

Alec laughed, then wondered if he should have done. Maureen's spending habits had long been a touchy subject. 'So,' he said, by way of diversion. 'Know anything about this *DI* Eddison we're meant to be meeting?' The truth was, Alec was curious too about Travers' involvement. Why did they need Alec *and* his DCI if all Alec was going to do was refresh a few memories of an old case, give his perspective on it? Travers had only just got his promotion at the time, and Alec couldn't recall that he'd been all that active on the Robinson business. He'd been off on some management course somewhere when everything came to a head and the arrest was made.

'I've met Eddison,' Travers said. 'He was a speaker on a conference I went to, if I remember right. He delivered a paper on steganography.' Travers laughed. 'Until then, I thought that was a type of dinosaur.' He paused again, waiting for Alec to say he still thought it was. Politically, Alec probably should have done, but as it happened—

'Hiding things in plain sight,' he said.

'Give that man a peanut.'

'Anyway, he's become the "go to guy" for anything technical.' Travers shrugged, but Alec could see he was reluctantly impressed.

They were out in the country now, driving a twisting road too fast for Alec's taste. Travers had always driven like a maniac. Alec remembered when they'd both taken the advance driving course and Travers had set out with the intention of proving just how good he was behind the wheel, only to be told at the end of the first day that he'd be thrown off the course if he didn't quiet down and focus.

Alec found himself switching attention between the now darkening road ahead and the little brown squiggle on the satnav map. 'What time are we expected?'

'When we get there. Why?'

Alec shrugged. From past experience he knew that any comment on the speed of Travers driving, any mild suggestion that he might like to slow down, would have the opposite effect. Silently, he cursed his failing car and hoped that Naomi *would* be taking the credit card for a walk and getting them a nice reliable one before he returned home. Harry could be trusted to ask the practical questions about insurance and petrol consumption, and Patrick and Naomi between them could be relied upon to make sure the purchase wasn't too dull.

'So, do we know what killed Robinson?'

'Not yet. Tox reports still aren't back. I understand you were familiar with that journalist woman?'

'Journalist? Oh, Jamie Dale. Yes, Naomi and I started in the force around the same time she started at the local paper. We got to know her quite well back then, but lost touch rather when she moved down south, as you do. Why?'

'Well, Eddison seems to think it may be helpful. That you knew her.'

'Very much past tense,' Alec told him. 'We liked her. She was funny and clever and very good at what she did. Committed, too. Even back then you'd have made a bet on her making it, whatever field she decided to go into.'

'Bet no one took odds on her burning up in a smashed-up car.'

'Burning?' Alec went cold. 'The news reports said nothing about a fire.'

'No, they didn't. The news reported it as an accident. Sad, but these things happen. The evidence says it was murder.'

'Murder?'

Travers nodded. 'So now we've got two bodies. It seems that your funny, clever reporter friend burned to death in her car. The keys had been taken, the child locks activated. She was locked in and left to die.'

THREE

It was funny, Gregory thought, the way some people were able to compartmentalize their lives. He doubted anyone in Jamie's circle knew about her friendship with Neil Robinson or many in his that he had a connection with her.

'We started chatting in a pub one night,' she'd said. 'I was supposed to meet a friend, and she was late and then she texted to say she'd been held up at work and probably wouldn't make it. Neil was there too, looking equally fed up, and we got talking.'

She had not, Gregory remembered, been in London all that long at the time and was probably just glad of the company. Neil could be engaging company. Smooth and charming and seemingly open: just the personality traits that made him such a good conman.

Not, so far as Gregory knew – and he knew a great deal – that Neil had ever tried anything with Jamie.

The two had become casual friends. The odd coffee, a film, an evening in the pub. It had been easy and appealing to a woman like Jamie, whose life otherwise was so intense.

Gregory, not an expert in personal relation-

ships, had always been interested when people spoke about theirs, and Jamie had been very easy to listen to. Like Neil she, too, was charming, smooth and open – though in Jamie's case she really was – and it made her pleasant company.

And Christopher had been right, Gregory thought. He had allowed himself to grow fond, to believe that the girl could be deflected from the dangerous path she had been taking. And so she had been, for a while.

He turned the little silver device in his hands. A digital recorder, quite high end and very pretty and compact. Then he looked at the number scribbled on the pad on his desk. Not that he needed to look; numbers he needed to know were committed quickly and retained, Christopher always joked, for elephant's years.

Reaching for the phone, and with his finger poised to play, he dialled the number.

Harry called around midnight. He apologized for the lateness, but said Patrick had told him it would be a good idea. Naomi smiled, amused at the parental buck-passing. The Harry–Patrick dynamic had certainly shifted in the past year. Harry would have missed him terribly if his son had decided to pick a distant university, but Patrick, despite offers of finance from his mother and stepfather, had elected to go to a local art college, which meant he could still live at home.

'Patrick was right,' Naomi said.

'No word from Alec?'

'Nothing yet. They should have arrived by now, but he probably won't get much time to call until later. You know how it is.'

'And you're all right?'

'I'm fine,' she lied.

'Because I can come over, you know I would.'

'Bless you, Harry. But I'm going to bed now, and I'll be *OK*. I've locked up everywhere.'

'If you're sure? Right then, we'll pick you up at half five tomorrow, if that's *OK*. The private view starts at six, and Patrick wants to meet up with his friends.'

Naomi smiled again. Friends hadn't really been dominant in Patrick's life when she first knew him and had definitely not been without their tragedy. They had both worried for Patrick for a while, but he seemed happy in his own skin these days, and she knew how relieved Harry was about that. 'Looking forward to it,' she said.

She had just put the phone back on its cradle when it rang again. Not Alec, she thought; he'd have rung her mobile just in case she'd already gone to bed. Had Harry forgotten something?

'Hello. Did you—?'

She knew at once that this was not Harry. The emptiness that greeted her words echoed as though she had connected with some vast space. No one spoke.

'Hello,' she said again. 'Who is this?'

A sudden click as though someone had flicked a switch. The sound of a voice, tight and panicked and speaking her name. Her unmarried name. 'Naomi? Naomi Blake? Do you remember me? This is Jamie, Jamie Dale.' The sound broke off, words becoming sobs so desperate that Naomi felt herself grow cold.

'Who is this?' she said again, trying hard to keep her own voice steady. You're dead, she thought. How can you be speaking to me?

Another click; she recognized it now, a tape machine being switched off. The voice had been recorded, but by whom? When?

'Who the hell are you?' Angry now. Fearful too.

Silence. Then the phone was hung up and the line went dead.

She stood for a moment, clutching the receiver in her hand, then slowly laid it back on the cradle. Light-headed and chilled, she felt as though all the blood and warmth had drained out of her. Jamie was dead. What the hell...? Briefly, she stood stock still, telling herself that whoever was doing this was just trying to frighten her, that she wasn't going to let that happen. Her resolve lasted only scant seconds. Whoever was trying to frighten her had damn well succeeded.

'Napoleon! Napoleon, come!' In a frenzy of activity she stormed around the house, barking her shins on furniture she knew was there but could not seem to avoid. She checked the locks on the windows, unfastened and then refastened the doors while the big black dog, thinking this was some new game, beat his heavy tail enthusiastically against her legs.

Finally, she stumbled up the stairs to her bedroom and locked that door too. Then stood, staring at a key she could no longer see and listening hard, as though any minute she might hear footsteps on the stairs and know that her carefully erected barricades had just been breached.

Down in the hall the phone rang out again, and Naomi jumped. Napoleon whined softly in sympathy, realizing belatedly that Naomi was not having fun. She counted. Five rings and then it stopped, as though whoever was calling merely wanted to make a point: *I know who you are; I know where you live.* She had her mobile in the pocket of her cardigan, and she almost gave in to the impulse to call Harry, ask him to come and get her and beg the use of his spare room for the night. She had the phone in her hand before she dismissed the thought. She wasn't going to drag Harry and Patrick into this, not unless she had to. Someone was trying to scare her. Someone was doing a bloody good job of it, and when Alec phoned she'd tell him what had happened and they'd figure out what she ought to do. One thing was certain. Neither Naomi nor Alec believed in coincidence. Alec had been called in to investigate a murder. The victim, Neil Robinson, had been in contact with Jamie Dale. Just what was going on here?

'Right, deep breaths, just stay calm. Doors are locked, everything is fine.'

Napoleon whined again, and she bent to stroke the smooth fur. She was still listening for any unusual sound, any little creak or groan that might not be the familiar noises of the house settling down for the night. After a while, she realized that she could hear nothing out of the ordinary. All was quiet, peaceful. Safe. She kicked off her slippers and curled up on the bed, shrinking back against the headboard, instinctively retreating from the bedroom door, and she listened again, then shook herself angrily.

'Dope. Do something about it!' The number for the local police station where Alec worked and Naomi once had done too was on speed dial in her phone, and she called it now. Got through to the desk sergeant and was utterly relieved to hear a voice she knew.

'Donald!'

'Naomi? Are you all right, love? You know he's not here, surely?'

'Yes, don't fret. He didn't go without telling me.' She tried to laugh, but it came out shaky and unconvincing.

'Naomi?'

'Don, I wonder if you could get a car to swing by, just take a quick look around. Nothing urgent, but...?'

'Naomi? I mean, course I will, but what is it?'

'I've just had a strange phone call,' she said, oddly relieved to have said it out loud.

'A nuisance call?' His turn to laugh now. 'What was it, a heavy breather?'

'If it had been, I wouldn't be bothering you,'

she said. 'I'd have got Napoleon to bark down the phone. No, Don, it was something weirder than that. You know that journalist that died?'

'Dale. That one?'

'Yes, well someone just called me and played a message from her down the phone. She sounded scared, Don. And whoever it was wanted me scared too.'

'Sounds like they succeeded. Right, love, I'll get someone to you. You spoken to Alec yet?'

'No, I'll talk to him later. There's nothing he can do right now. Thanks, Don, I appreciate it.'

She rang off and sat clutching the mobile as though it was a lifeline, keeping her connected to the sane and ordinary world. Listening again, she could discern no out of the ordinary noises, nothing that should not be there, but the sense of unease grew nonetheless, prowling like some solid, feral thing along the hallway outside of the bedroom door.

As it happened, the satnav got them to their destination. A lone house set back from a long, empty road.

'This is it?'

'Well, there's nothing else here,' Alec said. They pulled into the drive and parked up outside the house. Two other cars could be seen, tucked in at the side. The house itself was largely hidden from the road by a tall, unkempt hedge.

Alec glanced at the front door, illuminated by a small porch light. A sign above the door said

Police, in faded letters. A rural police station, then? Though the cracked paint on the door, the faded sign and the general untidiness of the front garden indicated it had been out of use for some time.

The front door opened as Alec and Travers got out of the car, and a tall, heavily built man stood silhouetted in the doorway.

'Someone's got a sense of the dramatic,' Travers muttered.

The figure stepped out into the arched porch and his features came into view, illuminated now by the scanty light. Alec noted a flat face and a broken nose.

'*DCI* Travers and *DI* Friedman, I presume? Nick, good to see you again. Good, come along in, apologies for all the mystery, I'll explain why we're meeting here if you care to step inside. Good.'

The word 'good' seemed to be a tick, Alec noted. The man's tone, however, noted no such approbation.

He turned, and Alec followed him – Travers, Alec noted, pausing to glance around before bringing up the rear. The stranger's voice was accented, a lilt that was vaguely Scottish, Alec thought, though with a touch of something more angular. Birmingham, perhaps? Alec gave up.

They were led into what looked as if it had been the front office, uncarpeted and with a scuffed desk and wooden chair filling most of the space, then back into the rear of the property, a large area with a small kitchen off to one side. Two others sat at a table, drinking tea. The walls were clad in pitted woodchip, which in turn was overlaid by maps and photographs and all the trappings of a crime-scene briefing room. Along one wall two desks had been placed, on which computers had been set, and a third desk was stacked high with box files and folders. It looked as though the trio had just moved in and not yet fully unpacked.

'So.' The tall man turned now and surveyed Alec and Travers. 'Nick Travers I know already; you I know by reputation.'

Worrying, Alec thought.

'*DI* Eddison,' the man said, extending his hand.

Alec shook, murmured something about being pleased to meet him. In truth, he was annoyed. What was going on here?

Eddison pointed at the dark-haired man still seated at the table. '*DS* Munroe,' he said and, indicating the blond, '*DI* Parks. Sit down and I'll get the kettle on.'

'Why are we meeting here?' Travers asked.

'Because it's private,' Munroe said. 'Because it's about midway between where Neil Robinson was in prison and where that journalist died, and because there are bigger concerns that don't need to be the subject of canteen gossip.'

Alec raised an eyebrow and glanced at his boss. Travers' face was expressionless, or at least would seem so to the casual observer. The slight tic at the corner of his mouth told Alec that Travers was as unamused as Alec.

Parks laughed softly, and Alec reviewed the man more carefully. Pale eyes set in a round face that, with the slightly waving blond hair, should almost have been cherubic but was in fact anything but. He was the sort of man, Alec found himself observing, who would have looked right with a crew cut and an earring. He corrected himself almost at once. That wasn't right either; there was something more behind the eyes than mere thug. Something feral.

Alec sat at the table and, reluctantly, Travers drew out a chair and plonked himself down close by. 'I'm told you want me to review the Robinson case. From my angle, I mean?' Alec let the question hang.

Munroe nodded; Parks sipped his tea. 'We've read your report, scanned the files. There were some loose ends when you signed off on it?'

'True, there were. It was decided that I'd taken things as far as I could, that we needed to bring in an expert eye. My then boss decided that as we'd got enough for a conviction for the con Robinson was running – that and a GBH – we should cut our losses and let someone else tie up anything left hanging.'

'A decision you didn't like,' Parks commented.

Alec smiled. 'I don't like unfinished business,' he said. 'It feels odd not to wrap everything up properly. Though,' he added, 'on this occasion I couldn't argue with the logic.' He glanced at Travers. His boss was watching

Eddison as he moved about the small kitchen. Watching as though the presence of the man upset him, made him uneasy. Alec, puzzled, wondered just what had happened when they'd last met at whatever conference it had been and if more had been delivered than a conference paper. Somehow, it was difficult to equate this big, rather slow-moving man, who looked like a long-retired rugby player or punch drunk heavyweight boxer, with an erudite presentation on some obscure element of cyber crime.

'I'm told Jamie Dale was murdered,' Alec said.

He felt, rather than saw, Travers flinch, and wondered if Travers was even meant to know that, never mind impart the information. And if not, why not?

'She was,' Munroe agreed. 'Nasty way to die. She tried to make a phone call, got through to emergency services but she was unable to tell them where she was.' He sniffed. 'Not that it would have helped. Operator stayed on the line till he lost the signal. He's still having counselling, apparently. They reckon he can't go to sleep, not without hearing her screaming over the phone as she died.' He met Alec's gaze squarely, and Alec felt he was being tested, his reaction assessed. 'Thankfully, the smoke got to her and she passed out before the flames took a real hold.' Munroe's voice was oddly soft. That softness somehow added emphasis to the horror of his words.

'It *is* a terrible way to die,' Alec said. 'I've

always thought it must be one of the worst.'

Parks emitted a soft grunt. Alec realized it was a stifled laugh. He let it go, not sure what to make of all this. Was it some test of machismo? Alec had little time for such displays and little patience with their practitioners.

'Is there a point to all this?'

Eddison came through with mugs of tea clasped awkwardly in one ham fist and a handful of sugar packs in the other. Alec noted that they bore the name of a motorway service station.

'The point is,' Eddison said, 'that you worked the Robinson case and you also knew the dead woman. That makes you potentially very useful.'

'Knew,' Alec emphasized. 'I'd not spoken to Jamie in years, not properly. We exchanged Christmas and birthday cards, the odd email, but that was about the extent of it.'

'Which in Miss Dale's world qualifies you and your wife as bosom buddies,' Parks said. 'She wasn't what you'd call one for making friends.'

'My wife? What does—?' He frowned. And that didn't ring true about Jamie Dale either. The one thing she had always been was gregarious. He said so.

Munroe shrugged. 'People change,' he said. 'She dumped her last boyfriend two years ago. He says he still doesn't know why. It was one of those "it's not you, it's me" conversations women seem to be good at and men don't understand.'

Parks grunted again; Alec assumed he was amused, in agreement or possibly both.

'He tried to get in touch a time or two, but she changed her number, moved away, let all her old friends know she wasn't available. Finally, they stopped calling.'

'I didn't know,' Alec said. 'That doesn't sound anything like the Jamie we knew.'

'When did you last hear from her? Get the usual Christmas card, did you?'

Alec thought about it and nodded. 'Yes, she'd changed her address. We couldn't remember when we'd sent her card, so we sent another one just to be sure she got it.'

'Say much, did she?'

'I don't think so. Just the new address and some comment about getting together some time. I think that was about it.'

'And that was the usual sort of message?' Eddison asked.

Alec took a swallow of tea. It was too hot and went down hard, burning his throat. He tried to remember what that last card had said. And the ones before. Truth be told, he had taken very little notice. Naomi would know; he read the cards out to her, and she told him what to put by way of reply. Left to his own devices, Alec would probably not even have got around to buying Christmas cards, never mind writing them.

'I think she said that most years,' he ventured. 'You know, the sort of casual remark people make about getting together when they know it won't happen.'

'And would you have minded if it had?' This from Travers. The first contribution he had made to the conversation since they had arrived.

Alec turned to look at his boss, wondering at the question. Would he have minded? 'No,' he said, 'why should I mind? Naomi probably knew Jamie better than I did. Before Jamie left for London they used to meet up a couple of times a month for a coffee or a drink. Not just them; they belonged to the same group of friends.'

'Unusual friendship,' Parks remarked. 'A copper and a journo. The two tribes don't generally mix it, do they?'

'I don't think their choice of profession impacted on their friendship,' Alec said coldly.

Parks laughed. Not just a grunt this time, but a recognizable sound. Alec didn't like it any better.

'Leave off,' Munroe said, and Parks shut up.

Alec sipped his tea more cautiously this time and surveyed the trio. It seemed to him that Eddison might be the senior officer, but it was this Munroe who was in control.

'It's late,' Munroe said, underlining Alec's assessment. 'What say we give you directions to your digs and then continue this in the morning? Say nine?'

Travers was already on his feet.

'Right,' Alec said. 'See you all in the morning

then.'

Following his boss out, he took a moment to scan the images pinned to the walls. Split into two frames, one for Jamie Dale and one for Neil Robinson, they showed both in death. Alec didn't look too hard; morning would be soon enough for that. A single image of each as they had been in life topped the collages. Neil Robinson in what Alec saw was a prison photo, and a picture of Jamie Dale, older than he remembered her. Still pretty, still smiling, though something behind the eyes was new. This Jamie was more worldly wise, less trusting, less exuberant – and, Alec would have sworn, scared. Or was that just projection on his part?

Travers did not speak until they were both in the car, and even then it was simply to direct him to program the satnav.

'What's going on?' Alec demanded as they drove away.

Travers shrugged.

'What is it with you and Eddison?'

Travers shrugged again. 'I barely know the man.'

'You know him well enough to hate his guts.'

'I barely know the man,' Travers repeated.

Alec gave up. He let the silence hang for a while and then asked, 'What about the other two? You know about them?'

'Parks I've heard about. Munroe is new to me.'

'*DS* Munroe,' Alec mused. 'Come off it, Trav,

he's no more a *DS* than you are. So what the hell—?'

'Alec, drop it,' Travers flared. 'We're here to brief the team then get ourselves back home. That's it.'

'So why all the secrecy? Why did they want you tagging along? Why bring two senior officers all the way over here when I could have handled the whole thing with a phone call? Look, we've known one another, what, close to twenty years? In all that time I've never seen you this rattled.'

'Who says I'm rattled? Alec, you're imagining things.' Travers laughed, but it was a hollow sound. 'Looks like we're here,' he added as they reached a traffic island and saw the signs for services. The satnav announced that they had reached their destination.

'I'm not letting this go,' Alec warned him.

Travers did not respond. He parked the car, and they retrieved their luggage from the boot. In the distance Alec could hear the roar of traffic. A motorway, he assumed. He could see the lights of the services just across the car park from the motel, noting with little enthusiasm that it was one of the large chains providing overnight accommodation to the weary motorist, then – with slightly more enthusiasm – that at least there appeared to be a restaurant. His stomach reminded him that the sandwich Naomi had made for him was a distant memory. He must call her.

Their rooms had been booked and paid for,

for three nights. Breakfast was included, but any extras would have to be settled up by them, the receptionist said. Travers nodded and took off in the direction of his room. Alec paused to ask about the restaurant, was told that it would be open for another hour. After that, food was available twenty-four-hours a day at the main complex across at the services.

Alec thanked her. 'Who made the reservations?' he asked. 'I need to know so the paperwork gets to the right place.'

She smiled and checked the records. 'A Mr Munroe,' she said. 'He said it would be for three nights initially and he'd let us know after that.'

Munroe again. 'Thank you,' Alec said and made his way to his room.

FOUR

The sound of a car pulling into the drive, wheels crunching on the gravel, brought Naomi to the window. It was as if, at moments of crisis, her sighted self took control, body memory from that time still dominant, so she behaved as though she could still see.

The knock at the front door startled her, and she unlocked the bedroom door slowly and stood uncertain at the top of the stairs, Napoleon pressed close to her side.

'Naomi.' A familiar voice calling through the letterbox. 'Naomi, it's Megan Allison. You going to let me in or what?'

'Are you all right, love?' Megan demanded when Naomi opened the door. 'Constable Watkins is trampling through your flower beds, by the way. He's a probationer. Nice lad, big feet yet though.'

Naomi laughed. Big feet was a Meganism for someone still learning about the diplomatic side of the job. Some people, according to Megan, had feet that just kept on growing no matter how long they were in the force.

'I'm all right, just a bit shaken. Did Don tell you what happened?'

'He did. What's all that about then? Would have freaked me out, I can tell you. Any chance of a cuppa?'

'Of course. Come on through to the kitchen, we can let your constable in the back way.'

Having something to do with her hands always calmed her, and the simple actions of filling the kettle and getting mugs from the cupboard made it easier to talk. Naomi told Megan what had happened, giving as much detail as she could and grateful that the other woman knew her well enough not to fuss around with unnecessary offers of help. She needed to be doing.

Constable Watkins joined them, and Megan made Naomi tell the story again for his benefit and also, Naomi understood, for her own. Megan was astute enough to pick up on any small shifts in the second telling. Any little changes of emphasis. Naomi would have done the same; stories become fixed with retelling, mistakes and misconceptions more firmly embedded, and that first recollection needed to be recorded and then checked. She could hear them both taking notes and Constable Watkins' nervous cough before he dared to ask her the odd question.

No doubt he knew about Megan's theory regarding feet.

'Um, you're sure it was her?' Watkins asked. 'I mean, excuse me asking, but if you've not spoken to her in a while, it could be someone, well, pretending.'

'Good question,' Megan approved, 'but go easy on the doubt. People don't like to feel you're doubting them.'

'Oh, right,' he said.

Naomi tried not to smile. 'I'm as sure as I can be,' she responded. 'True, I've not talked to Jamie in years, but we were good friends at one time. I recognized her voice at once, but,' she added thoughtfully, 'why did she call me by my maiden name? She knew Alec and I are married now. We invited her to the wedding.'

'But she didn't come?'

'No. She sent her apologies and a card, but no, she didn't come. I don't think we expected her to, really.'

'So, she knew you were married, but she still called you Naomi Blake.'

'Could she have been trying to tell you something?' Watkins asked. 'Like a secret code...' He trailed off. 'Sorry, that sounds dumb, doesn't it?'

'No,' Naomi reassured him. 'Not dumb.' She closed her eyes and concentrated; something in Watkins' suggestion had stuck a chord. 'She said Naomi, Naomi *Blake*, as though it mattered. As though—' She shook her head. 'I don't know.'

'As though whatever she was trying to tell you about had happened when you were still Naomi Blake?' Watkins said. Then he mumbled an apology as Naomi and Megan both turned to stare at him. 'I mean—'

'Watkins,' Megan said. 'I think you may be

on to something here.'

Naomi could almost feel the young man glow. 'Which creates even more questions,' she said softly. 'What was she trying to tell me, and why did she – or someone else – record her, and when? Megan, she sounded so scared. I think that's what freaked me out so much. Nothing fazed Jamie, and yet she sounded utterly terrified.'

'I suppose her death was definitely an accident,' Watkins said cautiously.

'I've not heard any different,' Megan said, 'but I think a little careful digging around might be in order, don't you, Watkins?'

The young man must be positively radiant now, Naomi thought. 'Just be careful,' she warned. 'Nothing about this is right, Megan. Just don't either of you make trouble for yourselves.'

Megan and Watkins left just before Alec called. Naomi had wandered back up to bed, feeling reassured now but still a little jumpy. Her mobile ring tone, irritatingly cheerful, startled her. 'Hi,' she said. 'How are you?'

'Pissed off.'

'Oh, why?'

'This is the strangest setup. Anyway, how're you? You sound a little tense – did I wake you?'

'No, I wasn't asleep. In fact Megan Allison and her new probationer have just left.'

'Megan? Why? Naomi, what's wrong?'

Taking a deep breath, she told him about the

phone call, trying not to let the tension back into her voice; knowing it was there anyway. 'I don't understand this, Alec. What's it all about?'

Silence for a moment. She wondered if she'd lost the signal.

'Naomi,' Alec said quietly, 'Travers told me tonight that Jamie Dale wasn't killed in a simple road accident. That's just what's been released publicly while the investigation goes on.'

'She was murdered?' Naomi asked. 'Oh, Alec. How?'

There was no easy way to say it, so he told her simply. 'She burned to death in the car. That's all I know, but they are definitely linking it to Robinson's death. Naomi, keep the doors locked, ask Harry or Mari if you can stay with them for a few days, please. I'd feel happier.'

'I'll think about it,' she said. 'But if whoever it was calls back and I'm not around to take the call – Alec, there has to be more on that recording that they played back to me. I think, for Jamie's sake, I need to be here, need to know.'

Silence again. He wanted to argue, but he knew her too well. Knew that would have been his reaction too. 'You can't stay in all the time,' he pointed out. 'You could miss a call any time.'

'True, but, well, you know.'

'I know. Look, maybe get someone over to stay with you?'

'What if they're watching the house?' She'd

said it. Voiced the fear.

'Anything to make you think someone may be?'

'No. Megan and *PC* Watkins checked thoroughly. There was no sign of anyone.'

'Naomi, don't take any risks. Promise me?'

'Promise you.'

'I'm hoping to be back before long, but you never know, do you?'

'I'll be fine,' she told him. 'Megan and co will keep an eye on things, and I'll see about getting some company.' She paused. 'Come home soon, Alec. I'm missing you.'

FIVE

Morning dawned bright and sunny for both Naomi and Alec. Neither had slept well. She took her morning tea into the garden and sat beside the pond; he ate breakfast alone in the motel restaurant. Travers had not appeared, and Alec wondered if the man had actually bothered to eat since the night before or if he had sneaked out at midnight and gone across to the services. Anything to put off Alec's promised questions.

Megan had called Naomi at seven o clock. She was off home, she said. Was Naomi all right or did she need her to call in? Naomi was touched but assured her friend and once fellow officer that she was fine. Surprisingly, she found that was almost true. She still felt shaken by the call, but experience and professional instinct had kicked in and Naomi felt sure that there was no immediate danger. Whoever had called wanted her scared and off balance but had also contacted her for some deeper purpose, and Naomi found that, of all the emotions gripping her, curiosity was standing head and shoulders above the rest. Curiosity, and a sense of outrage at the terrible way Jamie had died. If anything was going to give Naomi nightmares, it would be that.

Alec had called her just after Megan. He sounded tired, she thought, and seriously annoyed. He told her a little more about his encounter with Munroe and the others.

'Will you tell them about my phone call?'

'Yes, but I'll choose my moment. I'd like to talk it through with Travers first, but he seems to be avoiding me.'

'What's up with him, do you think?'

'My guess is pressure from above. A long way above, maybe; perhaps even external to the department. What was Robinson preparing to tell Jamie, and how many toes would she have trampled on to get to the nitty gritty? You know what Jamie was like when she had a hold of something, nothing could make her drop it.'

'I don't think she had a reverse gear,' Naomi agreed. 'Well, give Trav my best and tell him not to be such a grumpy sod.'

Alec laughed. They both knew Travers had a soft spot for Naomi. 'Will do, love. You take care now, and wish Patrick luck for tonight. I'll be thinking of him.'

'I'll take photos,' Naomi said. 'Well, I'll get Patrick to take them and I'll send them from my phone.'

'Maybe you should both do it. The results might be interesting. We could put them all together and create an installation. *OK*, love, I'll talk to you later. Bye.'

He poured himself another cup of tea and debated going back to the buffet for more breakfast. Something made him think that today was going to be a little light on breaks. What Naomi had told him about the phone call bothered him profoundly, and every instinct screamed at him to tell Travers he was off home to be with her. Had he driven over in his own car, then Alec knew he would not even have hesitated ... would he? Alec sipped his tea. Actually, he probably would have. Naomi would hate to think her anxiety was the cause of him rushing away from a job. She prided herself on her self-sufficiency and resilience – and, Alec acknowledged, in many ways hers was greater than his. He comforted himself with the thought that Megan and this *PC* Watkins seemed to be keeping an eye on her, and that Harry would look after Naomi any way he could. Alec was in no doubt at all that if he hadn't finally got his act together and asked Naomi to marry him, then Harry would have done so, and he was still slightly afraid that she might have said yes.

Glancing at his watch he saw that it was still only eight o clock. Travers was still significantly absent, and there would be no need for them to leave for at least another half hour. 'More breakfast it is then,' Alec said to himself and, asking the waitress if he could possibly have another pot of tea, he took his plate and went for seconds.

By ten they were at the prison where Neil Robinson had died. They had rendezvoused with Munroe and Parks back at the old police station. Eddison had not been there. He had a meeting, Parks said and suggested Alec went to the prison in his car and that Munroe could give Travers directions and travel in his.

Travers, who had barely spoken on the short drive over, had not looked happy.

'Have you worked with *DS* Munroe for long?' Alec had asked. Parks' car had surprised him. A small blue hatchback with a child seat in the back and a scatter of toys in the footwell. Parks saw him examining the debris and laughed. 'It's the wife's car,' he said. 'She's taken mine for a few days, gone with the kids and a friend and all the camping gear.'

'Didn't she need the child seat?' Alec asked innocently.

Parks turned his pale eyes on Alec and then laughed. The oddly cherubic mouth didn't seem designed for laughter, Alec thought. It was far too prissy and tight.

'We've got a seat in both cars for Nan. Nancy, that is. Luke is big enough to use a booster seat now.'

'How old are they?'

'Three and eight. You have kids?'

'No, not yet.' Both fell silent for a while, then Alec asked again, 'So you work regularly with Munroe and Eddison?'

Parks shrugged. 'Eddison, yes. Been my boss for five, nearly six years, since I got the transfer here from London. We wanted a better place to bring up the kids, somewhere with a big garden, and Phil's parents are here so – Philippa,' he added. 'She hates her name.'

'And Munroe?'

'Never met him until three days ago,' Parks said in a tone that told Alec he wasn't going to get any more than that.

The prison, Heathfields, was true to its type. A so-called open prison, though this, like most, did have high fences topped with razor wire along the perimeter. It enclosed a large area of grass and trees, and Alec glimpsed vegetable gardens. The gatehouse was little more than a wooden hut, and the barrier – flimsy and already up when they arrived – seemed totally at odds with the high fence and twisted wire that cordoned off the grounds. Alec had visited many such establishments in his time. Many of the prisoners here were close to release, Parks had told him. Many after serving very long sentences. Heathfields housed a number that were on day or community release programmes. The prison had a good relationship with the local farmers and growers, Parks said. They often gave inmates close to their release a taste of work and a reintroduction to the wider community before they were finally thrown back on to their own resources. It was considered a model prison in many ways, with an inspiration governor, Michelle Sanders, who, from his tone when he spoke of her, Parks actually seemed to admire – a rare attitude from a serving officer, in Alec's experience.

They were shown to Robinson's room in one

of the accommodation blocks furthest from the gate. The view from the window was of grass and trees, and the room was basic but comfortable. He had stayed in worse hotels, Alec reflected. Establishments like Heathfields had come in for a lot of flak in the media of late, their so-called liberal regimes attracting censure. Alec was more measured in his attitude. He had seen too many men and women released straight from Category A or B prisons with little preparation or concern or support, and far too many had been back there within the year. In Alec's view, if places like Heathfields dropped the recidivism rate, he was all for them.

Usually, however, he kept such views to himself.

'The room's not been touched,' they were told by the prison officer who'd taken them there. 'But we really could do with it being released as soon as. We've got a new batch coming in tomorrow.'

Munroe had gone straight to see the governor; Travers had not been invited, despite the fact that he outranked the other officer, and he had shown no sign of protest at that. It was, Alec thought, almost as though he was determined to be invisible.

Alec glanced at his boss. Travers stood looking out of the window, seemingly oblivious to the rest of them. Parks was watching him, a look of puzzlement on his face. He doesn't understand this setup any more than I do, Alec decided. He tried on the thought of Parks as provisional ally; decided it was still too early to tell. He turned back to the prison officer still hovering in the doorway.

'Care to give me the tour?' he asked, noting the slight look of annoyance that replaced puzzlement in Parks' expression. Alec wondered at the cause: because he didn't want Alec to go off alone? Or simply that he did not want to be stuck with the taciturn Travers? Used to an easygoing man who chatted easily to anyone, Alec was still flummoxed by Travers' sudden descent into silence and sulks.

He followed the prison officer back out into the main body of the accommodation block.

'This was an old army base,' the officer told Alec. 'The huts date back to the fifties, but the whole lot was renovated when the base closed in the eighties.'

Looking at the state of the decor, Alec decided very little had been done since.

'This is the main recreation area.' The man indicated the open space. Chairs, small tables screwed down to the floor, a half-sized pool table and table football that looked, from its vintage, as though the army might have left them behind. A dozen men presently inhabited this space; the rest were already out on work detail, the prison officer said. These others were about to join them.

'Neil Robinson have particular friends, did he?'

'He was close to one Freddie Gains. Armed robbery – Gains was the driver – but he left us a month before Robinson died.'

'Did he have many visitors?'

The officer shook his head. 'His sister came when she could, but she's got a young family and lives in Wales, I think. Somewhere that way. She spoke to him on the phone once a week, and I think her husband had a job lined up for Robinson. The rest of the family had given up on him, but she still did her best.'

'Think it would have worked? The job, I mean?'

The officer shrugged. 'Maybe,' he said. 'Robinson seemed excited about getting back to his family, I know that. Then about a week before he died he seemed ... I don't know. Anxious. Jumpy.'

'Anyone ask him why?'

Again, the shrug. 'I think we thought he was just a bit overwhelmed. It can happen when the release date gets close.'

'Anyone he might have confided in?'

'After Gains had gone, no, I don't think so. Robinson got along with most people, in that he knew how and when to keep out of the way. He played pool most evenings.'

'Any friction there?'

'No, not that I'm aware. Your colleagues have already asked all this.'

'I'm sure they have,' Alec said. 'Thanks, then, I'll not take up any more of your time.' He watched as the officer joined two of his colleagues and the knot of prisoners waiting to leave for their work. All looked at him with varying degrees of hostility and curiosity as they left, but only one met his eyes. A young man, tall, freckled, sandy-haired, who contrived to bring up the rear and dropped something to the floor at Alec's feet.

Little seemed to have changed when Alec returned to Robinson's room. Parks was poking aimlessly at the few paperbacks on the shelf, and Travers now perched on the window sill, looking back into the room instead of out of the window. Other than that, the frosty silence remained.

Alec moved to take a closer look at the bookshelves. Tattered paperbacks, mostly of the variety written by ex special forces, interspersed with the odd crime novel and, more surprisingly, ten slim volumes that Alec discovered were classic westerns by the likes of Zane Grey and Louis L'Amour. Alec had gone through a phase of reading these when he'd been just a kid, and the books looked to be of around the same vintage. Curious, he picked a couple off the shelf and flipped them open. Inside the flyleaf of each the same name was neatly printed.

'Eric Robinson?' he asked.

'Neil's dad,' Parks told him. 'The sister sent him the books,' he added.

Thoughtfully, Alec flicked through the pages. The old paperbacks were in excellent condition. Read, yes, but loved and cherished. He knew they would already have checked, but could not resist riffling the pages to ensure that nothing had been hidden, skimming the text for comments written in the margins or on the fly-leaves. Nothing.

'We already did that,' Parks said.

'Force of habit,' Alec told him. He pulled out the drawers and rummaged through Robinson's meagre possessions, but there was little apart from spare clothes.

'What did you think of him?' Parks asked.

'Robinson?'

'You interviewed him.'

'Yes. At length. What did I think of him?' Alec frowned. 'My main impression was that a man like Robinson could have taken any path he wanted, so I couldn't understand why he'd chosen the one he did. He was highly intelligent, personable, seemed to have a moral code, of sorts. I mean, he didn't pick on anyone who couldn't afford to lose.'

Parks laughed, mockingly. 'So he was a better class of criminal because he didn't try and rip off little old ladies?'

Alec nodded. 'Yes,' he said. 'I suppose I did think that.' Truthfully, under different circumstances, Alec could have liked the man, but he didn't share that impression with Parks.

'Alec's moral compass has always pointed northwest,' Travers growled.

Surprised, they both turned to look at him. 'And what did you think of Robinson?' Parks asked.

'That he had no excuse,' Travers said. 'He had a good brain, came from a stable home. No one pushed him into it. Like Alec said, he could have done something with his life. Instead, he chose to rip people off. Robinson was a turd.'

Parks cocked an eyebrow and pursed the cherub lips. 'So a slight difference of opinion there, folks,' he said, clearly amused.

Alec frowned, puzzled by this sudden animation from his boss and also by the comment. So far as Alec could recall, Travers had only met Robinson the once, when he had sat in on a final interview.

'So we can tell them to pack his stuff up now?' he said, more for want of something to say than because it was relevant.

'If you've finished looking,' Parks agreed. 'The governor wants to see us all before we go, once Munroe's finished briefing her.'

'Briefing her?' Alec asked. 'What about?'

Parks shrugged and wandered out into the rec room. Alec watched him go and then turned on Travers. 'What the hell is up with you?'

No response.

'Oh, for Christ sake, Trav, stop behaving like a sulky toddler and talk to me.'

Travers opened his mouth, and for a moment Alec expected a reprimand: a reminder that Travers was senior officer here and Alec should watch his mouth. He would almost have welcomed that. At least it would have been a response of sorts. Instead, he shut his mouth and shook his head. 'We'll talk later,' he said. 'I'm sorry, Alec, you're right, I am behaving like a prize prat.'

The sudden climb-down caught Alec off guard, and he wondered if his boss was just placating him. If the *later* would actually happen. 'We'd better,' he said angrily. 'Trav, I don't have a clue what this is all about, but it's spilling over in ways I really don't like.'

Travers frowned. 'What do you mean?'

'I mean it's involving Naomi, and I won't have that.'

'Naomi? How?' The sulky look was gone now, replaced by instant concern.

Alec glanced out into the rec room. Parks was chatting to one of the officers across on the far side of the room. Quickly, he filled Travers in on the events of the night before and the recorded phone call from Jamie Dale. Watching his boss's face, he saw the concern replaced by shock.

'Is she *OK*? Alec, if you want to go home—'

'She says she's all right and I'm to stay. I'll go along with that for now, but if you know more about this setup than you've said so far then you tell me. You owe me that.'

Travers hesitated, then nodded. 'We'll talk later,' he reiterated. 'Alec, I'm not—' He broke off as Parks wandered back into the room. Behind him stood a prison officer carrying a couple of cardboard boxes.

'You all done here?' Parks asked. 'I've told them if you have then they can pack Robinson's things away. His sister wants them back.'

'We're done,' Travers said. And Alec concurred. There was nothing here – not now. Anything relevant was long gone. Apart, maybe, from the whatever it was that the prisoner had dropped at his feet before he left on the work detail. Alec felt in his pocket, trying to discern what it might be from the size and shape. A small slip of card with a fold in it. He had glanced swiftly at it before pocketing it, and, judging from the blue and white print, it had been torn, he guessed, from a cigarette pack. He knew he should say something – and now, while there was still a chance of speaking directly to the man – but instinct told him that would be a bad thing: certainly for the tall, cropped-haired prisoner who had dropped the slip of paper, and maybe for others too. Alec could not shake the sense of unease and wrongness about this whole setup, or the feeling that he should tell Munroe and company to stuff their investigation, and then go home.

SIX

They were shown into Michelle Sanders' little office. Alec took in the scene: Munroe sitting opposite the prison governor, across a light wood desk that had certainly seen better days and on which a tray and coffee mugs had been set.

Munroe looked relaxed, leaning back in his chair and smiling as they entered. The governor, small and, Alec guessed, in her late forties, stood up and reached across to shake hands. She looked annoyed, Alec thought. Irritated, and trying to hide it; she wasn't doing a very good job. Munroe, he observed, seemed to have that effect on people.

He studied the prison governor with interest. Michelle Sanders had short fair hair with touches of grey showing at the temples and creases round her eyes seeming to indicate that she smiled often. No wedding ring, but an expensive watch. Alec liked watches and identified a Patek Philippe. She was dressed almost casually in black trousers and a lilac shirt, untucked. Closer analysis told him that both items were tailored, fitted and in good quality fabrics that required little embellishment. She indicated that they should sit down, the plastic chairs the same as Alec had seen throughout the prison and which had obviously been hastily assembled. Close packed in the small room, it made for an intimate experience. Travers, last in, chose to stand by the door.

'I'm not sure what more I can tell you,' Michelle Sanders said as she directed them to help themselves to coffee. 'Neil Robinson's death was a tragedy. He was a success story, someone who might have had a future, and the Lord knows we see few enough of those go out through the gates.'

'You sound as though you are taking his death personally,' Alec said.

'And why shouldn't I? Every success here is hard won.'

'And it must irk you to know the poison that killed him was probably prepared here. In the prison.'

'What do you mean?' Michelle demanded.

Yes, what *do* you mean, Alec wondered, looking at Munroe; this was news to him too.

'The tox report came through an hour ago. I had it sent to my phone. He died of nicotine poisoning, administered via a syringe. It only takes half a pack of smokes to get enough to kill.'

She stared at him. 'Then there will be an investigation.'

'The team will arrive later today,' Munroe confirmed.

'I meant an internal investigation.'

'And I remind you that this is a murder enquiry.'

'And I'm sure Michelle will be cooperative,' Eddison said.

There was a brief pause. Stand-off.

Alec broke it. 'I know you've already talked to my colleagues,' he said, 'but if you wouldn't mind me asking a few questions?'

She sighed. 'Go ahead.'

'Visitors. I understand he didn't have any?'

'His sister came three times; his brother-in-law came alone, once. Apparently, he had a business trip that brought him this way, and Robinson's sister had sent some books over. He came, dropped the books off and saw Robinson briefly. She called him once a week, and I believe he only ever used his phone privileges to call her.'

'So his contact with the reporter, Jamie Dale—'

'Was made via the sister, I believe. He certainly didn't call her from here; the calls are all logged.'

'Recorded?'

A withering look from the governor. 'This is an open prison. The last stop before freedom. Some measure of privacy has to be permitted.'

'Of course,' Alec said. 'Did he have close friends here? Enemies? Did he cross anyone?'

She leaned back in her chair. 'You lot obviously don't talk to one another,' she observed. 'The only person he seemed to get close to was Frederick Gains. They came here at the same time, but Gains left a month ago. He sent Robinson postcards, and I assume they planned to meet up when Robinson got out.'

'Postcards?'

'Which seem to have walked,' Munroe said heavily.

'When?'

'It seems no one can tell us that.' Munroe again. Across the desk, Michelle Sanders glared at him.

'What was Gains in for?' Alec asked. Parks had told him, but, perversely perhaps, he wanted to hear it from the governor.

'He was the getaway driver in an armed robbery. Had a record of petty theft and burglary as long as your arm. Driving was a step up the career ladder for Gains.'

'Short ladder,' Munroe said.

'Quite.' The governor's tone was icy.

'And has he been in touch since? He must have seen Robinson's death reported.'

'So far as we know, not. He wasn't close to any of the other inmates. Gains was an oddball; Robinson looked out for him.'

'Oddball?'

The governor shrugged. 'Bright, though you would never know it to look at him.'

'Does any of this matter?' Munroe said. 'It's all in the files, Alec. You can have access as soon as we leave here.' He stood. 'Now, if there's nothing else, we can leave these good people to get on with their work.'

Michelle Sanders stood too, obviously glad to

be seeing them off the premises.

Alec did not move. There was an uncomfortable silence as they all stared at him. 'Enemies,' Alec asked again, as though there had been no interruption. 'Did Robinson cross anyone while he was here?'

The governor's hands rested on the top of her desk. They clenched now, curling into fists. 'He kept a low profile,' she said stiffly. 'The other inmates in Accommodation Block Three were also close to release; none had a particular history of violence. It isn't the place you usually get trouble.'

'Usually?' Alec asked casually.

Michelle Sanders sighed in exasperation. 'Look,' she said. 'Robinson was an educated man. Something of a snob at times. He rubbed a few people up the wrong way, but nothing came of it beyond the odd bad-tempered spat and a bit of conflict over a game of pool. Gains was a hustler, played like a pro; it could cause a bit of friction.'

'So you've told me what the flashpoints were regarding Freddie Gains,' Alec observed. 'What was Robinson's tipping point? Or rather, what was the tipping point regarding Robinson and the rest?'

'There wasn't one,' Michelle Sanders told him coldly. 'As I said earlier, Robinson was a model prisoner. He was a potential success story.'

'Whose superior attitude caused offence sometimes? We all know that what might seem like a small spat, as you call it, in the outside world can fester in a place like this. I've seen men knifed because they used a word someone didn't understand and it was misread as an insult.'

'Nothing like that happened here,' Michelle Sanders asserted. The hands relaxed now, and so did her tone. So he'd moved too wide of the mark, Alec thought.

'Enough, now,' Munroe said. 'We've taken up enough time. Michelle, thank you, we'll get ourselves out of your hair.'

She looked relieved, Alec thought. For that matter, so did Travers.

Alec stood up, prepared to go, shifting position so he could see both his boss and the prison governor. Travers held out his hand, and Michelle Sanders shook it automatically, but Alec was watching her face. The anxiety was unmistakable, as was the question in her eyes when she looked at his boss.

Travers shook her hand and turned away, and Munroe hustled them out of the door.

Naomi had spent the day with her sister, attending Sue's first antenatal class with her and then going for lunch at a local pub they both liked.

'I don't know why I bother with the classes,' Sue said. 'I mean, this is the third time, I should know what I'm doing by now.'

'Habit,' Naomi told her. 'It's what you did before, so you're going through the same process now. Habit is reassuring.'

'Are you analysing me?' Sue laughed at her older sister. 'You could be right,' she admitted.

'You going back to work after?'

'Oh, I think so. Just part time, like I'm doing now. The agency said they'd be happy to have me back, and several of their clients ask for me by name now, so that's good. Though I had a chat with Harry, did he tell you?'

Naomi shook her head. 'What about?'

'Oh, the whole self-employed thing. School holidays are a nightmare and are not going to get better until this new one is old enough to look after herself.'

'Herself??'

'Or himself. I just think this one is a girl. It feels different, somehow.'

'Are you going to ask when you have the scan?'

'Um, don't know. We keep talking about it but can't decide if we'd rather know or if we like the surprise. Anyway, working from home might be a good idea, don't you think?'

'What would you do?'

'Ah, that's the thing. It's going to take a bit of thinking through. Did Alec tell you when he'd be back?'

'No, he hopes only a couple of days.'

'You *OK* in that big house on your own? I can move the boys into the same room and you can stop over for a day or two.'

Naomi was tempted. The thought of returning to what she usually regarded as her sanctuary was unnerving her. She loved the house she now shared with Alec, but after the events of the previous evening, she also felt as though it had been invaded, her sanctuary violated.

'I'll let you know,' she promised. 'We're all going to Patrick's exhibition tonight, so I might stay over with them or with Mari.' Mari was Harry's mother.

They left it at that and conversation moved to other things. Usually, Naomi reflected, she would have confided in her sister, but today – which was all about the celebration of new life and new plans – it seemed inappropriate. She was desperate not to spoil the mood or to cause Sue anxiety – though she also knew that Sue was going to be furious with her if this all came out later and she discovered that Naomi had been keeping important and potentially threatening things quiet. The sisters had always been close, and since Naomi had been blinded, Sue and her family had given her so much strength.

Resolving to talk to Harry first, Naomi let the matter lie. Later though, having taken a taxi home from her sister's house, the anxiety seemed to escalate, and when they pulled up in front of the house, Naomi almost asked her driver to turn around and take her back. George Mallard, the taxi driver, was an old friend. His family had run the small taxi company she regularly used for years.

'George, do you mind helping me in with the shopping?'

'Course I don't, my dear. Everything all right, is it?'

She managed a laugh. 'Yes. Why?'

'Because you've been very quiet today. Not yourself, if I may say so.'

'I suppose it's with Alec being away.'

'He's been away before,' George Mallard said pointedly. 'Naomi, if you're worried, there are people you can tell, you know that.'

'George?' Naomi questioned. 'This sounds more than speculation.'

George Mallard laughed. 'Got me there,' he admitted. 'Look, he meant no harm, but the wife's cousin's boy, he joined the police just under a year ago.'

'PC Watkins,' Naomi guessed.

'That'll be the one. Anyway, he happened to mention he'd been over at your place last night, knowing as how we know you. He knows we're fond of you, you see, and the wife, she thought ... well, she thought I should make sure you were all right.'

Naomi laughed. Unexpectedly, she found tears pricking at the corners of her eyes. 'Thanks, George,' she said. 'It's kind of you all, and he seems like a nice young man. And yes, I'd be grateful if you'd go in with me, just have a quick look around.'

Inside the house all was very quiet and very still. George did a circuit, checking the windows and the doors and looking out into the garden. 'Looks like you've got a couple of messages,' he said as they returned to the hall and Naomi prepared to say goodbye. She felt her stomach tighten.

'Probably just Alec,' she said, even though she knew that Alec would call her mobile and not the home phone. Few people did; all her friends knew that she kept her mobile close to hand almost all the time.

'You want me to...?'

'Thanks, George, I think I'd like that.' She pressed the button to replay the messages, but was met with only two dense blocks of silence.

George came over and pressed 1471. *Number not known*, they were told.

'Naomi, maybe it would be better if I took you back to your Sue's.'

She shook her head. 'I'm not going to be scared out of my home, George,' she told him firmly. 'Anyway, Harry will be here soon. I'm going to Patrick's exhibition. I'll be fine.' He'll be on the phone to Watkins as soon as he leaves here, she thought. The idea soothed her a little, but she still made double sure that the door was locked when George Mallard finally left and the silence of the empty house settled around her.

More silence as Alec and Travers drove back to their hotel. Alec had spent the day looking over Robinson's files, briefing Parks, Munroe and the now returned Eddison on the Robinson affair as he had seen it from his angle and looking at background information on Freddie Gains. Travers had said little. He had set to work collating information, creating databases both on the board and on the computer, busying himself with tasks Mac doubted he'd done since he'd been a sergeant in uniform. He'd done a good job, Alec admitted grudgingly, but it had not escaped any of them that Travers was doing anything and everything that did not involve him in direct interaction with his colleagues.

'So,' Alec asked him when they were finally alone. 'You know Michelle Sanders then?'

'And you think that, why?'

He hadn't denied it, Alec noted. 'The way the pair of you were deliberately trying to give the impression this was the first time you'd set eyes on one another.'

Travers laughed; a rare sound in the past few days. *'OK*, Alec. Yes, Michelle and I knew one another. Emphasis very strongly on the past tense. It was a long time ago.'

'Knew? In the Biblical sense? This before Maureen, was it?'

'Is that your business, Alec?' He sounded weary rather than annoyed.

'I don't know yet, do I?'

Travers sighed. 'There was some overlap,' he admitted. 'Maureen took a long time to understand just how demanding the job could be. In the early days I was never at home, and when I was we rowed about the fact, so—'

'So you went home even less.' Alec was familiar with the pattern. 'Where did you meet? Another bloody conference?'

'Actually, yes, it was. Eddison was there too,' he added. 'He was just another delegate, not a speaker. This was years ago. We were looking into computerization, use of databases across the police network. You know how much of a mess it all was to start with.'

Alec nodded. Computer systems had been set up piecemeal, really only getting any kind of priority in the late eighties, early nineties, and even quite recently there had been no truly centralized system. It took the deaths of two children and several other rather high-profile cases for a proper network covering all police forces and all levels to get prioritized.

'So you and Michelle Sanders were involved, and Eddison knew about it.'

'Yes, he knew.'

'And he made it his business, why?'

'Because that's what Eddison does,' Travers said bitterly. 'He collects the scraps and leavings from people's lives, and he stores them up just for the day when they might be valuable enough to make trouble.'

Alec looked sharply at his boss. 'Are we talking blackmail here?'

'What? Oh, not in the money sense, no. Nothing as crude as that. Eddison goes for the jugular in a far more subtle way, but once he has something he'll use it.'

'And he's used this affair against you how?'

'It wasn't an affair,' Travers snapped.

'So what was it then?'

Travers shrugged. 'It's hard to explain,' he said.

'Try me.'

Travers fell silent again. They had reached the hotel, and Alec knew he had missed his chance. Still, this was progress, of a sort. 'Meet you in the restaurant? Say, an hour?'

'Maybe.'

'You've got to eat.'

Travers nodded reluctantly. 'An hour, then. Have you called Naomi yet?'

'She spent the day with her sister, and she's out tonight with Harry and Patrick. I'll talk to her again later.'

'And she's all right?'

'Shaken, but she's all right, yes. Trav, why didn't we tell our esteemed colleagues about the phone calls? You can't pretend it's not relevant.'

'And I will, tomorrow,' Travers promised. 'Alec, trust me on this, there's someone I want to speak to first.'

Alec hesitated. 'This is Naomi we're talking about. Trav, if—'

'I know. I'd not risk anything happening to her, you know that.'

He got out of the car, and Alec had no option but to follow suit and then to follow in his wake as Travers stalked across the car park and into the hotel.

SEVEN

Naomi was ready to go out again long before Harry and Patrick arrived. She had made herself a sandwich and a cup of tea, and had showered and changed, all the time listening out far too intently for anything unusual, any sound that did not belong in her home. Listening so hard that she realized she was actually imagining things. Eventually, angry and impatient with such wimpishness, she grabbed a CD from the rock section of their considerable music collection and put it on. The sound of Bruce Springsteen filled the house, singing about hungry hearts and oversized motor bikes, and she sang along, defiantly and tunelessly – holding a tune was, she freely admitted, not among her accomplishments.

By the time Harry rang the bell and then tried the usually unlatched door, she was sitting on the stairs, waiting, Napoleon's head resting against her knee.

He rang the bell again as she crossed the hall. 'Naomi, it's us! The door was locked,' he added as she opened it and bent to fuss the dog.

'Yes, sorry, I forgot to undo it for you. All set then? Is Patrick nervous?'

'I think he is, rather. Is everything all right?'
'No, not really,' she admitted. 'But we'll talk about that later, if you don't mind. Let's not spoil Patrick's evening.'
'Naomi?'
'It's all right, Harry, we'll talk about this later. Promise. In fact, is it *OK* if I stay the night?'
'You know it is. Is that your bag?'
She could hear the concern in his voice, but knew also that he'd put it aside until she was ready to talk. She locked the door behind her, heard Harry check it – not because he didn't trust her to do it properly, but because that was what Harry did – then he helped her into the car. Napoleon, sensing that this was not a formal outing, was already in the back with Patrick.
'All set then,' Harry said. 'Cameras at the ready? Right, off we go.'

Alec had sat for some time in the restaurant, waiting for Travers to arrive. Finally, he had given up and ordered dinner, irritated with his boss, but not really surprised that he had not shown up. Who, Alec wondered, was the mysterious someone he'd needed to call before talking to Alec about his affair with Michelle Sanders? Alec was angry with himself, too; he should have pressed the point.
He probably should have mentioned the note slipped to him by the inmate at the prison too. Alec slipped it from his pocket now; he had sealed it in an evidence bag, but was still none the wiser as to the significance of this little slip

of card, torn from a cigarette packet. Like as not, he thought, it was a wind up, a laugh at his expense. Or had been dropped accidentally and would turn out to be the phone number of a girlfriend or some such.

That it was a phone number, Alec now knew. He'd dialled it from his hotel room, though there had been no reply, the phone just ringing out into emptiness. A local number, he thought; there had been no dialling code. Alec was still not even sure why he had failed to tell someone about it back at the prison. Simple dislike of his new colleagues? Maybe so, but that was still a deeply unprofessional attitude to have.

As unprofessional as Travers not mentioning the phone call Naomi had received, though that too, he felt, had been driven by the same ill-defined motivation.

It was a stupid attitude, Alec decided in the end. It had to stop.

A text from Patrick told him that they had collected Naomi and he should stand by for photos. Alec smiled, then frowned in irritation as he thought where he'd rather be tonight. Certainly not here, three hours away from home and effectively car-less.

Finally, irritation now at maximum, he returned to the reception in the motel and then went in search of Travers.

The reception area and restaurant were central to two long arms, two stories high, that stretched out and then folded back, forming three sides of a quadrangle, surrounding a garden area with an empty pond and bleached wooden seats. The fourth side was taken up with a second car park – marked staff only – and then gave on to scrubby woodland and neglected grass. Alec's room was in the left-hand arm on the first floor; Travers had been given a room on the opposite side, on the ground. Long corridors, with views looking out on to the unkempt garden, led to the guest rooms, the windows of which faced out on to neater lawns and the main car parks. Alec's afforded him a glimpse of the all-night services and the motorway beyond.

Alec knocked on Travers' door and, receiving no response, called out to his boss. 'Trav, it's Alec. You were supposed to meet me in the restaurant. Travers? Look, you've got to eat sometime. Trav, let me in.'

Still no response. Something was wrong; Alec could sense it.

He made his way back to the reception, checking on the way that Travers' car was still parked outside, then asked the girl at the desk if she'd seen DCI Travers go out. Alec knew that the fact they were both police officers had intrigued her when they'd checked in; he'd lay bets on her recalling every time either one of them had passed her desk.

'No, sorry. I saw you go to the restaurant, but I've not seen your friend since you both came back. Is something the matter?'

'Could you try calling his room?'

The girl frowned. 'Sure.'

Standing in the lobby, Alec could hear the

phone ring out, but Travers did not reply. The sense of unease was growing, moment by moment. 'Do you have a pass key?' he asked.

'No, only the duty manager—' Her eyes widened. '*Is* there something wrong?' she asked him again, her tone worried now, Alec's anxiety contagious.

'Can you get the manager, please? I'll wait outside the room. Number Fifty-One G.'

She nodded and was picking up the phone to make the call as Alec strode back out of the lobby. He was probably imagining things, Alec told himself. Trav had gone to sleep or left the motel when the girl at reception wasn't looking, or he was deliberately ignoring Alec.

The sense of dread now deep in his stomach told him Travers had done none of those things.

Back outside his room, Alec hammered on Travers' door again. Further down the corridor a man looked out of his own room and shouted at Alec to keep it down. Alec glared at him and the man ducked back inside.

'Please,' another voice said. 'Is it really necessary to disturb the other guests?'

Alec turned his attention to this new speaker, saw the duty manager, pass key in hand, regarding him with a mix of puzzlement and annoyance.

'Sorry,' Alec mumbled automatically. 'If I could have the key, please.'

The manager hesitated, then something in Alec's expression seemed to change his mind. He handed the swipe card over and then stepped back, as if to get out of range of whatever was behind that bland wooden door.

Alec took a deep breath and swiped the card. He'll be asleep, Alec told himself. Fallen asleep and I'll feel like a complete idiot. He swung the door wide and swore softly. 'Call an ambulance.'

'What!' The manager peered cautiously around the open door and then stepped back hurriedly. 'Oh my God, oh my God.'

'Call an ambulance,' Alec said again, though instinct and experience suggested it was far too late for that. Travers lay on the floor beside the bed, eyes open, his right hand reaching for something and—

So much blood, Alec thought. He had interviewed several finders of bodies during his career, and that phrase had been one he had heard many times. People saw the blood first, amplified the amount of it. Told him, even if the wound had bled little or been largely out of sight. *Oh God, there was so much blood...*

Alec thought it now, but he had no need to exaggerate. Travers was covered in it, the carpet sticky with it. Knowing he should stay back, wait for the medics to arrive, knowing he was interfering – probably needlessly – with a crime scene and that Travers was likely beyond anything he could do, Alec still went into the room and knelt beside his friend.

EIGHT

Past nine o clock, and the ambulance had long since driven from the scene. Eddison had arrived half an hour before, and Parks and Munroe had followed shortly after. Alec had called them, not knowing what else to do, and found he was pathetically grateful at the sight of familiar faces, despite his misgivings about these new colleagues.

Eddison had taken charge, managing the scene. 'You touched nothing else?' he asked again, his voice quiet and calm and surprisingly gentle.

Alec shook his head. 'I saw him lying there. I was sure he'd gone, but I needed to – I thought there might be something I could do.'

Eddison touched his arm. 'Any of us would have done the same,' he said. 'The human reaction takes over: we do what we feel, not what we know we should.'

Alec nodded. 'I knelt down there, and I touched his hand. Nothing else. When I left the room I back-tracked as near as I could remember.'

Eddison nodded. 'Good, good.' That verbal tick again. Alec hadn't noticed it so much that day. 'Go and get changed, get cleaned up. Then come back here to me.'

Alec nodded, suddenly horribly aware of the wet patches on his knees where he had knelt beside Travers. Knelt on carpet soaked with his boss's blood. He escaped to his room, closed the door and stood just inside the entrance, listening as though suddenly afraid that whoever had attacked Travers might also come for him.

'Stupid,' he told himself. 'Stupid.' But he still checked the locks on the windows and the latch on the door before going into the tiny bathroom.

He showered. The *CSI* manager had given him bags for his clothes. Gingerly, he emptied pockets and slipped the bloodied clothes and shoes inside. How often had he explained to those first witnesses on scene that they might have picked up something significant on their clothes and shoes as they bent over the body, that it was just procedure? How often had he heard them tell him, shamefacedly, that it made them feel like a criminal, handing their clothes over like this? He tried to shake that same thought now, but found he could empathize. It made him feel somehow unclean, blood on his clothes and shoes, those same clothes and shoes slipped now into evidence bags.

Dressed, and a little more composed, he carried the bags back into the reception, handed them over to the young woman responsible for collating and listing the evidence. He watched as she sealed and labelled his possessions and then got him to sign the forms, stating when and what he had handed over. Chain of evidence, Alec thought as he confirmed the time of hand-over and placed his initials beside hers. Then he returned to Travers' room. Eddison glanced up as he entered; he was crouched down beside one of the *CSI*s.

'Found something?' Alec was surprised but relieved that he sounded almost normal.

Eddison straightened up. 'A scrap of paper,' he said. 'When DCI Travers fell, it was trapped under his body. It looks as though our assailant tried to retrieve whatever it was, but a torn fragment got left behind. Cindy here's been trying to get it off the carpet without it falling to bits.'

Alec fought the desire to go closer. 'Any idea what it is?'

Addison shook his head. 'Whoever it was, they escaped out of the window,' he said.

Alec nodded. He had surmised as much.

'They left blood smears; likely, they were covered in it. Someone will have seen them. We've got people looking at the *CCTV* footage now. The way I see it, Travers left you at, what, six thirty?'

'More like six fifteen. I arrived at the restaurant at seven ten. I deliberately got there a few minutes early. I waited twenty minutes or so then thought – then thought bugger him, I'm hungry even if he isn't, and assumed he wasn't going to show. I ordered, ate and then came here.'

'What time would that have been?'

'I looked at my watch when I left the restaurant. It was twenty past eight.'

Eddison nodded. 'So, we've got a window of about two hours, give or take, though likely later rather than earlier. He had to have let them in. Smears of blood on the window lock indicate they unfastened it on the way out, so we can assume it was fastened when his attacker arrived. Did he say he was expecting anyone?'

'No,' Alec said. 'He mentioned a phone call he had to make.'

'He say who to?'

Alec shook his head. 'I think it might have been a personal call,' he said, suddenly reluctant to report the content of his last conversation with Travers to the man Trav had virtually accused of blackmailing him. His affair with Michelle Sanders could have no bearing on this. Surely.

'Right. Parks is in the lobby. The two of you go and get a cup of coffee, and you make your statement, then find that receptionist and the three of you start looking at the *CCTV* cameras in the lobby for the relevant period. Hopefully, she'll be able to tell you for certain who is a guest and who she doesn't recognize.'

'It might have *been* a guest,' Alec said absently.

'In which case, they'll still be here. Which I doubt.'

Ten o'clock, and Alec's phone vibrated. He glanced at the text as he walked back to the lobby to find Parks. It was from Patrick.

Alec paused to look at the pictures Patrick had sent of a long space that Alec recognized as the college assembly hall, now broken into discreet sections by large wooden screens. Patrick's display was on the wall at the far end. His pictures stood out from the rest, inspired in part by the graphic novels he loved so much, but with additions that Alec had not seen before. Alec scrolled through the images, glad of the momentary distraction, paying particular attention to these new scenes. There were two large landscapes, or, rather, cityscapes. One was vaguely familiar, but it took a moment or two to realize that this was a pastiche of Hopper's Nighthawks, the usually empty street now crammed with a procession of strange characters in carnival dress. It was painted not in Patrick's usual graphic style, but with a freedom and exuberance of brushstrokes that seemed to echo Hopper's.

The second was a place Alec recognized. A local view of the canal basin close to where Patrick and Harry lived and Naomi had grown up. The warehouses and quay were roughly as Alec remembered them, but the narrowboats usually docked in the safe harbour had been replaced by strange, ghostly seagoing galleons and tall ships, all crewed by what looked at first glance to be figures in historic costume. It was hard to tell from the rather low-resolution images on his mobile phone, but Alec was sure that, on closer inspection, none of the figures looked exactly human.

For a long time, Harry had worried about his son, seeing his somewhat weird art as unnatural and even an indicator that all was not well with Patrick's head. True, Alec thought, Patrick's work was as weird as it had ever been, but even to his untrained eye, it was evident that there was real skill here and an original if bizarre imagination at work. Patrick himself was one of the nicest and most balanced people Alec could think of – for all that life experience might have mitigated against that.

Sighing, Alec dragged himself back to present thoughts and immediate problems. He found Parks in the lobby and relayed Eddison's instructions.

'We've just heard from DCI Travers' wife,' Parks told him. 'She's on her way. I think a friend is driving her over.'

Alec closed his eyes. 'God, poor Maureen,' he said.

'You know her well?'

'Not really. She liked to keep her home life as separate from Trav's work as she could. Not that it was always possible, but, you know...'

Parks nodded. 'It's hard on families,' he said. 'My missus was an army brat, dragged all over the shop depending on where her dad was stationed, and even then she didn't see him for months on end. She reckons being a policeman's wife is a doddle compared to that.'

They settled themselves in the corner of the now almost deserted restaurant. It was officially closed, but the manager and a couple of the catering staff had stayed on to provide refreshments for whoever might need them in the hours to come, and Alec knew that was a very welcome decision. An informal base of operations had been set up, *CSI*s using one corner of the room to store their equipment and deliver their evidence to the collator. An officer close by prepared a space in which he could take witness statements from anyone in the rooms on Travers' corridor. By tacit agreement, Parks and Alec took their drinks across to the far side of the restaurant and settled at a table close to the window. Alec looked out at the still busy car park between them and the motorway services. Lights had come on, though it was still not completely dark, the year still building towards the longest day later in the month and the blueness of the summer sky not yet completely banished by what passed for dusk beyond the yellow of the sodium lamps.

'So–' Parks sat with his pen poised – 'where should we start? You'd arranged to meet DCI Travers?'

'Yes.' Alec hesitated. 'Travers hadn't been very happy about being here, about any of it. For that matter neither am I. It doesn't make sense.' He looked at Parks, waiting for the man to rise to the challenge.

Parks shrugged. 'I just go where I'm told, do my job, go home.'

'And who assigned you to this particular job? And why are you operating like a completely separate unit? Why is there no liaison with the locals?'

'I'm local,' Parks objected. He regarded Alec thoughtfully for a moment and then said, 'Yes, it's all a bit weird, and yes, we're not exactly keeping to the usual procedure, but Eddison says there's cause, and Eddison is the boss. Eddison, in turn, has been authorized by fuck knows who from who the hell knows where. Alec, sometimes it's best not to ask too many questions – not when you know no bugger's going to give you a straight response anyway.'

'And that doesn't bother you?'

'Ah, now, I never said that.' Parks glanced back towards the hotel reception, as though talking about his boss might be enough to make him appear.

'We both know that Eddison is just a front man here,' Alec pressed. 'It's Munroe who's calling the shots.'

Parks tapped his pen on the sheaf of paper in front of him. 'I just do my job and keep my mouth shut,' he said firmly. 'Alec, truthfully, I don't know what's going on, but I do know I'm glad my wife and kids are away just now. Let's just leave it at that, shall we?'

Alec scowled, shook his head. 'What are you afraid of?' he asked.

Parks hesitated but did not give a direct response to Alec's question. Instead, he said, 'Eddison told me Robinson was an informant. He'd got wind of something ... *political*, and he'd negotiated an early release on the strength of it and provided he agreed to disappear quietly afterwards and keep his mouth shut. But it looked like he was going to renege on that part of the deal as soon as he got out; that he'd suddenly realized he could get more out of it than a few months off his sentence. Munroe thinks this Jamie Dale was going to buy his story, that whatever it was he was going to tell her, well, someone got wind of it and didn't want it getting out.'

Alec frowned. Parks was obviously not comfortable with the explanation, but didn't know Alec well enough to express those doubts. From Alec's point of view, it didn't make sense. What early release? Robinson would have just about done his time anyway by now. 'Didn't want what getting out?'

'Ah, well, if we all knew that ... Look, Alec, I'm working in the dark too, and I've come to the considered conclusion that I'd probably like to keep it that way. Whatever it is Neil Robinson knew, it cost him. Whatever he told, or was going to tell, this Dale woman, it cost her. And now Travers.'

'Travers didn't know anything.'

'Didn't he?'

Alec shook his head. 'Travers was away on secondment when we broke the Robinson case. He came back at the very end of things, sat in on one of the interviews, but that was all. Robinson, so far as we were concerned, was a con artist. He ran insurance and investment scams. We got him on what we could, handed the case files over to the fraud squad.'

'And why exactly did you do that?'

'We didn't have the resources, or the skills, for the paperchase. God, he had fingers in more pies than he had fingers. It was like – like he got bored; if something was too easy, Robinson lost interest and shifted to the next big thing. We reckoned if he'd actually had the staying power to see any one thing through he'd have been a multimillionaire, but he just seemed to ... fizzle out.'

'Well, maybe he didn't fizzle out on whatever he was going to sell to Jamie Dale,' Parks said. 'Maybe this was one move too big and too far. Someone wanted to shut him up, and shut him up they did. Your reporter friend too, and now this.'

Alec nodded. He took a deep breath and did what he knew he and Travers should have done hours before. 'Naomi got a phone call last night,' he said. 'It was a recording of Jamie Dale's voice.'

Parks stared at him. 'Last night,' he said.

'I know, I know. I thought we should tell you about it, but Travers said to wait. I don't know why. It was like he was trying to work something out first.' Alec shook his head, no longer sure what Travers had been trying to do. 'Look, he's my boss, and I suppose—'

'You thought you'd keep your mouth shut, do your job and go home,' Parks said. He sighed, shaking his head. 'Look, Alec, Eddison isn't going to be a happy chappie, and neither is

Munroe, so how about we backtrack to last night and get this all on paper now?'

Alec nodded, still far from sure about Parks and the others but also relieved to be sharing the burden with someone. For the next hour they catalogued events as Alec knew them, starting with the call Naomi had got and then moving on to this present evening. There was not, Alec thought, very much to tell.

Munroe appeared in the midst of this. 'It seems the person Travers tried to call was Michelle Sanders,' he said. 'He got through to her voicemail but only left a message for her to call him.'

'Why would he call her?' Parks wondered.

Alec hesitated. 'They were involved, once upon a time,' he said. 'Maybe ... I don't know.'

'Right.' Munroe frowned but did not pursue the line of conversation. 'How's the statement coming?'

'Longer than we thought it'd be,' Parks said heavily.

'How so?'

Alec reprised his account. Munroe said nothing, but Alec was acutely aware of his disapproval, the dark-grey eyes fixed on Alec's face. Parks' already tight little cherub mouth seemed to have grown ever tighter as he wrote down Alec's account, and Alec could feel a sense of unease, coupled with increasing guilt at having kept so much from his colleagues, weighing down upon him.

Did he trust them? No, not at all. They were

unproven strangers, behaving in ways that Alec neither understood nor wanted any part in. Did he feel bad about not entrusting them with this information before? Yes, because perhaps that secrecy had led to this attack on Travers; perhaps, too, Parks was right and Alec would be happier if his wife, too, were well out of the picture.

'Anything else you've not been sharing?' Munroe said at last.

Alec hesitated, and then nodded. 'It might be nothing,' he said, taking the small strip of card in its evidence bag from his pocket. 'One of the inmates dropped this when we were at the prison today. I got the feeling he wanted me to pick this up, but—'

'And it didn't seem obvious that you should mention it. Preferably when we were still there and could have talked to him?'

Alec hesitated. 'I think that was precisely why I held back,' he said. 'If this was meant for me, then it was dropped in a way so no one else would see. I think the man who dropped this was scared of being seen communicating with any of us. I said nothing because I didn't want to expose someone else to the same trouble Neil Robinson got himself into.'

'You've had the rest of the day to say something,' Munroe pointed out drily.

'I have, yes. Look, it might not even be relevant.'

Munroe eyed him coldly. 'Can't have it both ways, Alec.'

Parks picked up the evidence bag. 'Looks like a phone number.'

'It is,' Alec said.

'You rang it?' Munroe said heavily.

'Yes,' Alec admitted. Munroe and the others had a right to be angry, he admitted to himself. In their shoes, he'd have been furious. 'I got no reply. The phone just rang out. It's got to be a local number,' he added. 'No code.'

'Nice deduction.' Munroe's sarcasm stung, for all that it was probably deserved. 'You should be a detective.' He got up, taking the piece of card with him. 'Looks like you'll get your wish, anyway.'

'My wish?'

'Your wish not to be here. Eddison hears about all this, you'll be gone.'

A few hours ago, that would almost have been good news. Now it was anything but. 'I'm involved,' Alec said, 'whether Eddison likes this or not. Travers—'

'Is irrelevant.' Munroe said coldly.

Not quite midnight, and Alec stood in the waiting area of the local hospital watching a doctor talking to Travers' wife. Another woman – a neighbour, apparently – stood beside her with an arm wrapped tightly around Maureen's slender shoulders. From time to time the neighbour glanced at Alec, her look cold and empty, as though she, too, blamed him for what had happened. Finally, the doctor left and the women returned, sitting down on adjoining plastic seats.

'What did he say?' Alec asked quietly.

Maureen buried her face in her hands and wept.

'He's still in surgery,' the neighbour said. 'It isn't looking good. The doctor says he'd have been dead within another few minutes if you hadn't found him,' she added, and Alec could feel the implication behind the bland words. If you'd gone to talk to him earlier, she meant. If you'd not chosen to eat alone, but instead gone to find him, none of this would have happened, would it?

Would it?

Another thought had occurred to Alec as he'd driven here in Travers' car. What if Trav had opened the door to his attacker, thinking it was Alec come to fetch him?

Maureen continued to cry.

Alec got up and walked back down the long corridor, out into the car park. He stood where the lights from the hospital windows still illuminated his phone, and he called Naomi. She answered on the second ring. She sounded happy, he thought, maybe even a little drunk. No doubt they had all been celebrating.

'You know I love you,' he said. Suddenly, that seemed like the only thing that mattered. 'You know I do.'

'Alec? Alec, what is it?'

'Where are you?'

'I'm at Harry's. I asked if I could stay the night.'

'Good, I'm glad. Naomi, stay there until I get back. Please. Promise me?'

'Alec, what the hell is wrong?'

'It's Trav,' he said. 'I'm at the hospital. God, Naomi, I thought he was dead. He was just lying there, and there was so much blood.' That phrase again; suddenly, he was merely a witness, not a policeman, used to dealing with such terrors.

'Blood? Alec, are you hurt?' She sounded frightened. He realized he was telling this all wrong.

'Not me,' he said. 'Someone got into Trav's room, stabbed him half a dozen times and left him for dead. He's in surgery now, but Naomi, it's not looking good.'

'Oh, God, Alec. Maureen—'

'She's here. A neighbour brought her over. Look, I've got to get back to ... back to the crime scene, so—'

'You're not stopping at the hospital?'

'Only till a family liaison officer arrives. Maureen, well, she blames me, Naomi. Doesn't want me around.'

'It isn't your fault, Alec!'

'Isn't it? How do you know?' Somehow the guilt was comforting now, a rapidly familiar blanket, settling on his senses, insulating him against the need to make decisions, to respond, to think what might have to happen next.

'Alec.' Naomi's voice was surprisingly sharp. It cut into him, slicing through the fug of self-doubt. 'Not your fault, Alec,' she said again.

'Look, can you come home, at least for tonight? Get some distance, talk about it?'

He was tempted. 'No,' he said finally. 'If I come home, I won't come back.'

'Is that such a bad thing?'

He didn't quite know how to respond to that one. Earlier in the year he had talked seriously about leaving the force, moving down south somewhere, starting something completely new. He felt the tug of that now, the temptation.

'I have to stay here,' he said. 'See this through. I owe him that.'

Silence on Naomi's end of the conversation.

'You understand, don't you?'

'Yes. I understand, of course I do. Alec, have you told anyone about my phone calls? I spoke to Megan this morning, they're taking it very seriously this end, but Megan says the feeling is they only have half of the story. They could do with some liaison.'

'I'll call the office tomorrow morning,' he promised. He managed a rather bitter laugh. 'Of course, I might not be given an option in the end. Eddison is threatening to throw me off the case.'

'Why?'

'Oh, the phone call among other things. Withholding information, he calls it, and he's right.'

'And you did that, why?'

He could hear she felt aggrieved. The thought that he hadn't taken things seriously enough to pass the incident on occurring, and then wounding.

'I spoke to Travers first thing, but he wanted to hold back. I don't *know* why.' He paused. 'Travers and Eddison have history; he's been behaving oddly ever since we got here.'

'Oddly? How?'

Alec glanced back towards the hospital entrance as a slight movement caught his eye. Maureen's friend stood there, beckoning to him. 'I've got to go, love, I'll call you later. I love you.'

'Love you too.'

Alec walked back towards the entrance. The feeling of dread cramping his guts must have shown on his face because the woman almost smiled. 'He's out of surgery,' she said.

'And?'

'He's been taken to the high dependency unit. Maureen's gone with him. I said I'd come and find you.'

'Thanks,' Alec said. 'Look, can I get you a cup of tea or something?'

That half smile again, and then a look of distaste. 'I think I've had enough vending machine tea. Or it might have been coffee, it was hard to tell.'

Alec nodded sympathetically.

'I wouldn't mind some company, though,' she added. 'I think it's going to be a long wait before I know what's going on and if I'm driving home alone or taking Maureen. I'm Sally, by the way. I don't think we got properly introduced.'

'No,' Alec said. They walked slowly back

towards the waiting room. 'Have you known Maureen long?'

Sally shrugged. 'We've been neighbours for years. Our children are friends, and we have the occasional barbecue, that sort of thing. I can't say we're close friends.'

'It's good of you to do this for her then.'

A withering look greeted that comment. 'It's what you do, isn't it? She needed help, I was there.'

Not everyone reacts like that, Alec thought. 'It's still good of you,' he said. His phone chimed, telling him he had a text. Excusing himself, he took it out. It was from Naomi. *Hang in there*, it said. *We're all thinking about you, and Harry says I can stay at his as long as I need.*

A pang of jealousy that Harry was with her and not him.

He was putting his phone away when a second text arrived. This one was from Eddison, summoning him back. Now. Alec sighed. 'I'm going to have to go.'

'Duty calls, and all that?' Sally smiled at him.

'Yes. Look, the family liaison should be here soon. Whoever it is, they'll stay with Maureen, so if you need to get home, she'll not be on her own.'

'Thanks,' she said. 'See you again, Alec.'

He was acutely aware that she was watching him as he walked away.

Alec arrived to find that Munroe had called a briefing for all the hotel staff still on the premises and any guest that cared to come along to the restaurant and listen. Eddison stood off on the sidelines watching. On the face of it all it was very informal, with police officers helping staff to serve hot drinks to guests in pyjamas and dressing gowns, who were looking both bleary eyed and fascinated. It was, Alec realized, looking at his watch, a little after two in the morning. Somehow he had expected it to be later.

'What prompted this?' Alec asked.

Eddison shrugged. 'We've had some calls from the media. A film crew showed up about a half hour ago. Parks has promised them a statement in an hour or so. We just want to make sure everyone is singing from the same page of the hymn book.'

'Including me?'

'Especially you.'

'You didn't ask how he is. Travers, I mean.'

'I know who you mean.'

Alec glanced at the battered, rugby player's face, but Eddison gave nothing away. The grey-blue eyes glanced at everyone, failing to settle, seeing and appraising.

'I know how he is. I've had someone calling the hospital every half hour. He dies and I want to be the first to know.'

Alec wasn't sure what to say. He started to speak, but Eddison motioned for silence. Munroe had taken up position next to the serving area and was about to begin.

'Ladies and gentlemen, this must have been a

very traumatic and difficult time for everyone. As most of you now understand, a man was attacked in his room, we think about seven p.m. yesterday evening. The man was a guest here and happened to be a serving police officer, here on secondment to an unrelated investigation. He is presently in surgery, and I believe the prognosis is better than we first feared, so that's the good news. I must stress, here and now, that we have absolutely no reason to believe he was targeted in particular, or that the fact of him being a serving officer had any bearing on this happening to him.'

The general murmuring picked up again, and Alec looked hard at Eddison. 'We know that's not—'

'Shut it, Alec,' Eddison hissed.

'How can you be sure of that?' someone asked.

Alec looked to see who it was; the voice sounded oddly familiar. He realized that the speaker was the young receptionist he had alerted when he couldn't rouse Travers. She was speaking to Munroe, but glancing at Alec, her puzzlement evident.

'Because,' Munroe said smoothly, 'we've had three reports from other guests along that corridor of someone knocking on their door. Fortunately, and for various reasons, no one else responded. We think our colleague might have opened the door because he was expecting someone he knew. Unfortunately, what he found was a bad man with a knife.'

'What the hell is he doing?' Alec whispered. 'There were no other guests involved. It's all—'

'And I said *shut it*, Alec. Leave it!'

Furious, Alec clenched his fists and clamped down on all he wanted to say. Eddison was right in one respect: it would do no one any good if Alec chose this moment to make a scene. But what good was it doing to plant the idea of some random attacker, threatening any guest foolish enough to open the door to him? The young receptionist was looking fully at Alec now. This isn't true, her expression said. That isn't what happened. You and I know that.

Guiltily, Alec tried not to meet her gaze.

'The bad news, of course, is that the attacker escaped – we believe through the bedroom window and out across the staff car park.'

Munroe paused, allowing the new tide of gasps and fearful little murmurs to subside. 'We are, of course, very concerned with where he went next, but the one major factor on our side is that the motel and its environs are very well covered by *CCTV* camera. He will be on one of them, and we will be able to track where he went, and it's very likely we will be able to get a good look at his face. Now, I know that's no comfort to you at the moment, but we'd just like to assure all of you that this is probably the safest place in the country right now.' He gestured to the uniformed officers. 'There are more of us, proportional to all of you, than you're likely to find anywhere outside of Buckingham Palace.'

Uncertain laughter at that. Maybe not the best of examples, Alec reflected, given the rather high-profile security breaches there in past years.

'Who would do such a thing?' someone asked. Alec looked for the speaker: a man in striped pyjamas and a red dressing gown, sitting uncertainly on the edge of his chair.

'Some nutter,' someone else muttered. 'I mean, got to be, hasn't it?'

Sounds of agreement, approbation, nervousness.

Alec watched as Munroe allowed the speculation to continue, the seed of the idea to grow. Of course, Alec thought – let the idea spread that it was some random nutcase, some escaped mental patient. Easy answers. Acceptable and digestible.

Munroe cleared his throat, and expectant eyes turned back to him. His timing perfect, he interceded just before the speculation could drift into other, less manipulable explanations. He was good at this, Alec thought grudgingly.

'Of course, there is no evidence of that being the case. We really can't speculate. I can only assure you that we have officers mobilized from three counties and full cooperation from the *CCTV* providers. Technology really is on our side.'

'So tomorrow, or the day after, we'll be hearing about an arrest then,' Alec said bitterly. 'Some unknown, unnamed non-existent—'

'The police don't do that sort of thing, Alec.'

'Don't we? But I'm forgetting Munroe isn't police, anyway, is he?'

Eddison's jaw tightened, but he gave no other sign that he had even heard.

'In the meantime,' Munroe continued smoothly, 'I suggest you all try to get some sleep. Those of you that haven't yet spoken to one of the officers, please make sure you've at least checked they have your name and address, and please, if you think you might have seen or heard anything – anything at all, however seemingly insignificant – don't be afraid to come and tell one of us. Please, don't be worried about it being nothing, we'd much rather know about it.' He smiled, a surprisingly warm smile ... provided you didn't look at his eyes, Alec thought.

'Are we free to leave?' a woman asked.

'If you've spoken to one of my officers, then certainly. Though I really would urge everyone to try and get some rest before they go. It's late, and I'm sure everyone is exhausted.'

He'll be telling them next that tiredness kills and they should take a break, Alec thought angrily. Munroe's soft, patronizing attitude was jarring on him, or maybe what was jarring was that people were responding to it. He was telling them what they wanted to hear.

'You called me back from the hospital for *this*?'

'Best you're present at the briefing, Alec,' Eddison said smoothly. 'Best we're all kept in the loop, don't you think?'

Alec grimaced at the implied rebuke but didn't rise to it. 'So, what now?' he asked tightly.

'You get some rest and we talk in the morning, decide what your position is going to be in the ongoing investigation.'

'If I still have one, you mean?'

'Not my call, Alec,' Eddison said and wandered off to join Munroe.

Alec stood impotently for a moment, wondering what to do. If it wasn't Eddison's call, then whose was it? Munroe's? He caught sight of Parks chatting to some of the guests. His blond head tilted sympathetically to one side, the cherubic little mouth tight with concern. He nodded briefly in Alec's direction and then turned back to the anxious little group.

'It didn't happen that way, did it?'

Startled, Alec turned towards the speaker. The receptionist. 'Didn't it? I don't think any of us are clear what happened yet.'

She said nothing, but her expression spoke of betrayal. She had been sure he would listen to her, tell her what was going on.

Alec sighed. He hated this. But two people were dead, he reminded himself, and another almost so. Instinct warned him that the best thing he could do for this young woman was to toe the party line.

Gently, he took her arm and led her aside, aware that Eddison had seen and was now headed back their way. 'Look,' he said quietly, 'sometimes we have to give out half truths in order to keep what really happened out of the media. If the media get hold of too much then the criminal will know exactly what we know. Sometimes we have to deliberately mislead, hold certain things back, certain things that might only be known to us and to the killer. You understand?'

'I think so.' She still looked doubtful. 'So whoever it was really *was* out to get your friend?'

Alec hesitated for a second and then nodded. 'We think so,' he conceded.

Oddly, she looked relieved then. 'But you want the killer to believe that you don't know that. To think you've not made the connection?'

'That's exactly it.' Alec was glad to resort to at least a half truth. 'So, even though you know different—'

'I don't say anything.' She nodded, half smiled. It would please her, he thought, to feel she was privy to some secret thing. That she was helping out by staying silent about her doubts. Hopefully, silence would also help to keep her safe. He noticed Eddison observing them and assumed he had heard. Alec excused himself and walked past the senior officer towards the lobby.

'Good move, Alec,' Eddison growled.

Alec ignored him and walked on, heading towards his room. It took all his self-control not to just get back into Travers' car and drive away.

NINE

Gregory sat at Christopher's bedside and watched the old man sleep. The light was dim in here, and the nurse had covered the lamp with something that filtered the light and turned it fragile and pink.

She had no idea who Gregory was and had been doing the job long enough not to ask. She entered now, touched Christopher's hand and checked his pulse, tucked the frail hand back under the covers and asked Gregory if he needed anything.

He shook his head. 'How is he?'

'Comfortable. That's the best we can offer.'

He nodded. He wanted to ask 'how long?' but he was afraid Christopher would hear, and that seemed wrong, somehow. His boss, his mentor, his friend and, latterly, his protector, Gregory was still uncertain what this death would mean for him.

'We are dinosaurs, you and I,' Christopher said.

'Are we? What kind?'

The nurse smiled at them and left the room.

'Oh, something slow and heavy and about to become extinct. We must make way for the

mammals, Gregory. The world of the warm-blooded.'

Gregory laughed softly. 'Will they make the world a better place?'

A harsh chuckle from the old man. 'Oh, if I thought that, my friend, I could die more peacefully.' He reached a pale hand towards his one-time protégée. 'You should not keep coming here, you know that. Separation, Gregory, that's the key now, keeping yourself distant when the merde *begins to fly.'*

He took the hand. 'Too late for that,' he said. 'You know what pains me? It was that in their own way they were both innocents.'

Christopher laughed, and then choked.

Gregory looked anxiously towards the door, wondering if he should call the nurse.

'I'm all right. Innocents, you say? Well, yes, the young woman was guilty of idealism, no more than that, and I do believe we both suffered that affliction once upon a time, before the world got far too complicated for us. But Robinson? He was a career criminal, Gregory. He even tried to take you down.'

'He was an amateur,' Gregory said. 'Out for what crumbs I might have spilled. He didn't deserve to die for it.'

'Gregory, my friend, Robinson didn't die for that, as well you know. He died for what the girl may or may not have told him. And remember, too, he found out enough to know who you are. He was one of the mammals.'

Gregory smiled and nodded, and Christopher

closed his eyes. He stayed until he was sure the old man was sleeping, and then he laid the hand beneath the blanket and slipped away.

Some decision seemed to have been made overnight, and Alec was woken by a call from reception asking him to meet his colleagues for breakfast.

Alec glanced at his watch. Ten to eight. He had slept after all. How had that happened?

Alec could remember texting Naomi to tell her that he was *OK* and things were looking better for Trav, and then he'd lain down on the bed, fully clothed, still in half a mind to leave. Sitting up now, he realized that he was still fully clothed, stiff and crumpled and as muzzy headed as though he'd got a hangover.

Telling himself that Eddison and co could wait, he showered and changed his shirt. There was little he could do now about the crumpled suit. Then he headed for the restaurant. They were already there, halfway through their breakfasts. Parks indicated an empty chair, and Alec nodded then went to the buffet. He was hungry, he realized. Surprisingly ravenous, in fact. With a loaded tray he returned to the table and plonked his breakfast down on the already overcrowded table.

'I like to see a man who enjoys his food,' Eddison intoned.

Parks laughed. Alec ignored him and nodded acceptance as a waitress arrived with tea. 'Thank you,' he said, and then focused on his breakfast.

'So,' Eddison continued, as though Alec had already been there, 'that's David and Alec looking through the *CCTV* footage. We've already got a lead on that, so get yourselves briefed and then relieve the overnight team.'

Who's David? Alec wondered, then realized Eddison was referring to Parks.

'Phillip and I are going back to talk to Robinson's sister,' he added.

Phillip, Alec thought, almost surprised that Munroe had a first name. He couldn't recall Eddison referring to anyone by their first name until now. Was he trying to make like they were a proper team? 'Travers?' he asked.

'Spent a comfortable night and is stable. Family Liaison Officer Susan Moran is with the wife, and the friend is planning on going home later today.'

Alec nodded, satisfied. He had dreamt about Travers, he remembered now. An incident from when the pair of them had still been in uniform and had been called on to cover some kind of protest. He tried hard now to recall what it was about. A factory closure, maybe? Some kind of government contract that had been withdrawn and the workers were protesting.

He could not at this time and distance grasp at the details, but Jamie had been there too, reporting on the protest for the local paper. Alec remembered placards and shouting and – a sit-in, that was it. Workers had occupied the building, and it had made quite a splash in the local press at the time.

He'd not thought about it in years, but in his dream the memory had been clear as day, and now that he tried hard to recall details that were already slipping away, as dreams so often do, he was left with some scrap of a joke Jamie had been making about her new jacket. It had a blue striped lining, and she'd had the sleeves turned back because they were too long for her—

'Alec?' Eddison said sharply, and Alec realized he must have been speaking to him. He apologized automatically. Tried to catch up with the last bit of the conversation he remembered hearing.

'The sister? Neil Robinson's sister?'

'What other bloody sister have we been talking about?'

Alec shrugged. 'Why talk to her again?'

'Because she was holding back,' Munroe said.

'Holding what back?'

'If we knew that we wouldn't need to talk to her again!'

'No, I mean about what happened to Neil Robinson, or, I don't know, whatever she told Jamie on his behalf.'

Munroe shrugged. 'Why?' he said.

'I don't know. It's something no one's talked about much. How did he know about Jamie in the first place? He wasn't local to Pinsent, so he didn't know about her from when she started out. So what made him choose her? And how did the sister make contact? No one's told me that either.'

A beat of silence.

'Maybe you didn't bother to ask,' Eddison said.

Maybe he hadn't. Maybe he'd been waiting for Travers to ask that sort of question. Maybe he'd just been caught up in Trav's concerns to the extent that he really hadn't been doing a proper job. 'I'm asking now.'

'We don't know, is the short answer. Clara, Neil Robinson's sister, says she got a message from him. One time she said he called her, another she said she thinks he wrote her a letter telling her to get in touch with Jamie Dale and say that her brother Neil had a story for her.'

'She'd know the difference. If he'd written her a letter she'd have kept it. That would be the natural thing to do. People ... *families* don't throw away personal letters.'

'Ah, thanks for the insight, Professor Friedman,' Parks teased. 'No, we figured as much too.'

'And someone like Jamie Dale wouldn't get in touch with anyone just because they said there might be a story. When she worked the local paper she reckoned she got a dozen calls a day like that. Usually, it was just a vindictive neighbour or a lost cat.'

Munroe nodded agreement. 'And since she started to make a name for herself, it is reasonable to assume she got even more "hot tips".'

'So what did the sister tell her that was sufficient bait? Neil Robinson must have offered something very specific. Something Jamie would have recognized; known about already. Have we looked at what she was working on? Looked to see if there was a link?'

'Course we bloody haven't,' Eddison said irritably. 'We've all been sitting here waiting for you to come up with that one.'

Alec ignored the sarcasm. 'So?' he asked, slicing into his second sausage and layering it with bacon before dipping his fork into his egg. 'What was she working on?'

Parks and Eddison exchanged a glance. Munroe just shrugged. 'On the face of it, nothing that would have got Neil Robinson's juices going,' Munroe told him. 'She was almost done with filming a documentary, a two part exposé thing on how many ex servicemen end up as rough sleepers. Especially those from special forces.'

'Not news, surely?' Alec said. 'I've seen a couple of films like that in the past few years.'

'No, but she was doing something on comparative care. Here, the USA, some of the old Soviet Bloc countries.' He shrugged. 'Previous to that she'd been part of a team, each making a kind of personal reflective thing on the changing face of Britain or Britishness or some such. It seems to be the fashion at the minute from what I can gather. You know, who we are and if multiculturalism works or is some kind of myth put about by politicians.'

I guess you could say it worked for Jamie, Alec thought. Her mother had been Welsh but working in Pinsent when she had met and married a man who was, if Alec recalled correctly, half French and half Nigerian. Jamie had spoken about half a dozen languages, largely because of family connections. How had Jamie thought of herself?? Alec realized he hadn't the foggiest idea. She'd just been Jamie Dale, a pen name she'd adopted so early in her career that he found he couldn't recall what her actual family name was.

He thought hard while attacking more of his breakfast. Fouquet, that was right. Or was it Foucault? 'Have you seen the films?'

Parks shrugged. 'Bits of them. Neither was a finished product yet.'

'So we're back with the original question. Why contact her, and what hooked her?'

'Which is what we're going back to ask the sister. Again.'

Eddison got to his feet and stretched, the movement untucking his shirt enough to expose a small area of hairy belly. Munroe followed his example, but he didn't stretch. Munroe, Alec found himself thinking, was not a man who would stretch. Such extravagance of motion was available only to those people who were capable of relaxing. Munroe was not one of them.

'So that leaves us,' Alec said to Parks when the others were gone.

'Looking at *CCTV* footage,' Parks confirmed.

They both accepted the offer of more tea, and Alec pushed his now empty plate away. Hunger had been replaced by incipient indigestion. 'So I've not been thrown off the investigation.'

'It would appear not. But don't relax, Alec. I think it's more a case of keeping your enemies closer, than hanging on to your friends.'

'And who views me as the enemy? You, Munroe or Eddison?'

'I already told you. I do my job and then—'

'Go home. Yeah right. What's going on here? What am I not being told?'

'That's just it, Alec,' David Parks told him. 'No one's keeping you in the dark. You're not being told because we just don't know.'

They relieved the uniformed officers who had spent the last several hours looking through the feeds from the cameras closest to the motel. Alec figured that he was still in disgrace, even if he had been permitted to stay; this was a job for uniform, not for detective inspectors and their sergeants, who could reasonably be expected to be off investigating, not drinking yet more tea and looking through hours of random comings and goings.

Eddison and Munroe were just keeping him on hold and out of the way, Alec figured, and Parks was there to make sure he didn't have any ideas they hadn't sanctioned.

Initial images of Travers' attacker had not been hard to find, and they were shown *CCTV* pictures of the suspect crossing the scrubby area of gravel and lawn and going into the staff car park. He got into a car that had been parked there, into the passenger side.

'A light blue saloon,' a uniform told them. 'We don't see the registration number at any time as they drive out, and we don't get a look at the driver either.'

He skimmed through the footage they had isolated so far, and Alec watched as the car, viewed from various cameras, took a circuitous route through the main car park in front of the hotel and then, instead of taking the most direct exit, snaked through the car park at the motorway services. At no time were either the registration plate or the driver and passenger fully visible.

'I think it's safe to say they know their way around,' Parks said. 'They've got to know what each of the *CCTV* cameras is seeing.'

'Are they all fixed camera angles?' Alec asked.

'Mostly. The majority of them concentrate on the lorry parking. There's a history of thefts. The cameras in the car park are mostly just to make the punters feel more comfortable. Half of them are dummies, the rest are fixed, and at least one was offline last night,' the uniform explained.

'So much for our surveillance society,' Parks joked. 'But what about when we get on to the motorway?'

'I'll show you.'

The blue saloon could be seen on the slip road leading from the services, and for a brief second or two the number plate was visible, but so dirty as to be unreadable. The car then left the slip road, tucked in close behind a lorry it had followed down and effectively disappeared from the next set of cameras.

'He comes off at the next junction, takes the first exit at the roundabout and then we lose him. It's all country roads from there. No cameras.'

'Search teams out looking for the car?'

'Soon as it got light. Nothing yet.'

'They'll have dumped the car,' Parks said.

'And probably torched it,' Alec predicted. '*OK*, let's go back to where we see him crossing the grass at the back of the hotel.'

The officer reset the system, made sure they knew what to do, and then he and the remainder of the night team took their leave. Parks and Alec were left alone.

'Not much doubt about it being him,' Parks said, nodding at the screen.

'No,' Alec agreed. He stepped through the footage frame by frame. The suspect was, he guessed, in his thirties, casually dressed in jeans and a T-shirt that seemed to have some kind of logo emblazoned across it – though it was rather hard to see what it was, for the shirt, the jeans, and the man's bare arms were all heavily stained with blood. His face, though, was always kept turned away from the camera.

He was on camera for maybe fifteen seconds, Alec counted. Long enough to walk quickly across the patchy lawn and into the car park. The car engine was already running. He got in, and they drove away.

Alec shook his head. 'White male. Thirties, would you say? Short cropped sandy hair. Some kind of logo on the back of his T-shirt.'

'Something on the front too, but, well, it's hard to see what. With all the blood. Maybe it can be enhanced?'

'The original image is pretty poor.' Alec wasn't hopeful.

Slowly, they tracked back through the rest of the footage. Then began the slow trawl through camera angles that hadn't yet been examined.

'We can hope someone in the main car park got a better look. Put out an appeal.' Parks sounded discouraged.

'Who's handling the press call? I thought Munroe said the media had started to arrive last night.'

'Get with the programme, Alec. Eddison did his bit to camera first thing ready for the breakfast news. The motel will be officially closed today, hence the excellent service at breakfast.'

He hadn't noticed, Alec thought, only belatedly recognizing that the dining room had been practically empty, the space inhabited only by the odd remaining guest and breakfasting police personnel.

'Eddison's promised the scene will be released by tomorrow – all except Travers' room and the corridor it's on.'

'Are they expecting anyone to want to stay?'

'Well, I expect the first few days it'll be media types, but it'll get back to normal after that. It's the only half-decent place for thirty miles. The next services are a long way up or a long way back.'

Alec nodded. In his experience people were oddly pragmatic about such things. Once the shock had worn off, a spot of notoriety could be good for business. Especially if the news was soon released of an arrest. He wondered how Munroe was going to stage-manage that. He could imagine the story courtesy of the sergeant – or whatever he actually was. Police find a burnt out car linked to the hotel attack. Body inside, possible murder-suicide scenario. A suspect with known history of mental health problems, who, coincidentally, none of the local hospitals would admit to having had as a patient, never mind having released.

He pushed the idea aside. Conspiracy theories, he thought, but he could not shake the idea that his appraisal of the situation might turn out to be close to the truth.

'Have you met the sister?' Alec asked, returning to what he thought might be safer ground.

'Once. I was there when Eddison told her about her brother being dead.'

'Eddison told her? Not the local police?'

Parks shrugged, as if to emphasize that he'd stopped asking questions.

'Tell me about her.'

'Not much to tell. She's a bit older than Neil Robinson. Big sister trying to keep little brother on the straight and narrow and not quite managing it. Married to a guy called Paul who is a used-car salesman, runs a little showroom and garage. He said he'd offered Neil a job. Like *that's* an appropriate career move for a conman like Robinson. They've got two kids, eight and ten, both girls. I didn't see them; they were at school.'

'And she was shocked?'

'What do you think?'

'I mean—'

'I know what you mean.' Parks stared at the computer screen, watching cars and pedestrians as they crossed the car park in front of the motorway services. 'She was shocked that police of any sort had come knocking at her door.'

'Occupational hazard, I'd have thought, with a brother like Neil Robinson.'

'No, that was the thing. It's like he kept family separate. His sister, anyway. I think the rest of them had long since written him off, so it was kind of academic, but the impression I got was that he tried hard to keep her out of that part of his life.'

'And yet he asked her to contact Jamie on his behalf.'

'True, but there's a world of difference between passing on a phone message and getting yourself involved in your brother's life of criminality.'

'Is there?' Alec thought about it. He supposed it was like everything else in life, just a matter of degree. Ordinarily, he didn't involve his non police friends in police business, but there were times, like now, when he asked favours of those whose connections dragged them part way into his sphere of influence. Like asking Harry to look after Naomi.

'You said she was shocked. What shocked her most?'

Parks frowned, running events through his mind. 'Not that he was dead. It was as though she'd almost resigned herself to the fact he would come to a bad end. We told her that Neil had been found dead, and she asked how. At that time we still weren't sure how, so we said it had been a heart attack. Which, technically, it was.'

'As in technically we all die of heart failure,' Alec said. 'Look, what's that?'

'Back up a few frames. Yes, that's our car. What's it doing going through the lorry park?'

'I don't know. You were saying that you told her he'd had a heart attack.'

'Yes, and she seemed almost relieved and, I'd say, surprised. Then when Eddison said we suspected foul play she just went kind of quiet, like that was what she'd been thinking all along. Like it hadn't ever occurred to her that Neil would die of natural causes. Look, back up again. How slow can we replay?'

Alec fiddled with controls he only half understood. 'There,' he said.

'He changed vehicles!' Parks leaned forward excitedly. It was so easy to miss, a shadow where there should not have been a shadow, the hint of an opening door as the car moved around the back of the lorry, one scant glimpse of a booted foot as someone climbed into the cab.

'Any chance of a better angle?'

Alec flicked through the camera positions, was not surprised to find that the answer was no. They returned to the original footage. The lorry moved off about a minute later, the car now looping back into the main car park and taking the snaking route on to the slip road they had previously observed.

'There's the lorry.' Parks pointed. The HGV, having taken a much more direct route, was also on the slip road, ahead of the light-blue saloon that had interested them before. The lorry pulled out, and the car tucked in behind, as they had previously observed, but when it swung out past the final camera – now they were looking for it – it was just possible to see that there was only one person aboard.

'Fuck,' Parks said softly. He fumbled for his mobile phone and called Eddison. 'Can you get a reg number for the lorry?' he demanded of Alec.

Alec was already on to it. Minutes later he handed the number, make and model to Parks, who relayed them to Eddison. When the car turned off, the lorry did not.

'He made a frigging mistake!' Parks was exultant. 'Got you, you bastard.'

Not yet, Alec thought. The footage was, he glanced at his watch, more than fifteen hours old; that was a massive head start. But he allowed himself a moment of pleasure. It was something. More than they'd had overnight. More than they'd had an hour ago, and in this desert any kind of something was an oasis.

TEN

Naomi had originally only packed an overnight bag. If she was to remain at Harry's for long she would need clothes. Harry drove her back to her home late in the morning, leaving Patrick in charge of cooking Sunday lunch under his grandmother Mari's supervision. Even though Patrick'd be living at home when he went to university, Mari had decided that he should at least in principle be able to fend for himself.

'He's growing up so fast,' Naomi said. 'You should be very proud, Harry. You've done a great job.'

'I am proud,' Harry said. 'But I do think that the shoe is on the other foot. I think Patrick has done a good job with me. I'm a bit of an old stick in the mud, Naomi, I know that. Having Patrick around has at least kept me from taking root.'

'Are you looking forward to Florida?'

'In a perverse way I suppose I am. I get on far better with my ex-wife now she's an ex than I ever did even when we were supposed to be happily married, and I do like the two boys a lot. I've even sort of forgiven the affair. Anyway, I think I owe it to Patrick to be grown up, don't you?'

Naomi laughed out loud. 'You're actually looking forward to this, aren't you? What's the angle, Harry? Showing her you can manage just fine without her?'

'Well, there might be a touch of that,' he admitted. 'But the rest is true, and I really am looking forward to going to New York with Patrick. It feels like a farewell to his childhood. This is the last summer of school, the last summer of my son being ... well. You know.'

'I can guess.'

'So I want to enjoy it. I want us to have really special memories.' He pulled into the short drive and cut the engine. 'You all right?' he asked.

'Is it that obvious?'

'Naomi, it's *OK* to be human. It's understandable that this business has unsettled you. It's fine *not* to be all right.'

'Then, I'll admit it. I'm not all right.'

He took her hand and squeezed it tight. 'I could go in and get what you need.'

'And have a strange man rummaging through my knicker drawer?' She giggled, happy to be able to break the tension. 'I'll be fine, Harry. But I'm glad you're here.'

Harry unlocked the front door, and Naomi unset the alarm. They stood in the hallway, listening to the silence and feeling the difference in the house. The sense of absence was somehow tangible, and Naomi felt almost like a stranger, an invader in this usually familiar space. She knew she would never forgive whoever it was that had made her feel this way.

Harry bent to pick up the mail.

'What have we got? I expect the bill man's been.'

'A lot of junk mail, and what looks like a gas bill,' Harry confirmed. 'And ... and there are messages on the machine.'

'Right.' Listen now or later? Should she get it over with, or should she gather her stuff together first so they could get away quickly after the messages had been played? She shook herself. Oh, for goodness' sake, Naomi, she told herself. Don't be such a wimp. 'Harry. Do you think you could come up and lift a case down for me?'

'Of course I can.' He touched her arm gently. 'Right, let's raid that knicker drawer and then get off home for lunch.'

She laughed. 'Thanks,' she said.

Naomi packed quickly. When she had first been blinded, her sister had taken over management of the day-to-day practicalities. She had helped Naomi learn to do her make-up, had sorted her clothes into outfits that she could assemble quickly, and later, when her confidence had grown, had taken her shopping and then rearranged her wardrobe and drawers into a logical sequence that Naomi could continue for herself.

Naomi could tell by touch that this was her favourite pink blouse and knew that her old jeans, washed until they were peach soft, lived in the second drawer down. Harry paced as she sorted through what she needed and then carried her case downstairs. She stood reluctantly in the hall while he checked over the rest of the house, returning quickly to deliver a verdict of security. Then she pressed the button on the phone.

The first message was from a friend hoping they could meet for coffee. The second from the centre Naomi volunteered at, wondering if she could do an extra session to cover sickness. Then two more, and Naomi knew at once that they were calls from Jamie even before a sound was made.

'Naomi, Naomi Blake. Naomi, are you there? Oh God, Naomi, please pick up.'

'Harry!'

'It's all right. I'm here.' He took her hand and held it tight as the second message played.

This time just the sound of a woman screaming. It filled the hallway, seemed to fill the mind. Someone in pain, someone so very scared they could no longer shape the words to express that fear.

'We need to report this,' Harry said quietly. She could hear his voice tremble, for all his outward calm. 'Naomi, how do I get the tape out?'

'You don't, it's digital. Um, just unplug it from the wall. We'll drop it into the police station on our way.'

She drew in a deep breath, or tried to. Her chest felt so tight it was as though her body no longer remembered how to process air. 'Oh God, Harry. What did they do to her?'

She knew what had been done to her. That was the trouble. Hearing the screams, she could imagine Jamie locked in that car, the flames taking hold and Jamie unable to get out.

'Naomi.' Harry's voice, stern now, teacher-like. He took her arm and led her from the house, locking the door.

'I didn't set the alarm.'

'Does that matter at the moment?'

'No. It doesn't. No. Just take me away from here.'

He helped her into the car and deposited the phone on the back seat. She was horribly conscious of it, as if her fear and horror now sat behind her. A physical presence she could not just drive away from.

Jamie, her friend Jamie, was dead, and Naomi was now convinced that whoever had killed her had recorded her dying screams.

ELEVEN

Nick Travers drifted. Sometimes he heard voices; once there was a voice he thought he recognized. Mostly, he just dreamed. Sometimes he dreamed of being in a hotel room and hearing a noise outside the door. He opened the door and someone came in. Someone who looked so familiar that Nick was sure he knew the man's name, and yet also knew that it was impossible. That man was dead, wasn't he? It was a dream that looped round and back in his consciousness, round and back and always ended the same way, in excruciating pain. After the third or fourth or fifth loop – he found he was unable to keep track of it – he concentrated on trying to break out of the cycle to focus on it *not* happening, and for a brief while he would think he had succeeded. Other dreams would float randomly into the space he had temporarily created, and he would allow himself to relax for a brief while. Then it would be back again and the pain would start over.

'He keeps almost starting awake,' Maureen said. 'Then he moans in his sleep, and he moves his hands like—'

'He's dreaming,' the nurse told her. 'That's a good sign.'

Sometimes the dreams were more pleasant. He remembered another hotel room, high up in a modern hotel looking out over a city he could not identify. A woman was with him. She was not his wife.

'He talks in his sleep,' Maureen said.

'What does he say?'

'He calls out a name. A woman's name.'

'It could be anyone.' The police liaison officer had seen all this before. The sick, the dying, those whose normal social controls are switched off, so often talked about things and people even those closest to them were ignorant of. *Especially* those closest to them ... 'It's nothing, Maureen, just the brain firing at random. It's a good thing. It means he's regaining consciousness.'

'He doesn't call *my* name.'

Sometimes the dream was tactile, sensual. Sensory overload, as he touched the woman's skin and kissed her mouth and felt the softness of her breasts as they pressed close against his body. 'Michelle,' he said. 'Michelle.'

Maureen leaned close and listened. Listened to his breathing, listened to his words and shed painful tears. Never mind what they were telling her. This was not and could never be a good thing. 'Who is Michelle?'

'It could be anyone,' Sally told her. She exchanged a glance with the police liaison, and Susan Moran nodded approval.

'Anyone,' Susan agreed. 'A work colleague.'

'He doesn't call *my* name.'

* * *

Sally slipped away and found the business card Alec left her. He answered on the third ring, just as she was about to decide this was a bad idea.

'Is everything all right?'

She knew he meant with Nick Travers.

'He's doing *OK*,' she said. 'It's Maureen I'm worried about.'

'What's wrong?'

'He's talking in his sleep. He keeps saying a woman's name.' There was a hint of silence, of withdrawal on the other end of the phone. *He knows*, she thought. *He knows who it is*.

'He's talking about someone called Michelle,' she said.

'A work colleague,' Alec told her. 'She's involved in the investigation.'

'Right,' she said. 'That's what we thought.' She rang off then and turned back towards the ward. Sitting at the bedside, Maureen was complaining sadly that Nick still hadn't called out her name.

'Problem?' Parks asked.

Alec shook his head. 'Maureen's friend from the hospital, just letting me know how things are.'

'And how are they?'

'He's getting better, apparently.'

'Good.' Parks cast him a quizzical glance. 'Look, I'm going to get the *CCTV* footage over to the tech team. You stay out of trouble while I'm not here to mind you.'

Alec watched him go and made up his mind. He got into Travers' car and drove back to the open prison where Neil Robinson had died and Michelle Sanders was governor.

He talks about someone called Michelle, Sally had told him. Was that just because Trav's mind had escaped to a safe place? A good memory? Or was there more to it than that? Alec still knew nothing about the prisoner who had dropped the phone number at his feet. Who was he, and what was his association with Neil Robinson? As far as Alec knew, no one else had followed up on it either. He told himself that events had rather overtaken earlier concerns, but the answer did not satisfy.

He announced himself at the gate and asked to see the governor.

Driving up to the main building, Alec took a proper look at his surroundings. The main building was an old house – Georgian, he thought – though with modern wings attached at the sides and a Portakabin parked on what must once have been a sweeping drive. Long buildings, those left over from the days when this was an army base, stacked up in a herringbone pattern on either side of a gravelled road, and at the back of these were areas of cultivated garden and then mature trees. He caught sight of the freckle faced prisoner who had dropped the phone number. The man glanced his way and then turned his back and walked purposefully on.

Michelle Sanders met him on the steps. She

didn't look happy, arms folded across her body and a frown creasing between her eyes.

'*DI* Friedman. What brings you here?'

'You can spare me a few minutes.'

'Can I?'

She turned and led the way, not to her office this time, but into what seemed to be a comfortable sitting room at the front of the house.

'Staff room,' she said, in answer to his unasked question. 'Coffee?'

'Thank you.'

'Have a seat. There'll be no one here until lunchtime. Then the admin staff will want their space back.'

'You have a lot of admin staff? This is a big room.'

She cast him a look that was half puzzled, half amused. 'Yes, we do,' she said. 'It's also used for some classes. We've got a writer in residence here two days a week and – look, what are you here for?'

Alec took a seat close to the window. This had once been a grand room, with its elaborate plaster cornices and a very large marble fireplace. Old rugs covered most of the wooden floor, and the furniture was a mishmash of ancient easy chairs and a couple of sofas. He wondered who had donated them and doubted any would comply with modern fire regulations. On the walls were cork notice boards, pigeon holes and photographs of staff and inmates on what looked like important occasions. A trestle table along the back wall supported trays of mugs and hot water urns and the makings for tea and coffee. Michelle took milk from a small fridge set next to it. 'Sugar?'

'Two, please.'

She pulled a face. 'Too sweet.'

He waited until she had sat down in an opposite chair and then asked, 'You heard about Travers?'

'Travers? What about Nick?'

Of course, he'd not yet been officially named, Alec remembered. In the early morning bulletins he'd still been an unnamed guest. 'The news this morning, the stabbing at the motel.'

It took a second or so to register, then he saw the colour drain from her face. 'That was Nick? Oh my God.'

Alec reached across and took the cup from her hand before it slipped through her fingers. Her face was white.

'Look, I'm sorry, I kind of assumed—' Stupid, how could she have known? 'Are you *OK*?'

'Is he...? I mean...'

'He's going to be all right, we hope. We found him in time. *I* found him in time.' Only *just* in time. 'It was touch and go, but he's going to be *OK*.' He paused. Already, the colour was returning to her cheeks, but as he proffered the mug of coffee he could see her hands were still trembling.

She grasped the mug between them and held it tight.

'You care a great deal for him,' Alec said.

'I *did*,' she said firmly. '*Did*. We were close for a while.'

'You had an affair.'

'Is that any of your business?'

'Ordinarily, no.'

'So why did you come here today? If it was to tell me about Nick, then thank you, though I've got to say your people skills need some improvement.'

'True. But no, it wasn't just that. He spoke your name. He's still only semi conscious, drifting in and out, but he spoke your name.'

'Oh. So you're here because that upset Maureen?'

Alec laughed. She was recovering fast. If he'd had any hope of using her weakness to his advantage, that moment was fast slipping away. 'No. I mean, yes, Maureen was upset, and I've no doubt he'll have some explaining to do once he's well enough, but no. You were clearly on his mind. Why is that, do you think?'

She shrugged. 'How the hell should I know? If, like you say, he's not fully conscious, then it could have been some dream he had, some memory that got triggered because we saw each other again...' She trailed off, suddenly seeing where Alec was going with this. 'It's been years since we last met.'

'How many years?'

'Five? Six? No, five.'

'And the relationship lasted?'

She pursed her lips, looking mutinous; he didn't think he'd get an answer. Then she said,

'On and off for a while. Eight, maybe nine years.'

Alec blinked.

'Ah,' she said. 'He didn't tell you that, did he? It was serious, Alec. For a while I actually thought he might leave her.'

'They have kids.'

'Which, I believe, is why he didn't. I can't think it was for love of Maureen.'

'And what ended it?'

'*I* ended it. I, like all those before and since who have been the "other woman", realized that he liked to have the best of both worlds. I decided I had to get on with my life. The job came up here, so I applied. I told him this was a fresh start and I wouldn't see him again. And I didn't.'

'You sure about that? You seemed very uncertain about the last time the two of you had been in touch. I'd have thought if it coincided with coming here you'd have known practically to the day.'

'You're a hard man, Alec. I saw him once, *OK*. He came here, I sent him away. Nothing happened.'

He let it lie for a moment, sipped his coffee and watched her thoughtfully. 'Tell me about Eddison.'

'What?' The frown returned. She sat back, suddenly defensive. 'What about him?'

'You have history. The three of you.'

'Eddison is ... How can I put this? He is not a man you want as your enemy.'

'And is he yours?'

She shook her head. 'No, you see, that was just it. Charlie Eddison was a friend of mine long before I knew Nick. He warned me about Nick, warned him off. Not that I took any notice.'

'Warned you?'

She laughed bitterly. 'You don't think I was the first or only one?'

'There were other affairs?'

'Oh, Lord, Alec. You really don't know him, do you? I like to think the others all dropped away once I was on the scene, but after me? There were rumours. Always rumours.'

True, Alec thought. There were always rumours. But then, in the rather hothouse, incestuous world of policing, there were very few people who didn't attract the rumours. He'd been the subject of a few, as had Naomi. You learnt to view it as an occupational hazard and dose every one with a large pinch of salt.

'So tell me about Eddison.'

She closed her eyes. Her hands still grasped the mug tightly, and she had not yet even sipped at it. He wondered again if she was going to talk to him.

'Eddison and I go back a long way. Just friends. He was more a friend of my brother's, really. My brother died, then Eddison became a friend of mine.'

'What's his background?'

'You should ask him.'

'I'm asking you. It saves time.'

This time she paused to drink her coffee. Alec waited.

'Charlie and my brother, Ben, they were in the army together. Then they both went into the police together. Way back when the force really began to computerize in a big way, Charlie got himself on to every training course he could and gradually shifted into the specialist, intelligence-led side of things. I attended some of the conferences. So did Nick. Charlie took to all this like the proverbial duck. You'd never know it to look at him, but he's got a brain like—'

'Trav said he was an information gatherer. He likes to have something on everyone he meets.'

She laughed. 'Look, you make it sound like it's deliberate. I don't think Charlie can help it. Some people just *have* to know and have memories like elephants for trivia. Charlie's one of those. He remembers and he collates, and sooner or later, usually when you least expect it, he puts a whole raft of random stuff together and comes up with a conclusion. It's made him good at what he does, and it's made him a lot of enemies in his personal life.'

'Just his personal life?'

She shrugged. 'I don't know, maybe professional too. He's like ... You know how men always reckon a woman in an argument will remember every previous slight, practically since before they were born? Well, in Charlie's case he really does remember.'

'And he uses that?'

'I suppose he does.'

Alec paused and finished his drink. It was all starting to make a little bit more sense. 'And Munroe?'

'Him, I don't know.'

'Eddison say anything about him?'

'No.'

'Is that significant? Would he normally have told you something? Anything?'

'I don't see why. He introduced this *DS* Munroe as a colleague on secondment. He didn't say from where, and I didn't ask.'

'But you suspect?'

'Alec, what's all this about? Why don't you just ask them?'

'Because you know as well as I do I'm not going to get a straight answer.'

She considered that. 'I wondered if he was Internal Affairs,' she said. 'Just a feeling.'

That was possible, Alec thought. He changed tack, sensing that he'd mined out this particular seam. 'When we were here, one of the inmates in Robinson's hut gave me something. Well, gave is probably putting it a bit strong. He dropped a piece of paper at my feet and made it very plain he didn't want me to acknowledge the fact.'

'Oh.' Now she was interested, he thought. She leaned forward, elbows on her knees. 'What was it, and who?'

'A phone number,' he said. He fished his notebook from his pocket and flicked through, finding the number he had written down. Showed it to her. 'Does this mean anything to you?'

She shook her head. 'It's a local number?'

'It seems to be.'

'And the man who dropped it?'

'I'd like to speak with him.'

She appeared to consider, then shook her head. 'Why? You'll be able to find out who owns the number without involving him, so—'

'So why did he want me to have it?'

'Could be anything and nothing. Could be a wind up, you thought of that?'

'Of course I have.'

'Right. Look, Alec, if it becomes relevant then I'll consider your request. Until then, I'm sorry.'

'Your objection?'

'Presumably, you realized the man wanted to keep this quiet. You allowed him to do so. You could have brought it to my – our – attention at any time while you were here, so why didn't you?'

'One man is dead, and we still don't know exactly how or why.'

'And my reasoning is the same. I will not put someone else at needless risk.'

'You could isolate him. Protect him.'

'Does this look like a secure unit? No, Alec, we do good work here, and we spend a hell of a lot of time building trust and cooperation between staff and inmates. I won't—'

'If there's so much trust, why didn't he come to you? To a member of your staff? Why wait until an outsider came along?'

'And why choose you and not one of your

colleagues? Alec, my guess is this is nothing. Someone taking the piss.'

'And if it's not?'

'Come back to me when you've got something. *If* you get something. Which I doubt.'

She stood, and Alec realized he was being dismissed. Had he learnt anything new? He still wasn't sure.

She walked him to the door and then watched him get into his car.

Alec drove back down the gravel drive. The same work crew tended the allotments behind the huts. Alec slowed the car and watched, then pulled on to the verge and stopped the car. One of the guards watched him as he crossed the grass between the huts.

'Can I help you? You were here the other day.'

'DI Friedman. Yes I was.' Alec extended a hand, and the man looked momentarily flummoxed and then shook it.

'Boss know you're here?'

'I've just had coffee with her. What are you growing?'

'What are we—?' The guard looked puzzled, then shrugged. 'You name it,' he said. 'We keep the kitchen ninety per cent supplied for veg from the plots here. We've got links with a local plant nursery – they take some of the lads on day release.'

'Sounds like a good scheme.'

'It is. It works. We've got the lowest recidivism rate of any prison in our category. Our inspection was outstanding.' He was clearly proud of that. Alec could understand why. It was a rare thing to be part of a success story in the prison system.

Alec pointed at a row of tall stalks. The freckled faced prisoner was working close to them. 'Is that sweetcorn? We tried growing that last year, didn't get a damned thing.'

He began to walk towards the rows, and the prison officer fell into step. 'Last year was cold and wet; we lost half our crop even here where we've got shelter. We're lucky; this patch is south facing, so we get the sun coming round the back of the trees most of the day. Over that way it's a bit overshadowed, but the fruit trees do all right. We've also got a special bit of fertilizer for the corn, isn't that right, Griffin?'

So the man's name was Griffin. Good. That narrowed things down a bit. 'What's that then?'

'Pig shit,' Griffin said. He regarded Alec warily. 'From the farm next door.'

'We rot it down, add it to the compost, and see that over there?' The officer pointed at a row of tall green plants Alec did not recognize. 'That's comfrey, that is. Helps the compost to rot faster, release all its nutrients better. I didn't believe it at first, but one of the old boys from the village told me about it, and I got Griffin here to look it up on the Internet.'

Alec glanced back towards where he'd left the car. He was unsurprised to see Michelle Sanders now standing next to it.

'Thanks,' he said. 'Looks like the boss wants

another word.'

He could feel them watching him as he returned to the vehicle. Michelle was incandescent; only the awareness of the many eyes of the work crew watching kept her temper in check.

'What the *hell* do you think you're doing?'

'Picking up some tips on growing sweetcorn,' Alec said. 'Thanks for your time, Michelle. It's been a pleasure.'

She'll be on the phone to Eddison before I'm through the gate, he thought as he drove down the rest of the gravel road. He'd gone too far, he knew that. Eddison would be as furious as the governor, if not more so, and if Alec's hold on his position in the investigation had been stretched before, it was going to be broken, or close to, now.

He found it hard to care. Alec had never been one for games. He'd known many officers who had played politics, jockeyed for position, taken every opportunity for advancement they could. Made their own chances. Alec had never been one of them. He took pride in his work, but more and more he'd come to realize it did not define him.

Not sure what impulse drove him, he pulled on to the side of the road about a mile from the prison and dialled the number Griffin had dropped. No one picked up the phone; it rang out into empty space.

TWELVE

Clara Thompson and her family lived in an end terrace that had been extended to the side at some time in the seventies. The red-brick and picture window of the added lounge sat at odds with the Victorian formality, as did the fact that the older section of their home still celebrated its period features. So did the seventies bit, Munroe supposed, with its feature fireplace, complete with stone cladding.

This was evidently a family space. Kids' toys and books vied for space with a large television and two massive sofas. He had caught a glimpse of the original living room – front parlour, as his nan used to call it – on the way in. That was obviously more of an adult space: restrained furnishings and a very good hi-fi system. He hadn't spotted the make. Clara had shut the door defensively when she'd seen him looking.

'I've told you all I know.' Neil Robinson's sister had been alone when Munroe and Eddison arrived. She'd phoned her husband, and he was, apparently, on his way. She lifted her chin defiantly, back rigid and upright, not an easy posture on a sofa that was designed for lounging.

Munroe lounged, leaning back, relaxed and putting forth the impression that he could sit there all day if he had to. Eddison sat as neatly as it was possible to do at the other end of the large settee. Munroe could see he felt ill at ease. Eddison, bulky and tall, was not made for lounging.

'I don't think you *have* told us all you know,' Munroe said. Last time they had been here she had given them tea, opened biscuits. There had been no such offer this time. 'The letter you had from Neil, telling you to contact Jamie Dale, what did you do with it?'

'There was no letter.'

'Well, last time we talked you couldn't recall if it had been a letter or a phone call. I'm betting on a letter, and I'm betting you've still got it?'

'There was no letter. He phoned and told me to get in touch with her.'

'And tell her what? Oh, hi, Miss Dale, my brother, the convicted conman, he thinks he might have a story for you? Yeah, right, that's really how it was.'

He let the silence build. Most people, in Munroe's experience, folded; they had to fill the silence with sound. Any sound. And usually out of the resultant waffle something useful emerged.

Clara wasn't going to be one of them.

'What are you afraid of, Clara?' Eddison asked her quietly.

'Who said I'm afraid?'

'You did.'

A puzzled look, a swift denial. 'Look, I've told you all I know, and I'd like you to leave.'

'After we came all this way?' Munroe looked hurt.

'That was your choice, not mine.'

'So what did he tell you to tell Jamie Dale? What hooked her in, Clara?'

That look again. She wasn't going to bite. Neither was she going to give him some story that could be broken or disproved.

'Whatever you say, say nothing,' Munroe said softly. 'Is that it, Clara? You and that husband of yours, you've decided just say nothing and it'll all go away?'

A little tic at the corner of her mouth told him he was spot on.

'Well, you see, you're wrong, Clara, because we'll just come back and ask again, and if we don't come back then others will and they might not ask so nicely.'

Another little tic – more of a flinch this time.

Munroe stopped lounging and leaned forward. 'Someone has been here already, haven't they, Clara? Someone who wasn't nearly as nice or as understanding as we've been. Someone that scared you?'

'I'd like you to go now. Please.' She stood and pointed theatrically at the door.

Neither man moved.

Slowly, her hand dropped back to her side, and she lowered herself back on to the seat. 'Please, just go.'

'This husband of yours is taking a long time

to get here, isn't he?'

'He'll be here.'

Eddison glanced at his watch. 'What time do you pick the kids up from school?'

A flash of anger this time. 'Leave my kids out of it.'

'Oh, we will,' Munroe told her. 'But others might not be so willing to. You know that, don't you, Clara? My guess is you've already found that out.'

She looked away, no longer able to meet his gaze. Her lips trembled, and she moistened them with a quick, nervous flick of her tongue.

'Who's been to see you, Clara? We can protect you. Look after you and that husband of yours and those pretty kids.'

Eddison glanced again at his watch. 'How long did you say he'd be, Clara? It isn't nice, is it, him leaving all this to you. A man should be here with his wife at a time like this.'

'I don't need him here.' Vehement, furious.

'Just as well,' Munroe said, 'Because my guess is you didn't get through to anyone when you made that "phone call" just now. He's long gone, isn't he, Clara? He's been frightened off, hasn't he? Left you here with the kids to deal with whatever storm is coming.'

'It isn't like that.'

'No?' Munroe let the question hang, and then again allowed the silence to build. She was breaking, he could see that. One more push.

'It must be hard to feel you can't protect your kids,' Eddison said. He sounded so sad, so sympathetic that Munroe almost wondered if he meant it.

'I can protect them. My kids are safe!'

'Gone with their dad, have they? They've left you too, have they? Well, I think you're right to get them out of the way, but I mean, can you really trust their dad to look after them? I mean, not exactly hero material, is he?'

'I don't know what you mean.'

'Well, running out on you when the first sign of trouble comes along. Leaving you to fend for yourself here.'

'Maybe she thinks if she stays they'll leave her family alone,' Eddison proposed. 'Maybe she thinks they'll stop looking.'

Clara was shrinking into herself now, diminishing. Munroe knew she was on the point of total collapse. She stood up again, facing them down though he could see her entire body was trembling.

'What did they do to him, Clara? What did they threaten to do to your kids? Are you sure they're safe? We know you're a good mother, we know you'd do anything to protect them, and they are beautiful kids, Clara, it would be such a tragedy if anything were to—'

'Get the fuck out of here. Just get the fuck out!' She flew at Eddison, grabbing at his hair, scratching at his face, kicking out at him as he stood up and captured her hands, holding them both easily in one of his own. 'Just get the fuck away from here.'

'Or what, Clara?' Munroe, sitting back now,

observed the scene. 'Besides, you've told us nothing. You can always try and convince whoever's threatening you that you told us nothing. Of course, they may not believe you.'

He paused. She had ceased to struggle now, but Eddison still held on to her wrists. A slow trickle of blood from beside his eye showed that Clara had scored one point against him.

'How convincing do you think you can be? I mean to say, *we're* constrained by the law, I suppose, but other people might not have those checks and balances.' He paused again. 'But I think you already know that, don't you?'

Again, the silence. Few people, Munroe thought, really appreciate the power of silence.

Clara had begun to cry.

Munroe nodded at Eddison, who released her hands.

'We'll be off then, Clara,' Munroe said.

'What?'

'Well, seeing as how you don't want to tell us anything.' He took a business card from his pocket and laid it on the arm of the sofa. 'Just in case you change your mind,' he said and followed Eddison out of the door.

They had parked the car just down the road. Eddison slipped into the passenger seat and withdrew a little black box from the glove compartment, then inserted what looked like a Bluetooth device into his ear.

'Where did you position them?'

'One in the living room, one in the hall near the phone.' He flipped the box open, revealing a small screen. 'She's dialling out.'

'Put it on speaker.'

Clara's voice, the distress evident, filled the car.

'The police were here ... No, of course I didn't, but Paul, what am I supposed to do? I can't ... Yes, I know, but ... Paul, I can't cope with this, I can't. Please, I need help with this. *Please*, Paul!'

'He's rung off,' Eddison said.

'Think he's got the kids with him?'

'I bloody hope so.' He took the earpiece out and replaced it with his mobile phone. Dialled. 'Right,' he said. 'I need you to run a number for me, get me an address. Ready?'

He relayed the phone number Clara had called, reading it from the screen of the little black PDA. 'Quick as you can. Any news on that other number?' He listened and then hung up.

'Well?'

'The office is still unoccupied, no one near or by for the past week, though the landlord says the rent is paid up for the next three months. It's listed as an import-export business, dealing in fine arts. The phone's rung a couple of times, but no action otherwise.'

'So why would anyone give the number to Alec?'

'Why not? Given the choice of him or you, I'd have gone for Alec.'

'Thanks for the vote of confidence. But why give it to anyone? What's the link?'

Eddison's phone rang. It was Michelle Sanders, trying for the third time to get hold of him. Eddison listened. 'I'll deal with him,' he said. 'Michelle, listen to me, I'll sort it out.'

'What?' Munroe asked when Eddison slid the phone back into his pocket.

'Our friend Alec Friedman,' Eddison said. 'That is a man who just doesn't know what's good for his health.'

THIRTEEN

It was mid afternoon by the time Naomi and Harry had finished at the police station and returned to an anxious Mari and Patrick. Mari, by some miracle, had slowed the progress of lunch, and only the carrots had been overcooked. Mari fussed over Naomi, and Napoleon, sensing that all was not well, pressed his big head against her leg and snuffled till she took adequate notice of him.

'I'm all right,' she said for the umpteenth time. 'Harry, I'm really sorry to have put you through that.'

'That poor, poor woman,' Harry said softly.

'Sit,' Mari told him. 'Eat. We'll all feel better with some food inside us.'

They made a deliberate effort to turn the conversation to other things. The exhibition, the trip to America, university, but the memory of the phone call draped like a pall across the room. She had tried to get hold of Alec, but he wasn't answering his phone and she felt very much alone despite the wonderful company.

As the meal drew to a close and Mari served the apple pie, Naomi said what had been on her mind for the past hours. 'I'm worried,' she said.

'Scared I've brought this all down on your heads. Whoever is doing this, they had a hand in killing Jamie, and probably Neil Robinson too. I don't want any of you involved in this.'

'Naomi, you know we wouldn't leave you.'

'I know that, but I think you should. Harry, I couldn't live with myself if anything happened, not to any of you. I'm serious about this. I really am.'

'Gran should go away, anyway,' Patrick said.

'Oh, should I?'

'Yes,' Harry told her quietly. 'We are, at least, all together, but you're on your own in that house. Go and visit Martha for a bit. I can take you up there. Go and have a break somewhere, just for a few days.'

'You're all really scared, aren't you?' Mari said.

'I think we should be,' Harry said. 'Patrick, I'm going to see if I can get you on an earlier flight. I'll give your mother a ring.'

'Not without you,' Patrick said. 'And Dad, don't think of arguing, you can't force me to get on a plane.'

'Any chance of you both going?' Naomi said.

'And leave you alone? No, we won't do that.'

'Look,' Mari said. 'We need contingency plans, don't we? Yes, I'll go and visit Martha or something if it makes you feel better. I've been threatening it for months, anyway. But you lot need to talk to Alec and see what he advises. That policewoman friend of yours, Naomi.'

'Megan?'

'Yes, Megan. What did she think?'

'She's going to make sure we get regular checks, and if necessary Alec can arrange a safe house.'

'Good. Now, I know I'm not an expert in these things, but it occurs to me that if whoever it was that's making these phone calls actually wanted to do any of us harm, Naomi especially, then they could have done so very easily before now.'

'It's a good point,' Harry conceded.

'It is,' Naomi agreed. 'Which leaves us with the questions: what do they want? What are they hoping I will do?'

'Or what do they think you know?' Patrick suggested. 'They obviously think these phone calls will make you do something. Maybe they think you know what it all means.'

Naomi nodded slowly. 'You have a point,' she said. 'But I don't know anything. I don't know what they want me to do. They've got that wrong.'

'Or you don't realize you know,' Patrick pressed. 'When did you last see your friend? Did she ever send you anything for safekeeping? Did she ever ring you out of the blue and say something that seemed a bit odd?'

'I've already asked myself those questions, and I can't think of anything. We got the occasional phone call, but even those stopped a while back. We exchanged Christmas and Birthday cards, but they only ever said the obvious stuff. You know – how are you, what are you doing now? The truth was we'd all but lost touch with her.'

'The last time you spoke on the phone?' Patrick insisted. 'Or what did she say in her last Christmas card?'

Naomi thought about it. 'We got a card from her this past year with a new address. We'd already sent her a card, but we sent another to the new address, just in case she hadn't got the first.'

'Did you put anything different in the second one?'

Naomi laughed. 'Patrick, I just don't remember. I dictated our cards, Alec wrote, and when he got fed up I took them over to Sue and she helped me with the rest.'

'Had Jamie been moved for long? Did she give you a new phone number?' Mari asked.

'And was there anything unusual about the new address?' Harry added.

That set something off in Naomi's brain. Some casual comment from Alec. 'Yes,' she said. 'It was a strange one. She said in her card that this was a temporary address because she was between moves; there was some work being done at her new place, I think. It was an office; she said it belonged to a friend. And it wasn't in London.'

'Do you remember where it was?'

'Offhand, no. It will be in the book in the hall, near the phone. That's where Alec puts all the family and friends' numbers and stuff. St Albans, I think, but that was the thing. Alec wondered why she didn't just tell us to contact her at work. We'd done that before when she was moving about a lot, especially in the early days when she didn't seem to have a place of her own half the time. She was always sleeping on some friend's couch or whatever. Then she got a flat.' Naomi frowned. 'I'd not given it any more thought.'

'And the last time you actually spoke to her?'

'Was when we invited her to the wedding. She called us and said she'd be working and couldn't make it. She sent a card and ... something else.' Think, Naomi. Was it a gift token? Both of them having well-established homes and therefore not needing the usual wedding list, quite a lot of people had given them tokens. But that wasn't Jamie's style, was it?

'She sent a photo frame,' Naomi said. 'Alec told me it had been handmade, that it looked kind of arts and crafts. It had bees and flowers on it.'

'You're sure there was nothing inside it? Nothing hidden? Dad, Naomi, we should go and get it.'

Naomi laughed. 'Sorry, Patrick, I don't think there was anything mysterious about it. I think Alec put a picture of Sue and family in it. I think he might have noticed any secret messages.'

'Maybe we should look anyway?'

'Maybe we should, but not today. I think we should go through *all* of the stuff Jamie sent over the years, just to be sure, but I it might be better if we get Alec to help do that. You don't know what to look for, and I'm not sure where in the attic or wherever it might be.'

'You'll have kept it all though?' Patrick persisted.

'Of course she will,' Mari said. 'Our Naomi is a magpie, always was.'

'Right,' Harry said. 'We'll clear away and see to the dishes, and then I suggest we all find something pointless on the television.'

No one argued. Something ordinary and Sunday-afternoonish was, Naomi thought, exactly the right recipe after the tension and trauma.

'I'll try Alec again,' she said.

'Do that. I'm surprised he's not phoned. He must have noticed your missed calls.'

She was rummaging in her bag for her mobile when Harry's home phone began to ring.

'That might be him now,' Harry called through from the kitchen. 'Do you want me to get it?'

He bustled through, heading for the hall. The call cut on to answerphone before he could get there. Naomi froze, heard Harry's strangled gasp of shock.

'Naomi? Naomi Blake? If you'rc there please pick up. It's me. It's Jamie.'

'Pick it up, Harry. Pick up the phone and give it to me.'

She heard him begin to object and then think better of it. The message cut as he plucked the receiver from its cradle. She fumbled it from his hand.

'Who is this? 'Naomi demanded. 'Who the fucking hell is this, and what the hell do you think you're playing at?'

She was met with only silence and a faint click as though someone had flicked a switch.

FOURTEEN

'Where the hell have you been?' Parks demanded. 'Eddison is mad as hell over something, and your wife's been trying to reach you. She says your phone is off.'

It was. Alec hadn't wanted to be reached. He'd figured Eddison would catch up with him soon enough, and before that he needed some thinking time. Now, if Naomi had been trying to reach him he regretted that.

Ignoring Parks, he turned his phone back on and rang Naomi. Listened, aware that Parks was watching him closely.

'I'm coming home,' he said. 'Stay where you are, and I'll be there as fast as I can.'

'What's going on?' Parks demanded as Alec headed back towards his car.

Alec paused briefly to tell him. 'I've got to go,' he said. 'Oh, and tell Eddison to go spin on it.' He drove back out of the staff car park where the police vehicles had been congregated, grateful that the press cordon kept the media to the far side of the public car park and he could come and go with very little attention. Soon he got on to the motorway and was heading for home.

* * *

Nick Travers opened his eyes. The ceiling bore a grey stain as though something had leaked and left a mark behind. Their bedroom ceiling had a mark like that. A water pipe, not broken but just seeping moisture. He'd kept promising to fix it until Maureen had given up and just got somebody in. He'd been promising to paint the ceiling too, She'd probably get someone in to do that as well.

'Nick?' Maureen said. 'Nick, can you hear me?'

With what felt like a profound effort he turned his head and looked at his wife. 'Not much good at *DIY*,' he said.

Travers drifted, and some small part of his mind was grateful that the dream loop seemed to have been broken and the sequence ending with the pain of the stab wounds now felt distant and muzzy, as though someone had decided to film it in soft focus. The face, though. That was just as clear. The man who should have been dead, but patently was not, now appeared in sharper focus. Older, yes, but then they were all older. But it was him.

Travers opened his eyes and this time turned his head towards his wife. 'Gregory,' he told her. 'Gregory was there. Alive.'

'He's gone, boss. Headed home.' Parks expected an explosion. None was forthcoming.

'Why?' Munroe asked.

Parks told him. 'The local police called here

when she couldn't reach him on his mobile. The last call from "Ms Dale" came through to the house of a friend she's staying with.'

Munroe nodded, exchanged a glance with Eddison. 'Then he's made the right choice,' Eddison said, and that was that. Eddison strode off towards his room. Munroe shrugged.

Parks regrouped. Do the job, go home. 'Anything more from the sister?' he asked.

'Not yet. But she'll be in touch.'

'You sound very certain.'

'Wouldn't you, if someone threatened your family?'

Parks, truthfully, wasn't sure. Would he want either Munroe or Eddison anywhere near his family?

'Yours safe, are they?' Munroe asked.

'They'd better bloody be.'

Munroe smiled. 'Anything on the lorry?'

'Yes, it's registered to a company called Madigor. They run an import export business. Far Eastern arts or something. The lorry was reported stolen a week ago. We've been trying to reach the owner, but neighbours say he's away on business. One of them is feeding his cat.'

'Owner's name?'

'Penbury. Joshua Penbury. No form. Nothing irregular as yet.'

'Then we shall have to keep digging. Anything more from the hospital?'

'He's been waking up and then drifting off again. He's still in the high dependency unit, but the signs are good. The hospital want to know if the armed guard is really necessary.'

'Tell them yes it bloody is.'

'Oh and Susan Moran, the family liaison, says he's been talking in his sleep. Two names. One is our friend Michelle Sanders.'

Munroe laughed. 'Oh, I don't envy him when he's well enough to take the flak on that one. Who else?'

'Someone called Gregory. He woke and told his wife that Gregory was alive. Mean anything?'

Munroe shrugged. 'Not to me.' Not yet. 'Keep me posted,' he said.

FIFTEEN

The call came through late that evening. The lorry had been found. It was still on the motorway at services some fifty miles distant. No one had given it much thought until the warden checking for patrons staying more than their permitted free hours had noticed that the reg number was still on his list. He'd assumed the driver was on a stopover and merely noted the fact. Then, at shift change, a routine glance at the police list – checking for stolen vehicles – and the number had been there.

'So he parked up and changed vehicles again,' Munroe said. 'The lorry hadn't been reported missing,' he confirmed, kicking irritably at the lorry wheels.

Parks shook his head. 'The owner, this Joshua Penbury, he's out of the country on a buying trip, apparently. Passport control has him on a flight to Paris en route to God knows where three days ago. The usual driver is visiting family in Bournemouth, part of his annual leave. He drives for this Penbury and for an agency. He's clean, so far as we can tell, and well alibied for the night *DI* Travers was attacked.'

'Which suggests someone knew the vehicle would be available and not missed. So we wait and see if *SOCO* turn anything up.' Munroe scowled in frustration. 'Where the hell are they, anyway?'

'En route. You'll just have to be patient,' Parks told him. But it did piss him off too, standing there next to a suspect vehicle and unable even to take a look in the cab.

'When's this Penbury due back?'

'The neighbour feeding the cat has enough cat food for a week and cash for more if she needs it, so—'

'Regular arrangement, is it?'

'Apparently,' Parks told him. The local officer he'd talked to had said she had three cats of her own and thought Joshua was a 'lovely man' so was glad to help.

'Nothing more on the car?'

Parks shook his head. 'It could be anywhere.'

'So we're back to trawling through *CCTV*.' Munroe wasn't impressed. 'See what new vehicle our would-be killer and our lorry driver moved on to.'

'Or vehicles,' Parks suggested. 'I doubt they'd stay together.'

'True. Anything from our errant *DI*?'

'What, Alec? No. Eddison says to let him cool off and then pull him back.'

'You think he'll come back?'

'Wouldn't bet on it. I don't think I would. I'd rather be with my wife and kids at a time like this.'

Munroe nodded what might have been agreement. 'What I can't figure out,' he said, 'is why the hell Eddison wants him involved anyway. I mean, what more can he tell us? So far as Alec Friedman was concerned, he'd done his bit, put a conman away, end of story.'

Parks looked speculatively at Munroe, as though wondering if Munroe actually wanted his opinion or was simply trying to trip him up in some way. Would Munroe really question Eddison's judgement so openly, or was he playing mind games again? Munroe, Parks had observed, seemed to enjoy mind games. 'I suppose he has his reasons,' he said cautiously.

Munroe looked amused. '*DS* Parks. Keeps his head down, does the job, goes home.'

'There are worse things.' He could tell Munroe was expecting more. 'Maybe the boss wants a different perspective.'

'Well, it must be obvious by now he won't be getting one. Come on, let's get ourselves a coffee and start looking at the *CCTV*.' He nodded to the uniformed officer keeping watch on the vehicle, and Parks followed him inside.

'You think he knows more than he's telling?'

'What, Alec? No. No, I don't, but I don't think he's telling all he knows, if you see what I mean.'

'No, I don't see what you mean.'

'I mean, Alec interviewed Robinson at length, and he knew this journalist woman well at one time. He's bound to know more than he thinks he does. You get to pick things up, to log things in the brain, and it's only a matter of time before something jogs the memory out. I think that's what Eddison's hoping for. Why he's keeping Alec around.'

Parks had to laugh. 'Then he's clutching at bloody straws,' he said.

Munroe was looking at him intently. Parks felt uncomfortable, as he often did around Phil Munroe.

'He often clutch at straws, does he?' Munroe asked.

'No. No, he does not.' Agreed, sometimes he'd seem to pull a theory out of nowhere and you'd wonder where the hell he got it from, and then it would fit with something else and the whole damn pattern would fall into place. But that was what a good copper did, wasn't it? You put the bits together slowly and carefully until you saw the whole story. But sometimes, with Eddison, it could be hard to see the logic of the thing, where he got that initial impetus from, and sometimes, Parks admitted to himself in very private moments, that really bothered him.

He could feel Munroe's gaze on him.

'You don't like him very much, do you?' Munroe said.

Parks didn't see the sense in denying it. Munroe wouldn't have believed him, anyway. 'I'm not paid to like him.' He glanced across the car park at the white van heading towards the lorry. 'Looks like the *SOCO*s have arrived. Maybe we should head back.'

'Let's have a coffee first. They've got to set

up, get their kit out – it'll be ages before they're ready for us.'

Parks agreed, and they turned back towards the services and the *CCTV* control room.

Alec was in agreement with Patrick. It was possible there had been something Jamie had sent to them that had not seemed relevant at the time. He had taken Megan Allison and Constable Watkins with him back to the house, Naomi insisting he did not go alone.

'So, how's she holding up?' Megan asked. 'We heard that recording. Christ, I don't think I'm ever going to forget it. Never.'

PC Watkins looked uncomfortable, but nodded sagely. Alec decided Watkins was more concerned with saying the wrong thing right now than with worrying about remembering the sound of Jamie Dale's screams. Megan was having quite a profound effect on the young man.

'Naomi's *OK*,' Alec said. 'I'm just glad Harry was with her. Wish I had been. I'm grateful, Megan. She says you've been a great help, both of you.'

Watkins blushed, and Megan smiled proudly at him, which just turned the blush from carmine to crimson.

'Right,' she said. 'So what are we looking for?'

Alec knew approximately where he'd stored unopened boxes from Naomi's flat, and also approximately where they kept old correspondence and cards. Naomi insisted on hanging on to a couple of years' worth, so they knew who they needed to send the damn things to. He knew she was right, but he still regarded it as something of an imposition on his time.

Together they went through the boxes, sorting out cards from Jamie, old letters and pictures, a photo album Alec had almost forgotten existed. He flicked through the pages, gazing in amazement at the collection of images. Young Alec, young Naomi, younger Jamie.

'There's an address on this one,' Watkins said. 'And another on this.'

Alec took the cards and glanced at what Jamie had written. These were from when she had first moved down to London. She'd moved three or four times in quick succession and written lengthy correspondence about the good time she was having.

Took the night off and went to the theatre. You'd have loved it, Naomi, I saw Cats. *The actual musical at the actual theatre in that there actual London. You've got to come down and stay – soon as I've got my own place and somewhere to sleep, you've just got to come down.*

'I remember her,' Megan said. 'I was a probationer the year before she left. Naomi introduced us. She said I should watch my mouth around the rest, but that Jamie was all right. I even went out with them a time or two.'

'She was pretty,' Watkins said.

'She was,' Megan agreed. 'But we were none of us bad looking once upon a time, isn't that right, Alec?'

Alec smiled. In his opinion Naomi was even more beautiful than she had been back then.

'This the lot, do you think?'

'I'm really not the one to ask. Naomi will know if there's anything missing. Oh, there's a picture frame in the other room, I'll just grab that.' He went through to the front room, glancing around to check there was nothing else. The address book in the hallway, which had her latest address in it. Alec thought he should take that too, just in case he hadn't found the relevant card.

The little green book always sat on the hall table beside the phone. He went through and looked. No book. A quick glance under the table in case it had been knocked down, on the stairs in case it had been moved.

'Megan?'

'What's wrong, Alec?' She and Watkins, laden with boxes, came into the hall.

'Someone's been here since Naomi left.'

'How do you know?'

'There's a little green address book I keep by the phone. It isn't here.'

'That doesn't mean – Naomi might have moved it.'

'No, it always stays there. She hardly uses the home phone, anyway. She's got her mobile, and she doesn't use the book, obviously. I've kept it there since before we were married. It's never moved.'

'It had Jamie's latest address in it?'

'Yes. It did.'

'Right,' Megan said. 'We get these things into your car, and I'll arrange to get the *CSI*s out here. It might take a while. Obviously, it's not an emergency, but—'

Of course it would take a while, Alec thought. His suspicion that someone might have been in his home and might have taken just a little green address book would hardly be given high priority. But Alec knew it had gone.

Carefully, he packed the boxes into the car, grabbed some clean clothes and thanked Megan and Watkins for their help, his sense of unease acute.

Nick Travers was dreaming again. A proper dream this time, not the heavy fragmentary action sequences that had thus far dominated his slow return to consciousness. He was dreaming of a time long ago, when he had been a very young man. A very young squaddie, to be exact, conscious of his uniform and his gun and his responsibility and the prickle at the back of his neck that told him he should be afraid.

He was on point, up ahead of the others and dodging from shadow to shadow in some small, night dark village that must have had a name, but in his dream he could no longer recall it. It wasn't, Nick realized slowly, an actual location, rather a blurring of many places half remembered, feelings and fears conflated. The sense of dislocation, though ... He could remember that with such intensity. The 'this isn't me, I am not really here' mantra that had seen him through one of the most miserable episodes in his life.

Travers had known, from the moment he joined up, that he was not cut out to be a soldier. That he was there because he couldn't think what else to do and knew it would get his dad off his back. And at least he would be with his friends.

That night, Charlie Eddison was close by, second man. Ben Sanders was rear guard. Gregory and Flynn were somewhere between. Nick Travers knew he should have been more aware of them – Charlie would have sensed exactly where each man was, Gregory could have told him to the millimetre, and even Ben would have been better than him. Nick Travers, dreaming, felt the mix of hard-packed rock, baked earth and loose cobbles beneath his feet and the rough texture of the house wall as he tucked in close and it scraped against his hand.

He signalled the others to halt. Still not certain he had actually seen anything at all, if he had imagined that flicker of movement across the narrow street.

And then, all hell broke loose – Flynn was down, lost in a hail of gunfire; Charlie and Greg were beside him. Charlie had his hand pressed tight on Nick's thigh, and it dawned on him that he'd been hit and was bleeding ferociously.

It's the femoral artery, he thought. I'm gone...

Nick remembered waiting to die and being

astonished that he had not. Recalled Charlie Eddison and Gregory dragging him into a house, and then Ben was there too, shouting something that Nick tried hard to recall but found made no sense. He was told that it took no more than minutes for backup to arrive and no more than an hour before they were out of there and headed back to base. Nick, heading home. Lucky. The dream receded, memory back where memory should be.

He opened his eyes and saw Maureen's face. She smiled, but he could see the tension at the corners of her mouth that told him she was angry about something. What had he done this time?

'I'm not very good at this,' he said. He could tell she didn't understand.

'It's all right,' she said, but he knew it wasn't.

'Who is Gregory?' Another voice was asking him something he didn't want to remember.

There was pain attached to the memory – searing, sharp, stabbing pain that rent him.

'Nick, you said that Gregory wasn't dead. Can you tell me what you meant? Was it Gregory that attacked you?'

'Gregory,' Nick said, then realized he might be answering a question. That he might be getting it wrong. 'He was my friend.'

'Gregory who?' Maureen demanded. 'You don't have a friend called Gregory.' She sounded hurt and impatient, as she always did when he talked about things she didn't know or understand. But whenever he did try and explain, she didn't want to know. She found it too hard, too distasteful, he thought. Much too real.

Nick closed his eyes and drifted away from her. She doesn't really want to know, he thought. She never really wants to know...

Susan Moran left the little side room. *DI* Travers had been moved this morning; no longer in the main high dependency unit, he'd been shifted off to one side so the armed guard was less visible and fewer visitors could be upset. She walked to the end of the hallway and dialled out, calling Eddison.

'He's been talking about Gregory again. He says this Gregory was a friend, but Maureen doesn't recognize the name. I did what you asked and put it to Nick that this Gregory was the one that attacked him.'

'And?'

'Well, he's still pretty much out of it, but I think—'

Eddison thanked her when she had finished and rang off. No, he thought, Gregory would mean nothing to Maureen. He wasn't even sure she knew about Travers' stint in the army. He knew it was something Travers didn't talk about, not unless he was among ... 'friends' was putting it too strongly. People who had shared that time. Everyone, Charlie Eddison thought, had bits and pieces of their lives they'd prefer not to be reminded of. For most it was often a simple matter of embarrassment. They'd cock-ed up, behaved like a prize prat, or simply been screwed over by someone they thought should have been trustworthy. No one likes to admit to those moments, Charlie Eddison reflected. At least, no one likes to be publicly reminded of them.

Among friends, close friends, those same moments can become the ties which bind, the bonds of stupidity admitted to with those you come closest to knowing.

Though, in Travers' case, he hadn't really cocked up. He couldn't really have prevented any of it. When folk with guns go up against other folk with guns, someone is going to be on the receiving end of the bullets.

SIXTEEN

Ordinarily, Paul Thompson would have felt exposed on a deserted beach, but it was strange how your perceptions were changed by circumstance. And the girls loved it here, that was the thing. They felt free and safe, and thankfully they had not been at the house when the men came and so had no memory to carry with them out into the sunshine.

They had seen their father's bruises, of course. Or rather, they had seen the marks on his face, and they knew he'd hurt his ribs and that he'd been in pain when he'd driven the car, but, as kids do when told with conviction, they had accepted his story of a fall at work.

Paul watched them run, hair flying loose, summer dresses belled by the strong wind. Barefoot on the sand.

They had discovered this funny little headland one summer when he and Clara had just met. More than once, Tilly, who owned the nearest farm, had let them camp up on the bank overlooking the beach, first in a tatty little tent they had bought from a charity shop, and later, as lives and incomes improved, she let them park their caravan in the hollow behind the bank that held back the dunes. This time, Paul had pulled the caravan right in beneath the trees and tucked the car close behind it, pointing back towards the track, ready for a swift departure. He tried not to think that the track was barely wide enough for a single vehicle, and the idea of escaping from someone coming the other way was therefore a little pointless.

'You here without yer woman?' Tilly had questioned when they'd arrived unexpectedly the week before.

'I'm in trouble, Tilly. Clara sent us out of the way.' He knew better than to try and lie to Tilly. He had known how it sounded, though, and would not have been surprised if Tilly'd sent him away. Instead, she looked at his face, marked the bruises and the pain he was in, and told him to get his van parked up.

'You got food?' she asked.

'Some.'

'I'll see to it you're provided for. Who am I to expect come looking for you?'

'I don't know, Tilly. I don't know who they are.'

She nodded and then ducked back inside the door, came back with a shotgun. 'You know how to handle this? Your woman do.'

Clara could handle a gun? Paul didn't know that; he wondered how or why Tilly should. As if she read his mind, she said, 'She brought him over once, bid me look out for him.'

'Him?'

'That brother on 'ers. Stupid bugger if you

ask me.'

'He's dead,' Paul said.

She nodded as though that was to be expected, him being a stupid bugger, handed him the shotgun and a handful of cartridges. He took them without a word.

'Don't you leave it round them kids loaded,' she warned.

'When did Clara bring her brother here?' Paul was curious now. He didn't yet have the energy to be angry, he was far too bruised and battered for that – though that would surely come later, he thought.

Tilly shrugged. 'Be once about four year ago,' she said. 'Once again about three year ago. He look like you do that time.'

'Like me?'

She gestured towards his bruises. 'No one come 'ere we don't know about,' she said and with that went back inside.

So far as Paul could make out, no one had come here at all. No one except Bryn who worked for Tilly and who brought them food and other supplies and helped Paul set up the aerial for the portable TV, but he wasn't what anyone would call talkative. In fact, the worst thing about the entire stay, Paul thought wryly, was that once he'd stopped being balls out scared, he'd started to be bored.

What now, he thought as he watched the girls running along the beach. They couldn't stay here forever. Oddly, after the first couple of days the girls had stopped asking when mum would be coming or when they would be going home. And he'd stopped worrying about what could happen to Clara.

He knew that was wrong, but he just couldn't help himself. The anger he had anticipated would eventually come had arrived sometime on the second day, along with a new fear that she might guess where he had gone and tell *them* if they came back. *When* they came back.

She'd brought this down on them all, Clara and that brother of hers. Let her deal with it.

'Daddy, Daddy, we've found a jellyfish!'

Slowly, he limped down to where Jilly danced and Kay crouched, peering at their find. Tanned and sandy faces grinned at him. He noticed that their clothes were dirty, the summer dresses grimed with sand and seaweed and stained with sea salt.

Painfully, Paul bent down to examine the transparent creature.

'Can we put it back in the water?'

'We can try.' He took the spade from Kay and slid it carefully beneath the jelly, and together they carried it to the water and Paul lowered it into the shallows.

'Will it be *OK*?'

'I don't know, Jilly. It might have been out of the water too long.'

They watched it drift in the clear water, and Paul convinced himself, as it was sucked back by the wave, that it had swum away.

'Did Mummy phone again?' Jilly asked.

'No, not again. I think the signal is bad here.'

He waited for the questions – is she coming? When are we going home? – but his daughter just looked at him with her summer-blue eyes, and he knew, somehow, that she understood. Mummy wouldn't come; they would not be going home. Not even after all this was over would they be going home.

It was always strange sorting through the debris of an earlier life, neatly packed away in boxes or slipped between the pages of albums. It reminded you, Naomi thought, both of how far you'd come and also how little you'd really changed.

Harry was working in his home office. Patrick and Alec had spread letters and cards and albums across the dining room table and were talking Naomi through what was there. Patrick, predictably, was fascinated by the photograph albums, especially when he discovered images of his father as a young man and a few precious snaps of a very young Naomi standing with her friend Helen.

'I must have been about nine,' she said as Patrick described them to her. 'There was some big festival to celebrate the reopening of the canal basin. They'd spent the spring dredging. God, it stank to high heaven, we were all so glad it didn't stretch on into summer. We went with Mari, and I'm sure Harry was there, though he'd probably have been the one taking the pictures. He was never without a camera, your dad.'

'Really?' Patrick laughed. 'I wonder why he stopped.'

'He used to seal up his bedroom and develop the photos in there. That stank too,' Naomi recalled. 'It was quite an important hobby for a while. I think he even belonged to a camera club.'

'I never knew that. I wonder if he still has his pictures.'

More poignant still, in the present circumstances, were the pictures of the old gang and Jamie. Snaps taken on nights out and holidays and even on the job. Alec and Naomi attending an industrial dispute; Jamie interviewing workers. The local press photographer capturing them all in a quiet moment.

'She had four – no, five – different address in the first couple of years away,' Alec said. The days when she slept in spare rooms or on sofas, before she started to pick up regular work and could finally get a place of her own. A bedsit above a shop, if Naomi remembered right.

'Ah,' Alec said. 'I've found it. The last Christmas card.'

'With the last address?'

'In St Albans. I was right, and there's a phone number...' He trailed off, fetched his notebook from his jacket pocket. Swore softly.

'What is it?'

'The number. You know, I had a feeling it looked familiar, but without the dialling code it just didn't click.'

'Familiar?' Naomi asked, but he was already

on the phone, asking for Eddison, telling him:

'The number the prisoner, Griffin, gave me. It was the same as for the last address Jamie gave us. Some shop or other in St Albans where she collected her mail and—' He broke off. 'You already know that, don't you?'

'Not the connection to Jamie Dale, no. The shop is registered to Madigor. Same company that owns the truck our perp escaped in.'

'Madigor. That can't be coincidence. Anything on the lorry yet?'

'Oh, still interested are we?' Eddison's tone was sarcastic. 'The truck was found this morning at services fifty miles away. The *SOCO*s have just arrived. Parks and Munroe are on scene.' He paused. 'How's your wife?'

'OK, she's *OK*, but we think someone's been to the house.' He told Eddison about the address book, half expecting ridicule. After all, it was the only thing missing; it could easily have been misplaced. Except that Alec just knew that wasn't the case. But there was no comment from Eddison.

'Keep me posted,' was all he said, and Alec was dismissed.

Madigor, Alec thought. The assumption so far had been that the truck had been used without the owner's knowledge. This put a different slant on things. Why had Jamie been using Madigor's office as her letter drop? Had she and the company's owner been friends, colleagues? What?

And was the theft of the book someone's

attempt to cover that up? Something in that didn't quite ring true, but Alec couldn't put his finger on exactly what.

'Alec?' Naomi, reminding him she didn't know what was going on.

'Sorry,' he apologized. 'They've found the truck Trav's attacker escaped in. That and the address Jamie was using, they belong to the same man.'

SEVENTEEN

Parks and Munroe had collected their coffee and settled into the control room to begin the long task of examining the *CCTV* footage. The two security officers on duty had been co-opted to help, and through the control room window, Munroe could see the car park, the lorry and the Scientific Support Crew, who were now unpacking their gear and donning white coveralls. Munroe estimated it would be half an hour or so until they'd be allowed anywhere near the truck; longer, probably until they could get inside. He glanced at the two motorway staff and then at Parks. He hated this bit of the job. Necessary, but tedious in the extreme.

'Look,' he said, depositing cups of placatory coffee on the desk. 'You two pinpoint the time when the truck arrived, and we'll go and talk to the *CSI*s. Give us a call when you'rc ready.'

Parks rose with alacrity. Resigned looks from the security guys. Munroe led the way out before anyone could object.

Across in the lorry park, Denver Moore had just taken preliminary photos of the truck cab. It had rained in the night, and the exterior of the vehicle had washed streakily clean. The step was still lightly puddled with the remnants of the shower. Denver stood back and watched as his colleague brushed the wing mirror with dark grey powder and checked for prints. 'Anything?'

'Nothing worth having, I think,' she said. She took the partials anyway, lifting the prints with tape and folding the cover closed. She moved on to the door handle. 'Going anywhere this weekend?'

Denver shook his head. 'Only the parentals, both sets.'

Ellen laughed at him. 'Oh joy, oh rapture,' she said. 'What did the pair of you do to deserve that?'

'We've both got the weekend off,' he said wryly. 'And everyone and his cat wants a hand in planning the wedding.'

'Painful,' Ellen said.

'Oh, girl, you don't know the half of it. Ready for me?' he asked as she moved off the footplate. He hopped up and took pictures of the window and cab interior, context shots before the door was opened. 'It isn't locked,' he said, surprised. 'Ellie, girl, you won't get to do your clever bit with the naughty keys.'

He leaned back, pulling on the handle.

The world shook.

Munroe was running now, Parks close behind. He was across the car park even before the blast had receded and the flames taken hold. A woman lay on the floor, knocked back by the explosion, he couldn't see how badly she was hurt. Flames blasted from the cab of the truck. The door had landed on a car fifty yards distant, and he could see nothing of the other *CSI*.

Parks was on the ground next to the fallen woman, speaking into his phone. He was calling for the ambulance, but as he looked up and met Munroe's questioning gaze he shook his head. Munroe ran to the Scientific Support van. It had been knocked on its side by the blast, and he prayed that there'd just been the team of two on board. A quick glance told him it was empty, and that they had a small fire extinguisher on board. He grasped it and then looked back at the truck, the flames spreading now through the cab and into the rear.

It would take more than the mini extinguisher to put out the developing inferno. Dropping it, he ran back to Parks. 'Move,' he yelled. 'Move before the whole damn lot goes up.'

'What about her?'

Swearing to himself, Munroe helped Parks scoop up the dead *CSI* and run from the flames. 'I don't see the other one,' Parks yelled. The roar of flames was now unbelievably loud.

Glancing back, Munroe took in the scene. If the lorry went up, how big would the blast site be? Was there more explosive on board?

A man stumbled out of a nearby cab. Dazed and confused he gaped at Munroe, who was now yelling at him to run. Munroe gave him a push in the direction of the services. 'Get as far away as you can, tell everyone, just get the hell out.'

Others had needed no instruction. Motorists ran from cars, others accelerated away. Munroe thanked the god of designers that whoever worked on these services had positioned the lorry park well away from the petrol pumps.

'Oh my God,' Parks said. 'Shit, Christ!'

Munroe looked to where Parks was pointing. The right hand of the missing *CSI* lay on the ground. There'd be more, Munroe knew. But he doubted there'd be any bit of him as large as the hand.

'Move,' he commanded. They carried the woman between them and half ran, half stumbled away.

Munroe dropped the body behind a low wall that separated the car park from a small picnic area. He sprinted off, calling to Parks to follow.

'What now?' Parks yelled. 'What the hell happened? That could have been us!'

Munroe grabbed Parks by the arms. He could see the first signs of shock in the other man's eyes. 'But it wasn't, was it? So just be bloody thankful. What we do now is we get inside, get everyone to the back of the building, as far away from all that glass as we can.'

Parks looked. People crowded against the massive windows of the restaurant, staring, pointing, crying out.

'Christ,' he said again.

At Munroe's heels he sped inside, shouting to the crowd to get away, to get back. For a moment he thought they were going to ignore what must seem like two madmen yelling and gesticulating, but then someone took up the call, and then another someone, and then the crowd began to move and the stampede started. Parks was almost swept along. Instead, with a massive effort, he pulled himself out of the crush and helped to herd people, as Munroe was doing.

'Get out of the back, far away as you can.'

And then it happened. A bang, like a firework, and then a roar and then another bang and then the sound of glass shattering and crashing down and a wave of screaming that seemed to break over Parks' head as he fell and curled tight on the floor waiting for the noise to stop.

EIGHTEEN

Alec had to go back. The news broke on the radio only minutes after the explosion and was on the television within half an hour. A helicopter circling the scene carried journalists, who speculated about terrorist plots and many dead.

He spoke to Eddison, to Munroe. Parks was hurt, but not badly, and was refusing to leave the scene, so Munroe had patched him up and set him to taking names and addresses of the walking wounded and the merely shocked.

The services were perhaps a couple of hours away down the motorway. The now closed motorway. Eddison gave him directions to the incident centre they were establishing half a mile from the scene. There was no argument, no suggestion that Alec should stay away. Now, it was all hands to the pump.

'Do you think I'm making the wrong choice?' Alec asked, suddenly anxious lest Naomi felt he was abandoning her.

'Alec, in your shoes I'd feel the same. You have to go. I'll be fine ... but, Alec? Watch your back.'

So less than a day after deserting the investigation, Alec made his way south again.

The radio news was filled with speculation. Extended bulletins talked about the many injured and the rumoured deaths of two *CSI*s. Witnesses on scene had seen one of them open the cab door. The witnesses had driven away, terrified by the explosion and the fire ripping through the truck. But shortly after, distressed and confused, they had pulled on to the hard shoulder and looked back at the smoke billowing out. The second explosion, they said, had shaken the ground beneath their feet.

Listening to them, Alec could hear the shock and distress and the beginnings of outrage. The reporter, first near the scene and now with an unexpected exclusive as the media were being kept back behind police cordons, had been travelling from a routine job, covering a factory opening. He now had the scoop of his life, he, too, having pulled up on the hard shoulder when he spotted first the smoke and then the distressed family by the side of the road.

Shaky images filmed on a mobile phone displayed the pall of smoke still hanging above the buildings, and the report had been phoned through, the sound crackly and uneven, but that in itself somehow adding to the fearful atmosphere.

Terrorists. That was the watchword. Who else could cause such catastrophe?

Alec didn't think so. They were terrorists only in the sense that terror had been caused, he thought. But this was all part of the same pattern as Jamie's death and Neil Robinson's murder and the attack on Travers and whatever else it was that was going on here.

He called Naomi an hour into the drive. In the background he could hear the television. A rolling news channel repeating what he had heard on the radio.

'Are you all right?' he asked.

'I'm fine. Harry phoned Megan and told her you'd had to get back. She's promised to keep an eye on us.'

'I should be there.'

'You should be doing your job.'

He drove on, suddenly lonely, suddenly bereft, and he knew that whatever Naomi had said, a choice had been offered and he had made the wrong one.

Gregory watched the news on the television in his hotel room with interest and building irritation. It was all wrong. He was not responsible for this, any more than he had been responsible for the death of Jamie Dale or the murder of Neil Robinson. And yet, someone was attempting to tie him into this mess, using his vehicle, linking his name and his business to this situation.

Gregory had no problem acknowledging those acts for which he had been responsible; that was part of the deal, the risk that one day he might be called to task for them. He accepted that, much as he accepted the sad fact that no one seemed to want to let him retire in peace. It was, however, an annoyance. It had taken time and effort to set up Madigor and reinvent his past, and Gregory resented the fact that he would now have to engineer that all over again.

So, he thought, who might be behind all of this? There was only one name in the frame so far as Gregory could see, and he wondered now what he should do about it and what exactly this man who had once claimed to be his friend, but who was now acting like his nemesis, was hoping to achieve.

We old guard are dying, Christopher had said, and he was right. Those that weren't dying were getting old, or were at least getting tired and wanting to fade back into the background. And, as Christopher said, that left a vacuum.

Gregory lay back on the bed and let the sound of the television news wash over him as he thought about it. There was a chain here that linked Neil Robinson, Jamie Dale, Nick Travers and himself. He just didn't have the full picture.

A change in the television sound attracted his attention. For the past hour the reporter had been filling in, repeating largely the same information over and over again, speculating meaninglessly about causes and guilt. Now he heard something new.

Gregory sat up and listened. A statement was about to be issued, apparently, with a phone line for any relative worried about their loved ones. It was the name of the officer about to give the statement that had caught his attention.

Gregory watched the screen as the familiar

face came into view and the rest of the chain began to form. The links between himself and Jamie Dale and Neil Robinson and—

'Right,' Gregory breathed. 'So that might be it. That might be the way of things.'

He switched off the television and packed his bag. Back to see the old man, he thought, and just hope he hadn't decided to die in the meantime.

NINETEEN

Alec was almost at his destination when he got a call from Eddison. He was to divert to St Albans and join the team searching the offices registered to Madigor that had been the postal drop Jamie had been using. He was then to join the team currently searching the house of Joshua Penbury, Madigor's director.

He pulled off the road, reprogrammed his sat-nav and took the opportunity to phone Naomi again.

'I'm fine,' she insisted. 'It's all going to be all right.'

Then he drove on, still heading south, listening to the news of the aftermath of the explosion and the voice in his head that kept nagging at him, telling him that nothing was ever going to be the same.

Despite the satnav, he managed to get lost in the one way system, and by the time he got to the office in a small side street he was feeling flustered and annoyed. He was expected, sent to join the team going through the top office.

Downstairs was a flower shop, the owner very put out that her shop had been closed and hoping she'd be compensated for business lost.

She had the radio on in her shop and the commentary continued: '—speculation that this is the first of a possible spate of terrorist acts. The national threat level has been raised to—'

He went upstairs, noting that although the two businesses shared a front door, Madigor had a second entrance that cut it off from the florists below. Customers to the florist came in, did an immediate dogleg left into the shop, while the entrance to the Madigor office was straight on and up a flight of stairs.

'What do we have?' he asked the officer in charge. *SOCO* had finished their fingerprinting and photographing, and the scene was now in the charge of *DS* Frobisher.

'Not a lot,' Frobisher said. 'According to the florist downstairs, Madigor was moving and the office hadn't been used much for the past six months or so. She says Joshua Penbury just used it for storage.'

'Much post?'

'Not that we found. The usual junk mail, and a few letters addressed to Madigor. There's half a dozen shipping receipts and an electric bill.' He pointed Alec in the direction of a storage box part filled with plastic wallets containing the said letters.

'Nothing for anyone else?'

'Not that we could find.'

'No computer equipment, files, nothing else?' Alec looked around the bare room. A desk in front of the window, and filing cabinet which, as Frobisher observed, was empty. An electric kettle, but no mugs; a calendar from the previous year.

'She said it had been used for storage?'

'She said. I don't see much evidence. This Penbury had his own keys, came and went as he wanted. She said up until last year he'd used this office pretty regularly, but this is a final electric bill, so it looks as though he was definitely moving out.'

'So, where to?' Alec wondered.

Off the office were a small bathroom and a large storage cupboard. A green hand-towel had been left on the side of the sink, together with a bottle of bleach. Everywhere was very clean, Alec noted.

'Fingerprints?'

Frobisher laughed. 'So far, one partial under the window catch. We doubt we'll get a match from it.'

Alec was thoughtful. 'To find Penbury's prints here would have been normal. Absence of prints is distinctly not. So, does that mean someone else was here that Penbury didn't want anyone to know about? Or do we have his prints on file?' Alec frowned. That didn't make sensc cither. This place was registered to Madigor. It was official and above board. And they had this Joshua Penbury's home address, which, no doubt would, or should, be covered with his prints.

It was like the address book; almost as if someone was trying that bit too hard to make things look strange, to deflect investigation. But what, exactly, from?

He looked around the room again. Something was missing. 'Where have you put the telephone?'

Frobisher looked puzzled. 'There was no phone.'

'You're sure?'

'We'd have seen a phone.'

Of course they would, and yet, Alec thought, a phone had certainly been there until a couple of days – no, until the day before. He had called the number Griffin had given to him. The number registered to this office. It had rung out. There had been a phone here.

He used his mobile to take pictures of the shipping receipts and the one solitary bill, did one more swift sweep of the room, and then got into his car and headed for the home of the mysterious Mr Penbury, Madigor's ersatz owner.

The home of Joshua Penbury was in a modern cul-de-sac. It was technically detached, which meant about five feet of space between the garage of one house and the wall of the next. Red-brick, UPVC windows and a patch of front lawn bordered by flowers, it was supremely ordinary. To the rear was a small but beautifully manicured walled garden. Climbers supported on vine wires clothed the walls, flowering shrubs and bright flowers filled the beds leaving space for another postage stamp lawn and a compact deck just outside of the French windows. A solitary cast-iron chair set next to a small cast-iron table, protected by a white linen parasol that almost filled the deck space. This was not a place for entertaining, Alec thought, but for enjoying a sort of solitary splendour at the end of a day spent clipping the lawn with a pair of nail scissors. He truly had never seen such an exact and pristine creation.

The house had three bedrooms, one clearly occupied, the second set up with a futon and a single wardrobe, as though to give some semblance of it being a guest room. The third had a desk, computer and small filing cabinet.

Downstairs was a through lounge with a seating area and television at one end and a dining table – small, with just a couple of chairs – at the end with the French windows. The kitchen was, as he would have expected, pristine. Black counters, white cupboards, concealed fridge and freezer. A small utility room off the kitchen afforded room for the washing machine and dryer and a bright-red cat bed. Bright-red bowls for food and water had been set out beside it, and the rear door, which gave on to the side of the house, just to the rear of the garage, had a cat flap inserted into the UPVC panel.

'Where's the cat?' he asked a passing *CSI*.

'Fergie is next door with the neighbour.'

'Fergie? What kind of a cat name is that?'

She laughed. 'I've got two cats,' she said. 'Chintz and Amygdala.' She laughed again. 'Don't ask.'

‘I think I’d better not.’ He wandered back into the main room, wondering vaguely what he’d call a cat should he ever have one. He’d always viewed the name Napoleon as an odd one for a dog, but it sort of suited the big black animal. He stood in the lounge and looked around. Evidence boxes had been stacked on the small dining table, but Alec could see it was solid, well made and of very nice timber. He thought some kind of oak, but he’d never been good with wood recognition. The chairs matched. Chunky and solid and not very comfortable looking. The curtains were heavy. Damask fabric, lined, and with a darker border. They matched the cushions on the dark-grey sofa and light-grey chair. And the rug, set in the middle of the cream carpet, seemed to be from the same range. A tall bookshelf standing against the wall at the dining end matched the table and also the small unit on which the television had been placed.

No music, Alec thought, or the means for playing it. There had been a radio in the kitchen, one of the few objects left out on the counter, though the cupboards had been full of kitchen gadgetry and the fridge was well stocked. Oddly, Alec thought, the choice of food was the most human, normal and comprehensible thing about this place. He’d been in show homes or hotel rooms with more individuality. It was almost as though whoever had chosen the furnishings had looked at what other people had and figured out that to look normal they'd need a sofa and a chair and...

He wandered over to the bookshelves. Unsurprisingly, given that Madigor was supposed to be an importer of things oriental, there were books about Japan and Thailand and China. There were also books on antiques and glass and silver, but there were no objects in the room that spoke of any interest in collecting. Nothing from the business seemed to have made its way home.

He began to look earnestly for what might be deemed personal objects. Beside the chair was what he remembered was called a Canterbury. Harry had one he'd picked up at an antiques fair, and he used it for papers and magazines. He'd told Alec that originally they had been for music.

Unlike the other furniture, this one was in dark wood and heavily carved, at odds with everything else in the room. Alec squatted down and admired the intricate detail of the turning and the wealthy polish; the old wood glowed in the afternoon sun. Unlike Harry's version, which was usually overflowing with remnants of Sunday paper or magazines on art or boats or whatever Patrick's latest passion might be, this was distinctly empty.

On the wall above the fireplace was a very beautiful mirror. Heavy and clearly old and with what Alec recognized as a pewter repoussé frame, Alec felt it was oddly familiar. He stared at it for a moment, taking in the flowers and bees, and then it hit him. The photo frame Jamie had sent them was a miniature version of this.

Had she been trying to tell them something? Was there, after all, something hidden in the frame? Alec would have sworn not. Like all repoussé pieces, the back was hollow, showing the pattern of indentations that made up the external pattern in relief. There had been no space in which to hide anything. He frowned, remembering that it was now at Harry's place. He would have to ask them to take another look.

He beckoned to one of the *SOCO* team. 'Give me a hand to take this down?'

The mirror was heavy. They laid it face down on the floor, and Alec examined the back. Old paper sealed it, covering both mirror and the inside edge of the frame. There didn't seem to be any disturbance to the original manufacture.

A stained label bore the name of a gallery in Paris and also what he took to be a maker's name. Phillipe Gerard. It meant nothing to Alec. He ran his hands around the edges of the paper seal. It lifted easily from one edge, but he soon realized this was only where the glue had hardened and fragmented. He peeled it away and looked at the back of the mirror beneath. Some of the silvering had begun to chip and crack and peel away, but other than that there was nothing to see.

He propped the mirror against the sofa and went back upstairs.

'Anything?' he asked hopefully.

A uniform and a *CSI* both looked up and

shook heads. 'Not so far.'

'Hopefully, there'll be something on the computer.'

'Nope. He uses a removable hard drive.' She indicated an empty space in the front of the machine. 'He's taken it with him. Tell you what, though, he can come and clean for me anytime. There's barely a cat hair or a fingerprint.'

He was wasting his time here, Alec thought. He went next door to where a young female officer was interviewing the cat-loving neighbour.

'This is Fergie,' he was told. A rather handsome tortoiseshell sat on the woman's lap in pride of place. Three other rather put-out-looking felines piled beside her on the settee. They looked pointedly at Alec, as though it was all his fault.

'Tell me about your neighbour,' Alec said. 'How did you get along with him?'

She looked surprised. 'Oh, he's a lovely man. No trouble at all. No noise, and he does his garden. I wasn't sure about him when he moved in, you know–' she leaned forward confidentially, her tight permed grey hair bouncing slightly as she did so – 'him being a single man and all, but he's been fine. I said he ought to have a cat, you know, some company for him, and he said all right, if I could advise him on that, and so I asked around and I got Fergie for him. Poor thing, his lady died, you know, and he was looking for someone new to be with and

Mr Penbury was just perfect. And of course he comes over here and plays with my lovelies, don't you, Fergie?'

Alec left. So that accounted for the oddly named cat and the outrageously red accoutrements of cat ownership.

What more could he do here?

Nothing, he decided.

He called Eddison and told him he was making his way to the incident room. Called Harry and asked if he and Patrick would take another look at the photo frame and the rest of Jamie's stuff. Gave his love again to Naomi and got back in his car. Reset his satnav. Drove north and west this time, listening to the news.

TWENTY

Clara Thompson opened her front door and wished she hadn't. The man outside was not particularly tall, neither was he especially muscular, but once he had taken hold of her there was nothing she could do to escape, no matter how hard she struggled or how she spit and fought.

She screamed and cursed at him, hoping the neighbours would hear, but knowing almost for certain that there was no one in next door. They'd all be at work on a Wednesday. The man must have known that too; he held on to her very tightly, fastened her hands behind her back with something she vaguely recognized as a cable tie and then fastened that to another looped through the back of a kitchen chair. She kicked out as he grabbed her feet, but he caught them then tied them securely to the legs of the chair, but he didn't bother to try and shut her up. His movements were neat and efficient, almost casual. Clara had been afraid before. Afraid when those thugs had beaten Paul for information he didn't have. Afraid when the police had come. Afraid every day for her children. But that was nothing to what she felt now.

He's going to kill me, she thought. He'd made no attempt to hide his face. He didn't care that she might recognize him again.

He left her in the kitchen. He'd taken a small device from his pocket, and now he walked back down the hall, listening to the small hum it made and watching a tiny screen.

Since there was nothing to be gained by screaming, Clara shut up and watched and tried to work out how she could escape. The ties cut into her wrists when she tried to move them, and she was now so tense she could hardly breathe.

She watched as the man bent down to look beneath her telephone table and take something that had been concealed there. She watched as he went upstairs, strained to hear him moving about and struggled against her bonds so hard she could feel her hands begin to bleed.

He came back down, and she watched again as he went into the front room and then the big room in the extension. In all that time he never made a sound, never uttered a word.

Then he came back into the kitchen and laid what he had found on the table. Curious, in spite of her terror, Clara leaned forward and looked. 'What the hell are they?'

Tiny round disks, each with a little pin wire extending on one side.

The man did not reply, but glanced around the room. He noticed the tenderizing mallet in the rack hanging beside the knives and ladles and slotted spoons, and for a moment Clara thought he was going to use it on her. She screamed again and then once more as he brought the mallet down on the small black objects resting on the table, crushing them like insects.

'Off-the-shelf product,' he said. 'You can get them on the Internet or in half a dozen real world shops up and down the country. They work, but their range is short. I doubt if there's anyone out there still listening, and if they are, I doubt very much that they are concerned with your welfare, Clara. Certainly, no one came running when they heard you scream, did they?'

'What?' The information coalesced in Clara's mind. 'Someone bugged my house? Oh, my God, when? Who, and who the hell are you?'

He dealt with the final question first. 'Many people would consider me their worst nightmare,' he said. 'But for you, Clara, I'll only be a very bad dream. I've no wish to hurt you, but that doesn't mean I won't, not if you don't tell me what I need to know.'

She stared at him, stunned.

'As to who planted these, well, *you* can tell me that. Who has been here? What did they want to know, and when did they come?'

'Why should I tell you?'

'Because I'll hurt you if you don't. It's what I do, one of the things I have a talent for. Clara, I've no grudge against you, no reason to want you dead or even severely maimed, so I will promise to do no lasting harm. But I will hurt you all the same, so how about we make this easy?'

He gave her time to think. Like Munroe, he, too, knew the value of silence. Of non-action.

'I don't know who they were,' she said. 'Some thugs came here and beat Paul. They wanted to know about Neil, what he'd told us about that journalist.'

'Jamie Dale?'

'Yes, her.'

'And what had he told you?'

She shook her head. 'Nothing. Paul wasn't even here when Neil called. He was working late that night. Neil just wanted me to phone her and pass a message on. It wasn't even a message. Just to call her.'

'And it was about? She was to contact him about what?'

That rapid head-shake again. She was twisting her hands against the ties, and the plastic dug into her wrists. He could see the blood dripping to the floor, but she seemed unaware.

'About what?' he prompted.

'It was just one word. A one-word message.'

She thought that must be too simple an answer, he could see that. She thought it wasn't a big enough secret to warrant all this death, all this trouble. She thought he wouldn't believe her when she told him how simple it was.

'And the word?'

'Gregory. Just a name. Just Gregory.'

He nodded and could see the relief in her eyes that he seemed satisfied. It would be easy now; she wouldn't fight him any more. 'Who else came here?'

'Just the police.'

'The police?'

'Yes. To tell me Neil was dead, and then they came back. One of the original policemen came back, and another one, a different one.'

'Their names were?'

She shook her head. She was trying to remember. 'They left a card,' she said. 'One was called Munroe, and the other left a card.'

'You still have it?'

'Yes, in the big room. On the bookshelf. Behind the television. I was going to throw it away but—'

He went through and found it. One glance at the name confirmed who had been responsible for the listening devices. Though it wasn't like Charlie Eddison to buy off the shelf. He must have been in a hurry.

He returned to the kitchen and took a pair of cutters from his pocket. She flinched when he touched her, convinced this was going to be the promised pain. He released her hands, but not her feet.

'Tell me, did you call anyone after they had gone? Straight after they had gone?'

He saw the look of horror in her eyes. She stared at the remnants of the bugs still on the table. 'I called my husband,' she whispered. 'I called Paul.'

He nodded. He had expected that. 'And how long were you on the phone to him?'

'Less than a minute. He hung up on me. He

said I was stupid to be calling him.'

She bit at her lower lip. He could see little flecks of dry skin and small red weals where others had been chewed off.

'Have you called him since?'

An emphatic no. She had not. 'They were listening in, is that what you're telling me? They listened to my call. They'll know where Paul is, where the kids are.'

'If you didn't stay on for longer than you told me, then no. Not from that. The danger is that they may try and contact him again.'

'His phone's been off since!'

'So you *did* try?'

A rapid rush of blood to her cheeks as she was caught in the half lie, followed swiftly by an equally rapid draining of colour as she realized what she might have done. 'You hear about it in films, don't you? People being traced by their mobile phones. Oh God, he didn't even tell me where they'd gone. He didn't want me to know in case those thugs came back and—'

'Clara, listen to me. Paul and your children, they will *not* be safe. They never were.'

'What do you mean? He didn't tell me anything! Paul didn't tell me where they were!'

He sighed. How best to explain this? Few people were actually good at disappearing. They always left a trail, they always left too many links in the chain.

'Clara, Paul isn't me, he isn't even you. If you'd wanted to give your kids the best chance, then *you* should have taken them, far away from here. You'd likely have done a far better job. He'll have gone somewhere he feels safe, somewhere he knows. Somewhere familiar, Clara, and it won't take much working out where that is. Not for you, not for me, not for them.'

'How do I know you aren't *them* too?'

He decided to forgive her for the grammatical error. 'Some other time I might well be, but not just now. For a little time our interests run side by side. And you can trust me.'

'Trust you?' She laughed harshly. 'I don't think so.' She paused, considering, her eyes wide and her mouth tight. 'And if that changes?'

'If that changes you will never know.'

'Why?' But she knew the answer.

He leant close, deciding he would say it anyway. 'Because, Clara, you and yours would already be dead.'

Leaving her in the kitchen he went back to examine the house room by room. He could hear her sobbing. It occurred to him that now she had her hands free she might try and prepare herself for when he returned, get a knife from the rack, or the mallet from the table. He had left her feet tied to the chair, but it was possible she'd have freed herself by the time he returned.

He thought it unlikely though. He'd filled her mind with doubt, with renewed fears, and for a while she would be numb, inactive until the shock diminished.

The little girls obviously shared a room. Large, square and airy and decorated in pink and a rather acid green, as though they had both been allowed to choose a colour. Green and pink also on the beds. Books, boxes of toys, a small desk on which drawings and pencils had been spread. He opened the wardrobe door and tried to guess what had been taken. The hangers had been spaced across the rail as though to give an impression of fullness, when in fact half the clothes were missing. He opened drawers and found their sparseness similarly disguised. Clara had thought this through as best she could. He was right – she should have been the one to take the children. Fierce mothers were always a dangerous animal.

The master bedroom was tidy, clean, undistinguished. Pale lavender on the walls, and cream everywhere else apart from a splash of colour in the duvet. Family photos by the bed. The four of them in happier times, and the little girls. He took the picture of the children and put it in his pocket. The larger photo had clearly previously been hanging on the wall – a loop of string had been threaded through the little metal hook on the back of the cheap frame – but it now stood on the bedside cabinet, supported by the strut.

So she still cared for him, he thought. Paul, not just the children, figured in her fears. He wondered how the husband now felt. If he blamed his wife for having such an errant brother.

The third room had been converted to a home office. He spent a little time examining the paperwork, but it seemed to be a mix of household bills and items relating to the car dealership.

He took the laptop anyway and a stick drive he found in a drawer.

Downstairs, in the hall, a space where the larger photograph had hung. He checked the two rooms, noticing that there were several pictures taken on a long sweeping beach. A closer look revealed a ruined cottage on the headland. He took that picture with him back to the kitchen and laid it on the table. Clara hadn't moved.

'Where is this?' he asked quietly.

'I won't tell you.'

Carefully, he took the back off the frame and slipped the picture out. There was nothing written on the reverse, and he saw her relief and little triumph and then her shock as he put the picture in his pocket with the first one.

'Neil sent something to you,' he said.

'I don't know what you mean.'

'He sent you something not long before he died.'

He saw her eyes flick towards the doorway and the big room. 'I'd like it, Clara.' Until that moment he had been guessing. It was good to have confirmation. 'And I'd like to know where this picture was taken.'

No response.

'Clara, I can look, but that would just involve

a mess and would take some time. Do you really want me in your house longer than is strictly necessary?'

She tensed, and he saw she had some of her fight back. He could admire that, he thought, but her timing really wasn't all that good. He didn't have the time or the patience today.

He gave her one last chance. 'What did he send you?' Then he took her hand. She tried to pull away, then tried harder as he placed a thumb on the pressure point on her wrist and twisted the hand. He felt the joint give way, the wrist bend beyond what nature had intended for it. He released the pressure slowly. He could see in her face that she was close to passing out, and he didn't want to have to wait for her to recover.

But it was enough. He brought the envelope through to the kitchen and laid the contents on the kitchen table. Three postcards, one of a vessel he recognized.

'What are these?'

'You should frigging know. You sent them to him.'

She was cradling the injured wrist, glaring at him, trying not to let the tears come. Clara, he thought, was a tough woman.

'Why do you think I sent them, Clara?'

She swallowed nervously. 'I don't know. He said I had to keep them but he didn't say why. I was supposed to keep them and give them to Jamie Dale, he said they were something to do with this Gregory.' Her eyes widened as a thought struck her. 'Are you Gregory?' she said.

He didn't reply. Instead, he turned the postcards over and looked at the brief messages. 'They are signed with an F,' he said.

She nodded. 'Neil thought they were from Freddie. Freddie Gains, they were friends. Then he realized – realized they were something else.'

'Something else? What did he tell you about them?'

'Nothing. Really nothing. He just got someone out on day release to post them for him and asked me to give them to Jamie Dale. But then he died, and then she was in that car crash and—'

'Who else did you tell? About the cards. Or about Gregory?'

'No one. I wouldn't lie to you. No one. I told no one.'

He believed her. She'd gone beyond the will to lie; now all she wanted was him to be satisfied and then to go.

He left the house a few minutes later with the laptop and the pictures and the postcards, satisfied that he had learnt all he could.

He had placed a knife on the table, close enough for her to reach, and advised her how to look after the damaged wrist. She could free herself now, though he knew it would take her a while to gather enough momentum to do that, when the nausea had passed.

Leave here, he had told her. Pack a bag and

go. But he didn't think she would.

And he had gained one other thing. She had given him a description of those who had come to beat her husband. From the way she had described them and what they had done, Gregory was almost sure they would turn out to be just local thugs, paid by the job and knowing nothing about why they were commissioned to do it. His local contacts would soon come up with a name or two, he was pretty sure of that. And he would not be as gentle with them as he had been with Clara Thompson.

TWENTY-ONE

Suddenly, the tension had seemed to diminish. Nothing happened – no phone calls, no threats, nothing to fear – and it was odd the way this only seemed to add to the sense of menace. It was as though someone or something was drawing deep breath before returning to the attack.

Naomi had been surprised to be invited to Jamie's funeral and very surprised to find that her body had come home to Pinsent for burial. Somehow she had expected Jamie to be buried down south, where she had worked and lived for the past decade. To Naomi's knowledge only her sister now lived close to their old home; her father had died while the girls were still young, and the mother – a woman Naomi had met only a couple of times – had moved back to Wales, where she had spent her girlhood.

The invitation had come from Jamie's sister, Belinda, delivered via a mutual friend.

Jamie Dale had been dead for almost three weeks. It was five days since the attack on Travers, and four since the last phone call: Jamie's voice calling Naomi's name. Three since the explosion they now knew had killed five and injured many more.

She had barely slept in the intervening time, even though there had been no more calls, no more drama. The lack of contact, absence of continuity, getting to her almost as much as the calls had done. Anticipation frayed her nerves.

As Munroe had observed: never underestimate the value of silence.

Although the rolling news regarding the explosion had now ceased, every news bulletin still led with it, though as far as Naomi could tell, there had been no new developments. In the absence of facts, folklore manifested, and the number of terrorist organizations either claiming responsibility or denying involvement, dizzying as it was, only added to the sense of ongoing drama. Among the wild theories were that it was Al Qaeda, Irish terrorists, animal rights activists, anarchists...

The police denied each claim, each conspiracy, but replaced it with nothing concrete. Alec could tell her little more; alternating between being stuck in the office, following the Madigor paper trail and interviewing witnesses, he felt peripheral.

And now there was Jamie's funeral.

'Should I go?' she asked Alec when he phoned.

'Any reason why not?'

'I suppose not. Will you be there? I just feel so...'

'I think we all feel like that. Yes, I'll be there.

Munroe too.'

He didn't sound very happy about that, she thought. 'I'll ask Harry to take me then.'

'Do that. I'll see you there.'

And so she had. Harry drove her to the service at St Anne's church and then to the graveside at the local cemetery out on the main coast road. The day was warm, but a harsh wind blew off the sea as it always did and Naomi was glad she'd worn a jacket over her summer dress, a grey print she hoped was suitable for such an occasion. Black seemed too sombre for the Jamie she had known, but she didn't quite have the courage to wear the bright colours her one-time friend had so loved.

Alec and Munroe had not come into the church. They had arrived late, he explained briefly as everyone filed out and he met her by the door.

'If you want to go with your wife to the cemetery, I'll follow on,' Munroe said.

He had an interesting voice, Naomi thought. Such an odd mix of accents, as if he had lived in a great many places and assimilated just a smidgen of local colour in each one.

'Thanks,' Alec said briefly. He took her arm tightly, and they walked with Harry to his car. 'Napoleon not with you?'

'He's stayed home with Patrick. They're at Mari's house helping paint the back bedroom.'

'Ah. So what colour dog are we likely to get back?' He helped Naomi into the rear seat and then collapsed beside her with a deep sigh.

'Tough time?' Harry said softly.

'It has been, yes. I have to say it would have been tougher if I hadn't known you'd all been there for Naomi. I'm grateful, Harry.'

'No need to be, you know that. We're all family, Alec.'

She felt him nod. She wanted to ask about the case, about Munroe, about so many things, and, for once, she didn't think he'd be reticent about Harry listening in. Harry already knew so much. Naomi sensed, though, that he didn't want to talk right now. That all Alec wanted was to sit quietly in the car and forget for a few minutes. Instead she said, 'There didn't seem to be many in the church. I'd have expected it to be full.'

'A dozen or so people,' Harry confirmed. 'Maybe there'll be more at the cemetery.'

'A lot of the old crowd have moved away,' Alec said. 'And I suppose we're a long way from London. Will there be a wake?'

'No one said anything.'

'The mother wasn't there,' Alec said. 'What was her name...?'

'Gwenda,' Naomi said. 'I didn't get to speak to Belinda.'

'I said hello as they all came out. I'm not sure she knew who I was. Clive McAllister was there, with Josie and Terry Livingstone. Gaynor Hedges, and a man I didn't recognize. Others that seemed to be family.'

She reached for his hand and held it tight, feeling the weariness that suffused him. Weariness and something, she sensed, close to despair. 'Don't go back,' she said. 'Alec, you can always just walk away, you know that. No one will think any the less of you.'

'I will,' he said. 'I'll think less of me.' He squeezed her hand. 'Afterwards, we'll talk about it.'

The car turned into the cemetery gates, and the wheels crunched on the gravel surface. Harry stopped the car. 'We're here,' he said unnecessarily. 'Um, seeing as Alec's here and I didn't really know the deceased ... I'm happy to stay in the car if—'

'Harry, please come with us,' Naomi said.

'Besides,' Alec added, 'I'm sort of on duty. I'd better get back to Munroe. Look, if any of the family ask, I just managed to call in on the way to somewhere else and Munroe is simply a work colleague who got dragged along. Naomi, not even Belinda knows exactly what happened to Jamie in that car.'

'You mean it's still not an official murder enquiry?' Harry was startled. 'Alec, how can you all keep that from the family?'

'It's a murder enquiry, yes, but no one is saying that officially. Harry, this is not like any situation I've ever been involved in, and I'll admit I'm far from happy, but...'

'No, but it's so ... What will happen when the family have to be told? They will be told eventually, won't they?'

'Eventually, yes. I expect the official line will be that new evidence has emerged. Fortunately, that isn't my call, Harry, and I'm hoping I won't be the one to break it to them. All this came from well above my rank and pay grade.'

'And must have been decided practically on the spot,' Naomi said wonderingly. 'Alec, that's so irregular.'

'What isn't about this? You aren't supposed to know either, never mind Harry, so—'

'Secret is safe,' Harry said. He sighed. 'I suppose in a way it's better for the family to believe this was just an accident. That's bad enough, but to know your loved one was deliberately murdered, that's something else again.'

And Harry knew the truth of that, Naomi thought. His sister Helen, her closest childhood friend, had been taken from her family in exactly that way, and it had been years before the family knew the full truth of the matter.

'Who else is here?' she asked as they walked to the graveside.

'Only those who came to the church, by the look of things.' Alec laughed, but there was a sadness in the sound. 'I can remember the time when if Jamie called and suggested a night out there'd be—'

'Usually about twenty of us, even at short notice.' Naomi smiled. 'What happened, Alec? This is so not right.'

They stood beside the grave, Alec to her left and Harry on her right. Someone read a poem; the vicar, or so she assumed, repeated almost word for word the eulogy he had given in the church. Perhaps he, too, had expected there to be a new audience at the cemetery, or perhaps he hadn't been able to think of anything new to say. Belinda said a sad farewell to her sister. 'There's only me left now, sis. Dad gone and then mum and now you.'

Ah, the mother was dead too, Naomi thought.

'I'll miss you so much, and I'm so sorry that we drifted so far apart.'

Naomi felt the tension in Alec's body as he heard that. So Belinda had lost touch with her too? That sounded so wrong as well. The sisters were only a couple of years' difference in age and had always been very close. What had gone so wrong that she'd cut herself off from those she loved, and what had driven her to appeal to Naomi for help? An appeal that had reached out only after Jamie's death, and then with such a different intent.

The little party broke up. Naomi and Alec managed to speak to Belinda at last, offering condolences, though it was clear she barely remembered them. Gaynor Hedges, the friend who had invited Naomi on Belinda's behalf, sidled up to them as they moved off. 'Hi, Naomi, hi, Alec, glad you could make it.'

'There's hardly anyone here.'

'No, that's what we were afraid of. Bel asked me if I could round up as many old friends as possible, but so many of us live somewhere else, and I don't know any of Jamie's London friends. I thought some of them would be here though.'

'Didn't anyone come?'

'One guy, some producer fella she worked with. I'll introduce you.' Gaynor sighed. 'I'd never have pegged Jamie as the first to leave. She was always the last one out the door.'

Naomi nodded. Terry McAllister touched her arm and said how sorry he was, someone else expressed disbelief. She heard Belinda's voice thanking them for coming and expressing thanks to the vicar. It was obvious that everyone was drifting away, and no one seemed inclined even to suggest a visit to the local pub to have a drink in Jamie's honour. Just how far apart had the sisters moved?

Gaynor returned with someone in tow. 'This is Matthew Broughton,' she said. 'He was working with Jamie just before she died. Matthew, Naomi Blake. Sorry, it's Friedman now isn't it, doofus. And her husband, Alec.'

Where had Harry disappeared to, Naomi wondered as she shook hands with Matthew.

'Look, I've got to dash, got to collect the kids from my mum's. She picked them up from school.' She pecked Naomi on the cheek. 'I'll give you a ring next week and we'll have that coffee.'

'So,' Alec said as the silence after the first introduction threatened to become uncomfortable. 'You worked with Jamie?'

'I did, yes. She talked about the two of you. In fact I think you were the only friends she ever mentioned.'

'She had a lot of friends,' Naomi said defensively. 'Once upon a time,' she added sadly.

'Matthew, did no one else want to come for the funeral?'

She could feel him hesitate, and then he said. 'A few years ago if this tragedy had happened, there'd have been standing room only in the church, I can promise you. I knew her from when she first moved down, and the Jamie I first met was not ... was not the woman who died. Recently, Jamie had work colleagues, not friends. People she *had* to interact with to get the job done. I don't believe she saw anyone socially. She'd leave work, and while the rest of us might go for a drink, or stand around and chat for a few minutes before we went off home, Jamie was just gone. She seemed to go out of her way to alienate people, and that was costing her. I mean, not only on a personal level. Work-wise too.'

'Look,' Alec said. 'There's a pub down the road. The Black Horse. They serve reasonable food too. How about we all adjourn there?'

'Yes, that would be good,' Matthew agreed. 'I could do with a drink, and I drove up first thing so something to eat would be welcome. You're a policeman, aren't you? In fact I think—'

'I was too,' Naomi confirmed. 'Officer, not man, I mean. That's how we all met up. We found ourselves covering the same incidents. I liked her a lot. Alec, where's Harry got to?'

Alec looked around. 'Talking to Munroe,' he said.

'Oh?'

'Oh indeed,' Alec said.

* * *

Munroe had separated himself from the funeral attendees, standing off to one side in the shade of a cedar tree and watching the interaction. Or lack of it. Alec had seemed to know most of those present, briefing him on who was friend and who was stranger.

'Small turnout,' Munroe had observed, and Alec had agreed.

Munroe had been very surprised when Harry Jones wandered across to join him beneath the cedar.

'Feels a bit awkward,' Harry said, as though Munroe had asked. 'Not really having known the deceased. Don't you feel that too?'

Munroe found he was amused. 'I often attend funerals,' he said. 'I rarely know the one who died.'

'Well,' Harry observed thoughtfully, 'I suppose we all need a hobby.'

Munroe made no comment. He made himself comfortable leaning against the bole of the tree and continued to watch.

'I don't think I want a eulogy at my funeral,' Harry said.

'Oh, and why is that?' Despite himself, Munroe was amused by this balding, dumpy man.

'Because eulogies always seem to pick out the things people think *should* be remembered, not the things that are really important to the dead person. I can remember my sister's funeral so vividly. Well, her memorial, really. First time around we didn't have a body to bury.'

Interested now, Munroe glanced at the man beside him. 'So you had two funerals?' Something from the background reading he had done on the Friedmans, Alec and Naomi, clicked into place. 'Ah, so you'll have been Helen's brother. Naomi's best friend when they were kids.'

Many people would have been perturbed that he knew that, or would have asked if Alec had told them, but Harry merely nodded. 'Helen's brother, yes. You know, for a very long time I think that's how we defined ourselves. I was Helen's brother. The brother of the little girl that disappeared, who everyone knew must be dead but who everyone still talked about as though she might turn up one day and it would all be fine. And Naomi was Helen's friend. The one that *didn't* get killed, or go missing or whatever it was people chose to think had happened to her. I believe, you know, it even affected the way my son thought of himself. Helen was there, in the background. The ghost at the feast.'

Monroe nodded briefly. 'Often the way of it,' he said.

'And yet, I don't think it's going to be that way for this poor dead thing, is it?'

'I'm not sure I'm following you.'

'Jamie. Naomi tells me that Dale was a pen name. She was Jamie Foucault. She apparently thought that Dale was snappier – more tabloid, I suppose.'

Munroe laughed softly. 'That's a very snobby thing to say, don't you think?'

'Oh, probably. It wouldn't be the first time I've been accused of that. But don't you think it's sad?'

'I take it we're not talking about her choice of pen name.'

'No, we're not. I mean, Helen was, as I say, the ghost at the feast, but she was at least there, and there was at least a feast for her to be at. We celebrated my little sister. I don't think this poor young woman will be celebrated, do you?'

Munroe shifted his position and looked more directly at Harry. 'What do you *really* want to say to me?'

Harry seemed to hesitate for a moment, and then he said, 'I suppose I want to say that I am very protective of those I love. As is Alec.'

'And?'

'But the difference between us is that Alec also has a sense of honour. It's that sense of honour that made him agree to come back and work with you and the rest. Agree much against his better judgement, I might add.'

'And you don't have a sense of honour?' Munroe laughed again. 'Harry Jones, you are one of the most conventional—'

'Perhaps I am. But don't mistake that for—'

'Harry, are you trying to threaten me?' Munroe was truly amused now.

'Threaten? No. Look, I've known men like you before. My ex-boss was one, and I can make a pretty good guess about your background and what you can be capable of. I'm just telling you. So far you've been able to take advantage of Alec's sense of honour, of his sense of what is right. After Helen died, I realized something about myself. I'm not proud of having realized it, and it doesn't fill me with any sense of superiority, I've just learnt to accept it over the years. I discovered hatred and anger were very much a part of Harry Jones. That I had, if you like, a vengeful spirit. I discovered that, and I made myself a promise: that if anyone I loved were ever threatened, and it came into my purview to do something about it, something to protect them, I would take the part of myself that is angry and vengeful and I would turn it loose. I discovered that, at heart, I'm not a terribly honourable man, Mr Munroe.'

Phillip Munroe studied Harry with more amusement and then new interest. Harry might be balding, dumpy, and too flabby around the middle, but Munroe looked into his eyes and saw something of himself reflected back.

'Harry? Phillip?' Alec was calling to them.

Munroe nodded. 'Time to join our friends,' he said. 'Take my card, Harry Jones. Give me a ring any time your evil twin decides to break out.'

The Black Horse was an old hostelry. It had been a coaching inn and still retained the archway into the stable block, the cobbled yard and the massive fireplaces inside. The fires were not lit at this time of year, and Naomi missed the scent of wood smoke and the crackle of flames as they were settled at a table and handed menus.

'Come and order at the bar when you're ready,' a cheerful voice told them.

'I've never been here in the summer,' Naomi said. 'I've always thought of this as a winter pub.'

'It is certainly very charming,' Matthew Broughton commented. 'Do you know if they still do rooms? I'm not relishing the thought of the drive back tonight.'

'I think so. I'll ask when I go and order,' Alec said.

There was quiet while they all contemplated the menu. Alec and Harry went to the bar to place the order and get drinks. Naomi wondered what Harry and Munroe had been talking about, but didn't really know how to ask.

Matthew broke the silence. 'So, did you know Jamie?' he asked Munroe.

'No. I'm like Harry, just providing the taxi service. Alec's working with me on another case.'

'Lucky you could both be spared for the afternoon,' Matthew said. 'Wouldn't it have been easier just to let Alec drive his own car?' He sounded amused.

'Probably,' Munroe told him in a tone that stopped the conversation dead.

Matthew won't give up, though, Naomi thought. His curiosity has been piqued, and he'll press the point. She said, 'I understand Jamie was working on a story about ex service people. Were you involved with that?'

'I was, yes. It's going to be called *Rough Sleepers* – at least, it is at the moment, you can never tell what some exec producer will finally do with the title or the sales pitch. And I'll make sure there's a dedication to Jamie when it goes out. She started the groundwork for it four or five years ago, but we didn't get the final go ahead until last year.'

'Is that usual? To have that kind of delay?'

'It's not uncommon, but in this case there were a couple of rival programmes commissioned, and that put the brakes on. We were told we'd got to find a new angle, and Jamie did. She started looking at comparative care here and in America, and in countries in the old Soviet Bloc, and she'd managed to do follow-up interviews with several of those featured in earlier documentaries. What was unusual is that she'd got help from several earlier filmmakers, and our film was, in part, updating and collating information about what happened after all the interest had died down.

'Originally she wanted to do a second documentary off the back of this one that focused on other groups in conflict zones and what happened to them when they came home. I've got her preliminary notes for that, and I'm going to do all I can to move it on.'

'What kind of groups?'

'Oh, aid workers, medics, both army and civilian, media – that sort of thing.'

'I'm not sure I get the link,' Naomi said. 'I

mean, you said this was a related documentary. Surely there aren't as many of those people homeless as among the service group?'

'I think that might be the point,' Munroe said drily.

'Well, yes, in a manner of speaking. We tend to forget that some people are working either in parallel to the armed forces or mopping up after the conflict is officially over – and note, I said "officially" here. I spent years reporting on frontline operations all over the world, and usually the ceasefire was just the start of the bigger problem. Anyway, Jamie's question was: when you reckon there are really quite large groups of people living in war zones for probably as long a period as many of the troops, maybe even having to defend themselves on occasion, certainly seeing the death and mayhem first hand, what is it about the support systems for them that largely cushions them from the after-effects?'

Monroe snorted. 'Give them guns and a body count, see what happens then.'

'That's exactly the point,' Matthew persisted. '*OK*, you've got aid workers and the like who, often as not, are conscientiously opposed to armed conflict and therefore don't get directly involved in the shooting. But what about the mercenary groups, the private security, the intelligence agents? Where do they end up?'

'Bouncing at your local nightclub,' Munroe suggested.

Alec and Harry returned with drinks. 'I've

booked you in for the night,' Alec told Matthew. 'You've just got to fill in the register. I thought it might be best.'

'Thanks, Alec,' Matthew said.

'You said, back at the funeral, that she didn't really have friends.'

'No, she didn't, not now. It started a couple of years ago. She was seeing this guy called Dan Toon. He was a cameraman she'd worked with – well, we'd both worked with on occasions. We all thought there'd be wedding bells, or at least a bit of cohabitation. She'd always liked to go out, enjoyed a drink, a club, you know Jamie – or rather you knew Jamie. Suddenly, out of the blue, she dumps him, moves out of her flat and changes her phone number. She even threatened to get an injunction out if he tried to see her. And it wasn't just Dan – she dropped out of sight except for work, and even that was hit and miss. I'm afraid Jamie started to get a reputation for unreliability. After a time, the list of people that wouldn't work with her – well, let's just say it was a long one.'

'But what happened? Surely it couldn't have happened just like that. There must have been signs. Did this Dan hurt her in some way?'

'No, you see, that's what was so strange. There were no signs. It was that sudden. There was this Friday night, November, two years last November. She and Dan and a whole group of us were out celebrating a birthday. Jamie was happy, laughing, as much fun to be with as she always was. Dan was happy, talking about a flat they'd just been to look at. We all went our separate ways about two in the morning, then I got a phone call from Dan on the Sunday saying Jamie had dumped him.'

'So what happened between early Saturday morning and the Sunday?' Naomi asked.

'Did they spend that night together?' Harry asked.

'Well, yes, sort of. Jamie apparently went back to Dan's place. When he woke up late Saturday morning she'd gone. He didn't think anything of it, then when he tried to call her later that day her phone was off. He tried her home phone, but no joy there either. He went round that night, let himself in, but no Jamie. Then she called him the next morning and just said she didn't want to see him again.'

Their meals arrived, and conversation paused.

'So what happened after that?' Alec wanted to know.

'She broke contact with just about everyone. Stopped seeing friends, stopped calling, stopped taking calls.' He hesitated, and then said, 'I think at first we all made it easy for her. You know how people try not to take sides with mutual friends but inevitably do? Well, I think a lot of us were shocked and took Dan's part. The rest of us just thought we'd wait her out, see if they could reconcile or if she started to make contact again. I think we took the easy option. I'm afraid that's what happened.'

'And you?'

'Left for the Middle East the week after the

split, came back five months later and Jamie was no longer part of the scene. Dan said he'd gone to the flat, *her* flat, tried to let himself in, but she'd changed the locks. He kept trying to call her, but she changed her phone, only gave her number to people who absolutely had to have it. Then when he kept on trying to make contact she threatened to get an injunction. So he stopped. That was that.'

Naomi thought about it, trying to make sense of the sequence. Jamie had kept in sporadic contact with herself and Alec, had even called when they sent the wedding invitation. Had she sounded like her old self? No, Naomi decided, she'd said she was tired and in the middle of projects that were taking all her time and energy, and Naomi had assumed this was why she hadn't been her bubbly self. The card and photo frame had arrived and, Naomi realized, she had given Jamie little further thought.

'*You* stayed in touch though,' she said.

'Not at first,' Matthew admitted. 'I was home in London for a couple of weeks and then back in the field. It was the best part of ten, eleven months before I actually saw Jamie again, and that was only because I bumped into her one day. She'd been in to see one of the commissioning editors, and we ran into one another in the lobby. We chatted, had coffee, and I made a point of keeping in touch.'

'How did she seem?'

'Quieter,' he said, so quickly that Naomi realized he'd given this a lot of thought. 'Older.

Sadder, somehow.'

'Did she say anything? I mean, about what happened.'

'Naomi, I soon learnt to keep the conversation neutral. I could discuss work or the weather, even what was in the news, but the moment the conversation even looked like turning personal it was like I'd pressed the off switch. I heard she was having trouble getting work, and I did what I could to help, but she wasn't the same. She was as efficient as ever, sometimes, then she'd suddenly not turn up for work or she'd be so snippy with everyone that the atmosphere was terrible. I'm afraid to say I'd reached the point where – well, we had an almighty row. Later, I heard about the crash and that she was dead.'

Silence for a few beats. Munroe broke it this time. 'What did you fight about?'

Matthew laughed bitterly. 'Her behaviour towards the rest of the crew. She was constantly picking fault, utterly impatient, and yet she didn't seem to know what she *did* want. We'd been editing a sequence, some filming we'd done in Manchester, picking up threads from the earlier documentaries. It was going well, but suddenly Jamie was ranting, and I mean out of control ranting, just because someone put sugar in her tea. So, later on that day, I gave her an ultimatum. She either told me what was eating her, or she was finished so far as I was concerned. I couldn't go on covering up for her, smoothing things over—'

'And how long before the crash was that?'

'It was the day before. The next day she didn't turn up for work. I think we all breathed a secret sigh of relief and got on with editing the Manchester sequences. I got home that night and watched the news. She was dead.'

TWENTY-TWO

They left the Black Horse just after six with the intention of going to the house to collect clothes for Alec, check the post and pick up a few bits and pieces that Naomi wanted. Harry took Naomi and Alec, while Munroe followed on behind. Harry and Naomi would then go back Harry's, and Alec would return to the investigation with Munroe.

Matthew had, inevitably, asked them about that. Were they involved in the investigation, did they know anything? He probed for a while, but Munroe deflected him and Alec just watched with some amusement. By the time they left, Matthew Broughton knew no more than he had a couple of hours before. Alec found himself wondering if any of them did.

It was a bright, clear evening, though a slight chill to the stiffening breeze suggested that rain might be on the way. No one said much, the events of the afternoon had been unsettling and sad and an air of melancholy had descended that seemed resistant to conversation.

It was the first time Naomi had returned home since she had come with Harry, and she did not feel exactly comfortable doing so now. Megan had said she'd been getting a patrol car to do the odd extra run, but as Naomi wasn't there, focus had shifted to Harry's place back in the town.

'I'll wait in the car unless you need me,' Harry said.

'Just as you like,' Alec told him.

Munroe got out of his car and leaned against the wing. He looked as though he was enjoying the evening air, eyes half closed and his jacket off. Alec led the way inside.

They halted in the doorway, knowing at once that something was wrong.

'What is that smell?'

'You didn't leave anything out of the fridge?' Alec suggested.

'Alec, that isn't something left out of the fridge.'

'No, you're right, it's not. I think you should wait outside. Or wait here.'

'Alec!'

'OK.' He took her hand, and together they walked cautiously down the hall and into the kitchen. The kitchen door stood wide. The smell was overpowering now. Dead thing. Very dead thing. The buzzing of flies astonishingly loud in the enclosed space. Alec let go of Naomi's hand and moved to where he could see.

'What is it?' Naomi demanded. Then, suddenly understanding, 'Who is it?'

'I don't know.' Whoever it had once been, their face was now a bloody pulp. Something, Alec guessed close to a week's worth of decomposition, had done the rest. It could have been someone he knew and he'd not have recognized them. 'We should go.'

He led Naomi back out of the house and called to Munroe. Harry, realizing something was wrong, got out of his car. The smell was now following them though the house and outside, or was it just, Naomi wondered, that it had attacked the inside of her nose and fixed itself there?

'We were here only four days ago!' she said.

'He's been dead longer than four days. Harry, go home, please, I'll come to you there. Pack a bag and get ready to leave. Get Patrick and Mari to do the same. Munroe, get on to Eddison and tell him to get his backside over here.'

'Who are you calling?' Munroe wanted to know.

'People I can trust,' Alec said.

It was two hours before Alec arrived at Harry's place. He had called Megan Allison, and she had arrived with *PC* Watkins in tow and what looked to Alec like half the Pinsent force. *SOCO*s had been in evidence only minutes later, and Alec and Naomi's home, now a crime scene, was cordoned and isolated.

Alec waited until all had been set in motion, and then he got someone to give him a lift across town, leaving Munroe to explain to Eddison once he arrived.

'Do we know who it was?' Naomi asked.

'His name was Freddie Gains. He was a

friend of Neil Robinson. They served time together. Munroe recognized the tattoo on his arm.'

'So what now?' Naomi asked.

'I leave it to them. Eddison's been in touch, offered us a safe house. I've declined. I think I'm happier if we fend for ourselves. Harry—?'

'Taken care of,' Harry said. 'We're going to take Mum up to her sisters, and Patrick has been on the Internet and we've managed to bring our flights forward. We think Florida might be far enough away from trouble. What about the two of you?'

'Here,' Patrick said. 'I've charged these, so you can use yours right away. Then get another when you can. I've put the number of the other one in your phone.'

'What—?' Alec looked at the tiny phone Patrick had placed in his hand.

'We've got two. I take that one with me if I go out for the night. If I lose it, it's just a tenner gone and that includes top-up calls, and Dad takes the other one if we're out walking. I think it might be safer if, you know, we don't use our own.'

'I think you could be right. You've not registered either of these phones?'

Patrick shook his head. 'Gran's old car is in the garage,' he said. 'I've started it up and checked the oil and water. We thought it might be best if you use that.'

'You've thought of everything, haven't you?'

'Probably not,' Patrick said. 'But I think

we've got the obvious stuff.'

'Right, I think we should leave. Be careful, Harry.'

'You too.'

Minutes later and they were gone, headed in opposite directions, Alec setting out through Pinsent and then across country, watching in his mirror for any sign that they were being followed.

'You think they'll be all right?' Naomi asked.

'Yes, I think so. Eddison is convinced this all has to do with the original investigation. He thinks that's why Travers was targeted and why we have been.'

'But they tried to *kill* Trav. They seem to be just trying to put the frighteners on us.'

'And succeeding at that. Naomi, I don't pretend to know, but I think Eddison might be on to something. Neil Robinson said or did something that no one saw the significance of at the time. I don't think even Robinson knew he'd done it. Then, my guess is, he saw or was told something that made him realize he knew something important. So he tried to tell Jamie.'

'It must have been something she was involved in for him to make that connection. But what?'

'I'm guessing he must have confided in Freddie Gains, and maybe in his sister, Clara, too.'

'So why just scare us? Why kill him and Jamie and now this Freddie Gains and not us? It doesn't make sense.'

'It does if they think we have information. If they think we actually *know* what all this is about and can pass on whatever it is. Maybe they thought Jamie and Freddie Gains knew; maybe they tried to force that information out of them, but Jamie and Freddie simply didn't have it.'

'Neither do we,' Naomi pointed out, 'and ignorance didn't keep Jamie safe, did it?'

'Which is why we need to find whatever it is out,' Alec said.

'And how are we going to do that? And where are we going, anyway?'

'Wales,' Alec said.

'What's in Wales?'

'Oh, rain, sheep, hills, the odd mountain. And Clara, Neil Robinson's sister.'

TWENTY-THREE

If Jamie had simply kept to the brief she had been given, none of this would have happened, Gregory thought. She was a talented film maker and had a way with people; five minutes in her company and they were telling her their life story.

He paused, standing on the jetty and listening as he always did for sounds that might signal something not so ordinary. Gregory had been a little shaken when he'd recognized the image on the picture. His boat. She had never been registered as part of Madigor property. He had always filtered her ownership via other companies he had shares in. In fact, it had been with Neil's help that he had tightened this security, Neil's understanding of such things being broad and deep.

The Jeannie *was not a new or an attractive vessel – a converted collier, she had been little more than a transporter with a cabin until Gregory had purchased and converted her. From the outside she was still unprepossessing; inside, she was home, far more home than his current house was, than anywhere else he had ever lived had been.*

He had bought supplies, and he took them aboard now, started the engines and cast off before bothering to stow them. A sense of urgency affected him, and the feeling that he should put distance between himself and land. Between himself and those he now knew would be in pursuit.

Gregory was not afraid. It was simply that he didn't wish to be caught.

He chugged out into the gathering dusk, enjoying the last of the light, rounded the buoy that marked the harbour entrance and then followed the coastline around the headland before heading out into deeper water. The first stars emerged from a still pale sky. He loved this time of year with its long dusks.

Checking his charts again before dropping anchor, reassuring himself that he was in quiet waters here and hoping that no call had been put out to watch for the Jeannie, *he went below and put away the provisions he had bought.*

Gregory ate and then settled in front of his computer, searching through the files on Jamie Dale.

If she'd just stuck to the brief...

He recalled their first meeting: coffee, with a colleague of his, of Joshua Penbury's. Funny, he had now shed that persona so completely that it felt as though he was thinking of someone else. He had been employed as a technical adviser – not the first time he had taken such a role. Ex-military and with some experience in intelligence, according to his CV, Joshua

Penbury was just one of a list of 'experts' brought on board from time to time as advisers to film-makers.

Christopher had arranged it, of course, the original setting-up of that list. The careful selection of its members. He knew that if there was ever a vacuum, someone or something would move to fill it, and that someone might not be so easily controlled.

Of course, things had moved on since then, but some of the old guard still remained. Some dinosaurs to pick off the mammals. And he had liked Jamie. Loved her spirit and her idealism and her energy.

She should have kept to the brief.

The film she had been making, the issues raised, Gregory could have given his whole-hearted support to that – and he had. Getting her the introductions she required, even going with her to the homeless shelters in the UK and in the states and even in Moscow, where his fluency in the language had saved them a great deal of time and trouble.

Then, in Seattle, she had been introduced to a young soldier, a young marine who had told her about the game, and that had been that.

Gregory wasn't sure how he felt about the use of drones to carry bombs.

'But it saves lives, doesn't it?' Jamie had asked him.

'Does it? Or does it kill those who might not have died?'

'What do you mean?'

At the time he would not be drawn, but when Jamie came back she had filled in the gaps for herself.

'They call it Bugsplat,' she said. 'They treat it like a video game. I mean, not all of them, but some – and that's bad enough. They seem separate from it, like they're bombing little video people, not real live human beings.'

'That's always been the way of things,' Gregory had told her. 'You shut yourself off, keep it separate. Bomber pilots couldn't think of all the deaths they would cause. If you fire a missile, you don't know what it will take out. Even if you shoot a gun you can't be sure.'

'I know.' She had shrugged and smiled at him. 'But it seems like – I don't know, maybe every generation has its own version of night vision.'

'Night vision?' A little bell had rung in Gregory's brain. Something he had read about? Heard about?

'The new generation of drones. That's what the software is going to be called. It's deliberately been set up so it looks like game play, and that's what it will be called. The official line is that's so it's easier for kids who've grown up with computer games to assimilate the information in the training programmes, but ... I don't know, it all feels like it's designed to separate them even more from the real blood and guts of it all.'

'Where did you hear about this?'

She frowned, then giggled and refilled the glass of wine she had only half drunk. 'It's a

British company,' she said. 'I heard the name mentioned, and I did a bit of digging. Lots of palms being greased, Joshua. Lots of people going to make lots of money out of this one.'

Gregory closed his eyes and enjoyed the memory of Jamie, sitting on his boat, drinking his wine. It was the last time he could remember her being really happy.

'Don't push too hard,' he told her. 'Jamie, when there's big money involved there are big people.'

She had grinned that wonderful mischievous smile of hers. 'That's what I'm counting on,' she said. 'Pulitzer Prize, here I come.

And then she had discovered just what she was really up against and just how viciously big men protected their big money, and ultimately, she had died for that.

TWENTY-FOUR

The same night the *Jeannie* slipped her moorings and headed out to sea, Naomi and Alec headed into Wales and found a dog-friendly place to stay for the night. Harry and Patrick went north, depositing Mari at her sister's, and then, the house only being very small, finding their own place for the night in one of the big chain hotels.

Eddison had arrived an hour or so after Alec had departed and was far from happy to find that he had gone, even less sanguine to find that Alec's phone was not only off, but unobtainable.

Monroe wasn't quite sure why his boss was so riled. But he had other things on his mind.

'Why dump Freddie Gains here?' he wondered. 'Why kill him, for that matter? What did Freddie Gains ever know that was worth a damn?'

'Why assume that's why he was killed?' Eddison returned.

'Because they tortured him before they killed him. Why torture someone unless they know something?'

News came in the night that Christopher had died. Gregory knew his last protection had gone. 'I'm sorry,' the nurse told him. 'He went peacefully in the end.'

Gregory thanked her, and then removed the SIM card from his phone and threw it overboard before replacing it with another from his stock.

The night sky was the deepest of blues now, studded with little points of light. 'Goodbye old man,' Gregory said, and then went below.

Patrick had packed all of Jamie's cards and letters into a box and had brought them along. It seemed wrong to have left them back at home somehow. He and Harry had spread them out open on the bed. Patrick sat cross legged, leaning against the headboard. Harry had brought a chair and placed it at the side. Both cradled mugs of too-hot tea.

'Just Christmas and Birthday cards,' Harry said. The early ones had been filled with little notes and random chat, but as Jamie had become more established the notes had become shorter and the chat a little less informative. It happened, Harry thought, rejoicing again that Patrick had chosen to go to university but still live at home. He wasn't ready to be alone.

Patrick frowned. He picked up the last Christmas card again and looked more closely at Jamie's last address. The office owned by Madigor that she'd been using as a drop box.

Keep this safe, the message said. *So you can contact me*.

Keep this safe, Patrick thought. It seemed oddly emphatic.

'What the link was between Jamie and this criminal on the loose, I can't guess,' Harry mused.

'Maybe he isn't?'

'Isn't what?'

'A criminal. Maybe he's, I don't know, been framed.'

'Seems unlikely,' Harry said.

Patrick shrugged. 'I don't know, Dad, but think about it, if you wanted to blow something up and also commit murder and you didn't actually plan on getting caught, then surely you wouldn't use your own truck. I mean, think about it, it's not exactly the ideal getaway vehicle, is it?'

'Well, if you put it like that, I suppose it is odd. Maybe they were making a statement?'

'The email address is weird too.'

'Email?'

'Yeah, she sent them an email address too. Didn't you see?'

'No, sorry, I didn't notice. Why?'

'Well, when I first glanced at it I thought it was Jamie1948 at hotmail dot com.'

'I see,' Harry said doubtfully.

'But it's not. It's jeannie1948 at hotmail dot com. I mean, most people, if they're not making up something silly, use some variation on their own name, don't they?'

'I suppose so. Maybe it was the email at the office she had her letters sent to.'

'Maybe.' Patrick stretched and began to gather the cards together. In his opinion, Jamie had good taste when it came to cards. Quite a lot were famous paintings, but there were others that featured artists he didn't know. He would have to do a search, see what other work they'd done.

He packed them back in the box and switched the television on. *'OK* if we watch for a while?'

'Why not?' Harry said. 'Though I expect I'll fall asleep.'

'What's new?' Patrick grinned at his father. 'I'll text Alec, make sure everything's *OK*. We'll need to get some more credit tomorrow, just to be sure.'

He paused and looked back at the box of cards, frowning.

'What?' Harry said.

'I don't know, just the feeling I'm missing something really obvious. It'll come to me, I expect.'

Harry nodded and went to have a shower. When he returned it was Patrick who had fallen asleep in front of the television.

Harry stood, looking down at his sleeping son. He loved Patrick so much that sometimes the power of the emotion was like a physical pain in his chest.

In the pocket of his jacket was the business card Munroe had given him that day at Jamie Dale's funeral. Call me, he had said. Harry had the strangest feeling that the evil twin, as Munroe had described it, would probably be making that call.

TWENTY-FIVE

The day started with news that the pale-blue saloon had been found. The car that had conveyed Travers' would-be killer from the motel to the lorry park. It had, as predicted, been burned out, but part of the number plate was still readable, and the owner was known to the police. The car had been reported stolen the day after Travers had been attacked, but Eddison smelt a rat.

'Got a record of petty theft and a string of driving offences,' Munroe told him. 'Nothing major, but—'

'Bring him in then,' Eddison said. 'We'll head back this morning. I doubt there's more to be gained from stopping here; let the locals sort it out.'

Munroe couldn't fault the logic of that, but was slightly surprised by Eddison's sudden eagerness to depart.

Parks met them as they arrived. Tony Marsh was in Interview Room One, refusing to say anything to anyone till he had legal advice.

'And is that imminent?' Munroe asked.

'It'll be a while. Duty solicitor's en route, but there are two in front of Marsh wanting attention.'

'Let him sweat then,' Eddison said. He glanced at his watch. 'Lunchtime news,' he said.

'You expecting something new?' Munroe asked.

Eddison didn't reply.

The bulletin started with breaking news and a picture and a name. 'Joshua Penbury, also known as Gregory Meehan and Anthony Sharp. A wanted suspect in the motorway bombing, and also implicated in the murders of journalist Jamie Dale and convicted conman Neil Robinson, and the attempted murder of *DI* Nicholas Travers...'

Eddison looked pleased. Munroe was aghast. He exchanged a glance with Parks. 'When did this happen?' Parks wanted to know.

'I authorized it first thing. We've got enough to bring him in.'

'You're making it sound like it's all done and dusted. For all we know this Joshua Penbury could be lying somewhere with his head bashed in while someone else runs off with his truck.'

'No, he's our man.'

'You don't know that,' Munroe protested. 'Where did the intel on his aliases come from? And where did you get the picture? We searched right through his place, not a sign of a photograph.'

'That's not a photograph,' Parks said. 'It's a composite. It's just been digitized to make it look right.'

Eddison nodded, satisfied. 'And a good job

they've done too.'

'But you must have started with something. Where did you get his picture from?'

'Army *ID*,' Eddison said.

'And you didn't think to mention any of this?'

'I'm mentioning it now.'

'Gregory,' Munroe said. 'That was the name Travers gave us. You led me to believe it meant nothing.'

'I had to be sure.'

'And what made you sure?' Munroe demanded. 'Eddison, you're moving far too fast on this. It's all supposition. A house of cards. What if the whole damn lot comes crashing down?'

'It won't,' Eddison said. 'I know this man. I know what he's capable of. He's the one.'

'You know him?' Parks was just as bemused now. 'Boss, I don't get it. If you'd got all this intel then why not—'

'You questioning me, Parks? Right, we've got a suspect to interrogate. Interview Room One, was it?'

'Duty solicitor isn't here yet.'

'Then bloody well find him and bring him to the party. We've got a killer to catch, public opinion to placate.'

Parks and Munroe exchanged another glance when Eddison had marched off. 'What the hell is going on here?' Parks asked.

'Fucked if I know,' Munroe said. 'Parks, see if you can round up the brief and get him in with this Marsh character before the boss decides he's starting without him. Sit in, *OK*?'

'*OK*, but what will you be doing?'

'Digging,' Munroe said. 'And I think I'll start with a visit to friend Travers.'

Parks nodded. 'There's something else,' he said. 'It's been bothering me since we visited the prison.'

'Why has no one been and talked to this Griffin character that gave our Alec the phone number?' Munroe guessed.

'Yes, frankly.'

'Why indeed. Right, let's see if we can get ourselves a warrant. I doubt Michelle Sanders will let me in on spec.'

'How are you going to do that?'

'Trust me. There are ways and means. Meantime, keep an eye on things with this Marsh. I don't know what's got into our *DI* Eddison, but I don't like it one little bit.'

Patrick had woken knowing what was wrong with the cards. It was that last one Alec and Naomi had received, and in this instance it had nothing specific to do with what Jamie might have written.

He laid them out on the bed, face up.

'See,' he said.

'See what?'

'The pictures. What do you notice? Most people buy similar cards all the time. Friends often insult one another. Gran likes soppy and sentimental, so we buy her soppy and sentimental. Jamie liked art, and I guess she knew Alec and Naomi did too.'

Harry nodded. 'And. Ah, I see. This card. This last one. It stands out from the rest because it's different.' He picked it up and looked closely. 'I think this is what they call three-D découpage,' he said.

'Well, listen to you!'

'Of course, this is a commercially produced card, but your cousin Laurie is into all this card-making stuff, isn't she? You buy all these shapes on sheets and cut them out and then stick them on to cards with this sticky-pad stuff.' He prodded at the twin reindeer fastened to the card by what he referred to as the sticky-pad stuff and sent a little rain of glitter down on to the bed.

Patrick took it from him. 'Have you got your penknife on you?'

'Of course.'

Patrick took the knife and went over to the window where the light was best. He gently began to lever the sticky pad from the card and then pulled the reindeer off the other side.

'What are you doing?'

Patrick held his breath. 'This stuff should be flexible, shouldn't it?'

'I think so. Patrick, what is it?'

With the tip of the knife Patrick began to probe the sticky pad, peeling back the top layer and exposing – 'Look.'

'What is it?' Harry peered at the blue plastic nestled in the foam.

'It's a micro SD card. A memory card.'

'Ah, so it is. Can you get it out?'

'Yes, but I need something to get the gunge off.'

'Right. Ah.' Harry opened the minibar and found a miniature of Vodka. Carefully, he soaked the corner of his handkerchief and Patrick gently cleaned the remnants of glue and foam from the tiny, flimsy plastic.

'Can you put it in your computer? It looks smaller than the ones that go in your camera.'

'It is. I'll need an adaptor. We can get one at any camera or computer shop.'

'Patrick. This is evidence. Why would Jamie have sent it to Alec and Naomi if it wasn't?'

'Sure, but evidence of what? And if it was so important, why didn't she at least tell them about it in some way? For all she knew they might have done what most people do and put the card in the recycling.'

'She knew Naomi,' Harry said. 'And she knew that if there was information on the card they'd probably keep it. I would have done. Even if I'd put the new address in the book, chances are I'd also have slipped the card into a drawer or something. And anyway, think what she said in the card. Hang on to this in case you need my new address. Something like that?'

'Keep it safe,' Patrick corrected. 'And, like Gran says, Naomi is a magpie. It's still a hell of a risk, though. I mean, that was Christmas; it's June now.'

'I think she took a chance that Naomi would still have the same habits, or that she or Alec would realize something was unusual,' Harry said.

'Naomi might,' Patrick thought. 'I think it's a bit too subtle for Alec. It sounds desperate.'

'Yes,' Harry agreed. 'It does.'

The interrogation of Tony Marsh continued. Parks watched and listened as Eddison demanded he admit to having picked up this Gregory person from the hotel and Tony Marsh consistently rejected the idea. And Parks was pretty convinced the man was telling the truth. He had watched and re-watched the *CCTV* footage taken at the hotel so many times, and the man he had seen on camera was younger, taller, thicker set than this Gregory seemed to be.

'It wasn't him,' Marsh argued again. 'And I don't know who paid me. I just got a call – they wanted a driver, and if I wanted the job I should turn up at The Fox on the Sunday. So, like I told you already, I went to The Fox, I talked to the landlord, he said someone had dropped a letter in for me and I took the letter and did what it said.'

'A letter. Very civilized. And the landlord didn't know who delivered it, I suppose?'

'He reckoned it came in with the post. How the hell should I know?'

'Accommodating of the landlord, looking after your mail like that. Spend a lot of time at The Fox, do you? People normally just phone you up with offers of money, do they?'

Marsh looked away, doing his best to ignore Eddison.

'What did the note say?' Parks asked quietly. 'Was it typed, handwritten?'

'Printed, like from a computer,' Marsh said sullenly. 'Like I already said, there was five hundred quid in tens and twenties and a note that said be at the back of the motel at half seven on the Tuesday and there's five hundred more. I thought it were easy money, so I went.'

'And what happened?'

'I waited. I saw him coming out of the back of the hotel, over the grass, and then I saw the blood and I ... I thought, I'm out of here, then I saw he had a gun, pointed right at me, and I thought that was it. I'd had it. Then he got in the car and he gave me my money and he said to drive where he said to drive and we went through the car park in between the cars and then into the lorry park and that's all I know. He said to follow him out and keep in tight and I did that and then I started off home.'

'But you abandoned your car?'

'No. I went home, then I took another look at it. There was blood all over the seat. I tried scrubbing it off, but it wouldn't go. There were, like, smears of it in the fabric. I knew the wife would see, she'd want to know what went on. So I dumped the car and fired it, and I walked home across the fields, made like it had been stolen.'

'And this man.' Eddison tapped the photograph. 'This was the man you picked up.'

Marsh shook his head emphatically. 'I never saw that man.'

'*DI* Eddison, you are harassing my client. He says that was not the man.'

Eddison leaned across the table, face close to Marsh's. 'And I don't believe him,' he said.

Adaptor bought, they went back to the hotel and plugged the little card into Patrick's computer. Photos shot with a long lens, Harry thought. People meeting, talking, parting, meeting with other people. It meant nothing to either of them. Harry studied the people carefully, sure he had seen one man before.

'I know him,' he said. 'I've seen him on the television.'

'Really? When?'

'The day of the motorway explosion. I'm sure of it. Patrick, can we get the iPlayer here?'

'Sure. There's a Wi-Fi link.'

They spent the next hour trawling through the news reports and then found what they had been looking for. The first press conference on the day of the explosion at the motorway services.

'That's definitely him,' Patrick said. '*DI* Eddison. That's one of the police officers Alec's been working with.'

Harry nodded. 'I think we should let Alec know,' he said. 'Patrick, can we send him these pictures?'

'Not to the mobile he's using, no. It's just dead simple. Text and phone, it can't send or receive images. What do you think we should do?'

Harry thought hard. 'Talk to Alec,' he said. 'Tell him what we've found and see if we can make any sense of it. Then I think we should contact this *DS* Munroe. I've got his card in my pocket.'

'Why him?'

'I don't know,' Harry said. 'We had a bit of a chat at the funeral, and he seems to be – well, gut instinct, you might say, tells me he's all right.'

'*OK*,' Patrick said. 'Well, seeing as we're acting on instinct, I think there's something else we should do.'

'I'm not going to like this, am I?'

'Um, don't know. But I think we should send the pictures to that email Jamie put in the card.'

'And your reason?'

Patrick shrugged. 'No better than yours,' he said.

TWENTY-SIX

Clara was not so keen on opening the door this time. Her wrist hurt abominably, but stubbornness and shame had prevented her from doing anything about it in terms of seeing a doctor or asking for help. Resentfully, she had done as the man had said, applying cold compresses, bandaging it to give support and, when the pain grew too much, managing to tie a sling. She'd got through her own supply of painkillers and had eventually walked to the corner shop for more, but all the time she was out she'd felt exposed and scared.

But that was nothing compared to the fear for her children that had built and built since Gregory had left and now felt ready to explode.

She had tried to call Paul again, but he still wasn't answering his phone. She had tried to find the number for Tilly's farm, but either it was ex-directory or it didn't have a phone and her search was not helped by the fact that she didn't know the actual address. To them it had always been Tilly's farm, at the end of an unadopted road, up a long cart track. She wasn't even sure it had a proper name.

Peering out this time when the doorbell rang,

Clara was met with a strange sight. A man, a woman and a dog. A dog wearing a harness. A guide dog?

Her first thought was to wonder what religion they were selling, and she glanced up and down the road in search of their inevitable companions. Jehovah's Witnesses tended to go about in small gangs, in Clara's experience. As did chapel types and Seventh Day Adventists, whereas Mormons generally only went about in pairs. On bicycles.

The man saw her watching and waved encouragingly. She retreated from the window. He must have bent down and opened the letter box next, because she heard him calling, 'Clara, we need to speak with you. Clara, I'm—' Whatever he was, she thought, he obviously thought better of it, but his next words shocked her.

'Clara, we were friends of Jamie Dale.'

'Jesus!' That was all she needed.

'Clara, we just want to help you.'

She stood uncertainly in the hallway, cradling her injured hand across her body, and wondered what she had to lose. What could they do to her that hadn't already been done?

Quite a lot, she supposed, but somehow this man and woman and dog didn't seem so much of a threat. Reluctantly, but resignedly, Clara Thompson opened the door.

Patrick had been unable to get through to Alec's phone. He had sent a text telling Alec to call as soon as he could. 'Signal isn't always great with these phones,' he said. 'It could be that, or he might just be keeping it switched off. It just says the phone is unavailable.'

Harry had similar problems getting through to Munroe but had left a message on his voicemail. It was all, he thought, a little anti-climactic, just when they'd tried to be decisive. Patrick had sent the email and uploaded photographs to the 'Jeannie' email.

Now all they could do was wait.

The next decision was where they should do their waiting. They decided to head back south towards home.

'We fly out in two days,' Harry said.

'Do we?'

'That's what we arranged. Rearranged, rather.'

'I know, but—'

'Patrick, I think we'll have to take it as it comes, don't you?'

Clara sat on one of the overlarge sofas and stared at the people she had let in. She had taken in only part of what they had to say, but she gathered that he was a policeman and his wife had also been one. That they had known Jamie, and that the man had once arrested her brother.

'What happened to your arm?' Alec asked.

Clara shrugged. Then wished she hadn't. Every movement hurt.

'Where are your children, Clara? Your husband?' Naomi asked.

'They're not here. I sent them away.' Trouble was, *he* knew where they were, and Clara was not sure if that was a good thing or a bad thing. Would the man called Gregory do them harm? He seemed to be saying to her that they were under much greater threat from elsewhere.

Clara could no longer think clearly about any of this. She hurt. Physically, mentally, the pain consumed her.

'I want to see my kids,' she said. 'I want to know they're safe.' She made up her mind. 'You can take me to them.'

Alec began to argue, to ask if that was really a good idea.

Naomi laid a hand on his arm. 'Tell us where to take you,' she said.

Gregory had made better time than he had hoped. His boat now lay at anchor some way from the shore, but within the broad bay. The ruin on the headland matched the one in the picture he had taken from Clara's home, and he had seen the kids and their father playing on the beach.

He made lunch and thought some more about what he was going to do. Gregory was by nature a man who planned, but no action seemed ideally suited to the moment. He still wasn't sure what he intended to do.

He thought some more about Jamie too, about the time it had all come to a head. She had dug too deep, rattled the bars of too many gilded cages, and uncovered the fact of exactly which palms the Night Vision project had greased to get its contracts through the government hoops. And she had uncovered the name of the director of operations ... and it was a name Gregory knew well.

Even now, Gregory was unconvinced that Jamie understood what a dangerous game she had been playing until—

He had warned her to back off, warned her that this was not just business, it was life or death, but she hadn't believed him until the night he had told her that if she kept pushing he could no longer protect her. And had tried to convince her to what lengths certain people would go in the protection of their interests.

'People have died for less, Jamie.'

'You're just trying to scare me.'

'So, be scared. Make your film, just leave out the accusations. This isn't political, Jamie, this is criminal. This is corruption on a level you can't even begin to comprehend.'

'I won't be put off.'

'Then if you aren't scared for yourself, be afraid for those you love.'

He saw doubt in her eyes for the first time. 'They'll take it all from you. Everything you love, all you hold dear, and in the end you won't care if you die because you'll have nothing left that's worth living for.'

She had considered his words. 'You're serious,' she said at last.

'I'm serious. I've been told, Jamie, to keep you in check or stop you dead, and frankly I

know which they would prefer.'

She stared at him, disbelieving. 'You wouldn't hurt me.'

'Yes, I would. I have obligations that go back a lot further than knowing you.'

In the end, she had been right. She had, in consequence, died a terrible death, and that was something Gregory regretted more than he could say.

TWENTY-SEVEN

Michelle Sanders had been furious when he arrived but had eventually accepted that Munroe was going to talk to Trevor Griffin and that he had the clout to insist. An hour in and he knew no more than when he had first arrived. Except that Michelle was even more annoyed. She had tried to call Eddison and been told that he was unavailable.

'I don't know nothing about a telephone number.' This had been Griffin's line from the start, and he didn't seem ready to vary it.

'You're wasting your time,' Michelle Sanders said.

Munroe watched Griffin, the way his gaze kept skipping towards the governor and then back again.

'Neil Robinson didn't give you that number, did he?' Munroe asked.

Michelle Sanders shifted position, impatience conveyed in her every gesture.

'No,' Griffin said.

That was at least a change of line.

'Was it another inmate?'

That little sideways flick of the eyes again. 'No. I don't know. Look, I just picked it up somewhere. I thought it would be a laugh. Get one over, you know.'

'I told *DI* Friedman it was a wind up.' Michelle Sanders sounded triumphant. 'Enough now. We've wasted enough time.'

Munroe nodded, as if in agreement. 'Strange coincidence then,' he said.

'What is?'

'That Griffin here should happen to pick up a number that he should happen to decide he'd use in a wind up that just happens to have relevance to our investigation, don't you think?'

'What do you mean?'

'I mean, if it turns out Griffin here is being economical with the truth. If we find out, for instance, that he knew this was the number of the Madigor offices—'

'Madigor?' Michelle Sanders looked puzzled now, which was progress of sorts, Munroe thought.

'The bloke what blew up the van?' Griffin looked anxious. 'I don't have nothing to do with that. I just dropped the number. I didn't know what it was.'

'No?' Munroe persisted. 'Of course, then it might add up to a conspiracy charge. It might—'

'I only dropped the number. I don't know nothing!' Griffin was on his feet.

'Sit down,' Michelle Sanders ordered.

'She told me to,' Griffin shouted. 'Her.'

'Me?' The governor was outraged. 'You can't believe – right, I think that's enough.'

'You gave him the number? Why was that, Michelle?'

'I think you should leave now.'

Munroe agreed, oddly enough. Was Griffin telling the truth? Munroe could think of no reason why Michelle Sanders would have done such a thing, but neither could he come up with a convincing reason for Griffin telling that particular lie.

'Michelle?'

She said nothing but opened the door and motioned for Griffin to leave, then tried her phone again, frowning as no one picked up.

'Eddison still leaving you out in the cold?' Munroe said.

She slammed the phone down on the table and dropped into the chair Griffin had vacated. She seemed at a loss.

'Did Eddison give you that number?'

'Why would you think that? How would that make any sense?'

Munroe shrugged. 'It doesn't,' he said. 'But then, not much does right now.'

She closed her eyes, pinching the bridge of her nose as though a headache was starting. 'Charlie and I go back a long way,' she said at last.

'And you and Travers?'

'Alec told you then?'

'Not in so many words.'

'Charlie and I ... we go back a lot further than that. He's been a good friend to me, was a good friend to my brother.'

'Your brother was shot, wasn't he?' Munroe said. 'An armed robbery if I remember right. He got caught in the crossfire.'

She nodded.

'So you feel obliged to Charlie Eddison, is that it?'

'Like I say, he's been a good friend.'

'And that phone number?'

She hesitated, but it was clear she now knew something was badly wrong.

Munroe waited.

'He said he had intelligence, something linked to Neil Robinson. He didn't say what, only that it was big. He needed – he said he needed a nudge, just to get the investigation moving in the right direction, that he had to protect his source. So he gave me the number and asked me to find a way to get it dropped into the investigation. He said he knew the link was there but he had no way of, well, of making things happen, not now Neil Robinson was dead. That he couldn't make the links.'

'Links?'

She shrugged. 'I don't know, he said something about organized crime and computers. He said he couldn't tell me exactly what, just to trust him.'

'And so you trusted him.'

'He's been a good friend. I—' She gestured angrily. 'I had Griffin drop the number where Alec Friedman would see it. It seemed like such a simple thing. I knew it wasn't right, but I couldn't see what was wrong either. I was just doing a favour for a good friend. A good police officer.'

'And now?' Munroe asked.

'Now I feel like a bloody fool. Charlie used me, didn't he?'

'You *allowed* him to use you.'

'Yes, but I thought—'

'I don't think you did,' Munroe told her gently. 'That's just it – I don't believe you thought at all.' He paused and then asked, 'Did Eddison come here to talk to Neil Robinson?'

'You've seen the visitors list. He isn't on it, is he?'

'That wasn't what I asked.'

She shrugged.

'How about the day Robinson died. He come over for a chat that day, did he, Michelle?'

'Not to see Robinson. No.'

'Someone else then. Someone who may have done his dirty work for him?'

One look at her face told him she wasn't going to say anything more. No matter, he thought, he could guess the truth of it and there would be time later to put pressure on the Governor. Right now he had more urgent matters to attend to.

He left, feeling it was enough to have shaken the tree for now, though it would be interesting to see what fell out. Just what game was Charlie Eddison playing, and how far had he and Parks helped him along the road? What damage had they all done – for that matter, damage to what?

Checking his phone as he returned to his car,

he found a message from Harry Jones accompanied by half a dozen photographs. Two of which featured Eddison in deep conversation with someone Munroe did not recognize.

When Munroe returned the call, Harry was driving, so Patrick answered. Munroe listened as Patrick explained about the card and the memory card.

'I think we need to talk,' Munroe said. 'Where shall we meet?'

He heard the murmurs of a swift conference. 'Dad says anywhere we can get a decent meal,' Patrick says.

'I think your dad has a good set of priorities,' Munroe said.

Travers had been moved from the high dependency unit and into a side room on a main ward. He was still very weak, still slept a great deal, but he was definitely on the mend.

Maureen sat beside him on one side of the bed, the family liaison officer, Susan Moran, on the other, and they watched the television news.

Gregory's picture was on the screen. The reporter was reprising the list of offences for which he was suspect.

Including, the attack on *DI* Nicholas Travers.

'No,' he said. No one called him Nicholas. 'No,' he repeated, not sure if that last thought had been spoken out loud. 'It wasn't Gregory, it wasn't him.'

'What do you mean?' Maureen asked him. 'Trav, this is good, they've got his picture, they're out looking for him.'

'No, it wasn't him.'

Susan Moran leaned in closer. 'You're saying you know this is not the man that attacked you? Nick, are you sure about this?'

'I told you, it wasn't Gregory. I know Gregory. There was a brief moment when I thought – a superficial resemblance – then I knew it wasn't him. The man who attacked me was taller, heavier, it wasn't him.'

'Who is this Gregory?' Maureen was demanding. 'You don't know a Gregory.'

'It was a long time ago.'

Susan Moran left him to explain. She called *DI* Eddison and told him what *DI* Travers had said.

'He's mistaken,' Eddison said bluntly. 'He doesn't know what he's saying.'

Susan Moran was left staring at the phone.

'Where the hell is Munroe?' Eddison demanded. No one knew, but there were missed calls from Michelle Sanders, and soon the mystery was partly solved.

'And where is he now?' Eddison demanded.

'How the hell should I know?' Michelle said, over the phone. 'He left a half hour ago.'

'Damn.' He turned on Parks. 'Find out where the hell he's got to and get him back here.'

'How do I do that?'

'Just do it!'

'Right,' Parks said. 'Oh, there's a message come through for you. About some place in

Wales. Desk sergeant has it.'

Eddison left.

Parks tried Munroe's phone and then, unable to get through, sent a text. *Eddison got news from Wales. U R in deep shit. Trav says it wasn't Gregory.*

That, he figured, was about all he could do. He went back to talk to Marsh, convinced now that whoever had attacked Nick Travers, he was just a thug for hire.

'So tell me more about this man you picked up,' he said. 'We've got some pictures I'd like you to take a gander at.'

TWENTY-EIGHT

Gregory had come ashore to watch. The children were called Kay and Jilly. He hadn't known that. They ran on the beach, their father in tow, his stiffness of movement testament to his injuries. The little girls were tanned and lithe, their blonde hair flying out behind them. The father was dark-haired and olive-skinned, handsome in a fine boned way, Gregory thought. Clara was of more solid build.

The man was nervous, alert. Twice he looked towards Gregory's hiding place, as though sure he had sensed something unusual. Gregory did not move. An untrained eye on high alert was as likely to spot the unusual as any trained observer, especially with so much at stake.

What was he here for? Gregory asked himself. Just what was he hoping to achieve? Were Clara's family actually in any danger now?

That depended, he thought, on how the tide turned next. It might ebb gently and the matter be quietly forgotten, Clara and her children be left alone. Or the storm might break over them, as it had her brother and Jamie Dale, and that rather depended on what Eddison did next.

Had he drawn Eddison here? Had he made it

worse? That, Gregory acknowledged, was a major possibility. He had come here initially to direct Paul to leave, to take the children elsewhere until home was once more a safe place, as it should be if Eddison was finally rid of Gregory, and that would be easy. He had seen the news, heard the accusations, knew he was a wanted man, a hunted man, and that the one who hunted him knew all the tricks of the trade. Had been trained as Gregory had been trained. Another of the dinosaurs, Gregory had thought, but one with the skill to pretend to be a mammal.

Once the family had passed out of view, he took the opportunity to check his phone, logging in to the various web-based mailboxes he used, and he froze. His first thought was that Eddison had sent the message. Jeannie1948, that was the email Jamie had chosen – though to his knowledge she had never used it.

Noting there were attachments, he opened the message:

I don't know what these are, and I don't know who I'm sending them to, but Jamie Dale left this email address and she hid these pictures so we think they might be important.

Yours sincerely, Patrick Jones

For a moment or two Gregory just stared at the message, overcome by the absurdity of it.

Well, you're polite, Patrick Jones, he thought. And very, very foolish. Then he opened the attachments and he understood. When had Jamie taken these pictures? The boy said she had hidden them. Where and how, and how had they been found? The boy might not have known the importance of these pictures, but Gregory understood it the moment he saw Eddison in the photographs and recognized who he was talking to. He understood just what a threat Jamie must have become to them. And why she had died.

The armed guard was still at the hospital, the family liaison officer there too, and Travers' wife, Maureen, sitting by the bed. Ironic, Munroe thought, that he was at most risk from someone supposed to be on the same side.

'I need to talk to your husband alone,' he told Maureen. 'I'm sorry, but I have to ask you to leave for a few minutes.'

'Whatever you have to say, I want to hear it.' Maureen lifted her chin defiantly.

'It's all right, Maureen. Please, go, just for a little while.'

She looked daggers at her husband, but she went, along with Susan, the liaison.

Munroe took Susan's seat beside the bed. 'Tell me about Eddison,' he said, 'and about Gregory. And tell me fast, I don't have much time.'

Travers looked puzzled and then confused. He eased his position on the bed. 'There's not much I know,' he said.

'But a lot you suspect. So...?'

Travers closed his eyes. He still looked exhausted. 'It wasn't Gregory,' he said.

'Eddison is insisting that it was.'

Travers nodded. 'That would suit him,' he said.

'Why? Nick, I don't have much time. Eddison is way ahead of me.'

'Where's he gone?'

'Parks reckons he's headed for Wales. Neil Robinson's sister and her family are there. Maybe he thinks this Gregory is too.'

'We all served together. There were five of us. Flynn was killed, and I was sent back home wounded. I went back, briefly. Then, well, let's just say I found a way out.'

'That much I know,' Munroe said. 'You were considered unfit to serve, got discharge on medical grounds, spent some time in a psychiatric unit.'

Travers nodded. He smiled wryly. 'It's not the kind of record you want known. It's in my file, of course, but not many are aware either at work or at home.'

'Maureen doesn't know?'

Travers shook his head.

'But, of course, Eddison did.'

'Eddison makes sure he knows something about everyone. It's what he does.'

'It's what he's paid to do,' Munroe said flatly.

'Bit like you then. Does Eddison know who you are?'

'Of course he does. It flatters him.'

Munroe could see Maureen hovering outside

the door. 'Look,' he said, 'my guess is that whoever attacked you, Eddison arranged it.'

'Eddison? Why?'

'You don't sound all that shocked.'

Travers hesitated. 'If Gregory had wanted me dead, then that's what I'd be – and, believe me, I wouldn't have seen it coming. Charlie told me Greg had died – killed in action, he said – but I was always doubtful. Greg worked deep cover for years, I knew that. Eddison was the public face, always was. Greg was the executive–' he smiled – 'and I don't mean he wore a suit.'

Munroe nodded. He could see Maureen arguing with Susan.

'Charlie Eddison was ambitious. I suppose Greg was too, but in a different way. Charlie wanted, *needed*, to be seen, and Greg was a shadows man. All you ever saw of Gregory's work was the body on the floor. Gregory is a dangerous man.'

'So is Charlie Eddison,' Munroe said. 'Nick, what does the name Christopher Rains mean to you?'

'Christopher.' Travers seemed to grow paler. 'I told you I went back. Charlie, Greg and Ben they were still part of the same unit, but in the three months I'd been away they'd changed. Everything had changed. They'd moved on, and I was still the – well, I should never have been there in the first place. Two days after I got back to base a group of insurgents were captured and brought in. An interrogation team arrived. Christopher Rains was in charge. At that time, I didn't know his name, and I never did know his rank, or even if he had one. Talking to Charlie a long time later, he took great pride in showing me an article in some glossy magazine or other. There was Chris Rains, head of some government think tank on counter intelligence, and Charlie was named as one of the advisers. All jobs for the boys.'

Adviser could mean a lot of things, Munroe thought. In Eddison's case it had come to mean taking a more active role. Clearing the way for a number of very lucrative contracts as the war on terror spelt big profits for many of those Eddison had been 'advising'. The suspicion was that Charlie Eddison had been effective in removing the opposition or the alternate tender from those parties he did *not* advise, either with good intelligence gathering, by dealing in the inevitable dirt that adhered to the powerful, or by more direct means. Some very well-placed government contractors and some more shadily-placed dealers in arms and information had benefited from Charlie Eddison's skills.

As had Charlie Eddison. Soon to retire, and with some very discreet investments that would cushion his later years nicely.

'Tell me about Ben.'

Travers took a deep breath. 'Ben died in a police operation almost six years ago.'

'An operation you were in charge of.'

'Yes.'

'The official line is he was the victim of friendly fire. You had an armed suspect fleeing the scene and—'

'And I gave the order to fire. Yes. None of us saw Ben. He'd been ordered to stay low, not to engage the suspect. If he'd stayed where he was meant to be, or even reported his new position, he'd still be alive.'

'Which doesn't stop you from feeling responsible.'

'I'm not to blame.'

'But that doesn't always matter, does it? Alec tells me you and Michelle Sanders were more than friends.'

'We had an affair. It ended just before her brother died.'

'And your relationship since?'

'There wasn't one.'

Maureen was positively mutinous now. She flung open the door and stood looking pointedly at Munroe.

'I watched Christopher Rains work on one of the insurgents,' Travers said, and Munroe was surprised that Nick no longer seemed to care if Maureen heard.

'Gregory and Charlie, they were there, not all of the time, but for a lot of it. Charlie enjoyed it. Greg, he was just intrigued. Cold.'

'And you?'

Travers didn't respond.

Maureen returned to his bedside, eyes blazing. Defensive now. 'Go,' she said. 'I want you to go.'

Munroe left.

TWENTY-NINE

Harry and Patrick arrived for their meeting with Munroe a little early.

'You think he's here?' Patrick asked.

'I doubt it. Can you check your messages now?'

'I can try.' He had sent the email via his laptop, but now he dug his mobile out of his messenger bag. Harry glimpsed the sketchbook his son was rarely without and the tin of pencils and specialist fibre pens he had bought from some Japanese site online. Since leaving home he'd not switched his own mobile on, relying purely on the disposable one, but now he needed to get online.

Harry watched as he logged into his email.

'There's a reply.'

'Open it.' Harry found he could hardly breathe.

Patrick read, and then read out loud. 'It just says "call me", and there's a phone number. What do we do?'

Harry thought about it. Had Alec or Naomi been available, he would have relied on their advice. This was way beyond his experience or understanding.

Munroe's car pulled into the car park and eased in beside them.

'We talk to *DS* Munroe,' he said. Then, observing the mutinous look on his son's face: 'And then we ring this man.'

Harry found that all this excitement bred an appetite. He wasn't sure if to be ashamed of that, or just get on and order a larger lunch.

Munroe listened as Patrick explained how he had found the memory card and what they had done next. The remaining images were still on Patrick's laptop. Sitting in the cosy little dining room of the Radcliffe Arms, Munroe looked at pictures that not only implicated Eddison but also had the potential to crash some very major reputations. The CEO of a major telecommunications company in rather close proximity to a very high-up fixer. A government minister drinking with a man who was currently under investigation for seeking to bribe another minister.

'Do you recognize any of these people?' he asked.

Harry shrugged. 'Eddison, of course, and I think that bald man there is something in the government. I've seen him on *Newsnight*.'

Patrick was thinking. He touched the screen, as though that helped him focus. 'Him and him,' he said. 'And the woman. I mean, I don't know who they are, just the faces. I'm pretty good with faces.'

'I hear you're an artist.'

Patrick nodded. 'Trying to be. Who are they?'

Munroe hesitated. 'Where do you think you've seen them?'

Patrick thought about it, touching the screen again.

Harry looked uncomfortable. 'Patrick?'

'I don't know. Look, what do we do about the phone call? Do we call him?' He was still staring at the computer screen, as though something puzzled him.

'We make the call,' Munroe said. 'And we talk to Alec too, warn him that Eddison is heading his way.'

Patrick seemed to make up his mind about something. 'That man there.' He pointed to a figure tucked away in the background. Medium height, not heavily built, short sandy hair. Insignificant. 'I've see him,' he said. 'But I'm not sure where.'

'Are you certain?'

Patrick nodded. 'Like I said, I'm good with faces. I just don't remember where. You know, I think it was when you brought Naomi back to stay with us. Maybe he was in a car or something. Who is he, anyway?'

'It's very possible he was watching you,' Munroe agreed. 'Patrick, that's Gregory.'

To Patrick's annoyance, it was Munroe who made contact with Gregory, and they talked at length, Munroe standing in the car park and out of earshot. They talked about Clara and her children, about Eddison, about the images

Patrick had emailed to Gregory. I've set him and Eddison on a collision course, Munroe thought. Clash of the Titans. Problem is, who is going to get caught up in the collateral damage?

'We need to get the kids away,' Gregory said. 'Eddison won't care, you know that.'

'And you do?'

'And I do.'

'Look,' Munroe said. 'You're on the ground there, do what you can. I'll see who I can convince this end, but Gregory, things are moving at a rate of knots here. Eddison will reach you before I can.'

After Munroe hung up, he turned to Harry and Patrick. So, what now? he thought.

'Alec and Naomi have gone to see Clara,' Harry said. 'They may already have seen her, I don't know.'

Munroe could not hide his consternation. 'Go home, Harry. You've done enough now.'

'No,' Harry told him. 'We're going to where our friends are. If they're in trouble, we want to help.'

'And when you run into trouble, who's going to pull you out? Think of your son.'

'I always think of him. His opinion matters a great deal and I need to be able to look him in the eye and say I behaved as I'd expect him to behave. We'll hold back – I promise you we won't rush in, as it were – but we *will* be on hand.' He asked, as Munroe said his goodbyes, 'Where will you be going?'

Munroe shrugged. 'Same place as you,' he said. 'Just by a slightly different route.'

Gregory had long since known that you don't put all your eggs in one basket, all your apples in the same barrel, or all of your insurance policies in the same folder.

It had been Jamie who taught him about cloud computing, and from Eddison he had learnt the value of hiding in plain sight. He named his folders after books and, taking note of what Jamie had told him about people skimming initial paragraphs before deciding what to read, had added innocuous, even boring notes on the texts involved. She had been deeply amused, but that had been before she had learnt to be afraid. Now, he removed those excess notes. He wanted the recipients to read on.

The contacts he now selected as recipients for these little bomblets of information were from Jamie's contact book. He saw it as a tribute to her.

Newspaper editors, media groups, politicians ... He spread the net wide. And to the intel he already had on Eddison and his cohort, he added the photographs that Patrick Jones had sent to him. Much of this might be ignored at first, he knew, but it would take only one person to run with it, to ask the questions, to make a challenge and the rest would follow. He just hoped it would all happen fast enough.

THIRTY

Alec, Naomi and Clara had arrived at the farm and driven down the narrow track to where the caravan was parked. Paul and the children were just returning from their walk when they arrived, coming over the bank that separated the farm from the beach.

Paul halted part way down the slope and stared at them in horror. 'What the hell are you doing here? Who the hell are *they*?'

The girls had seen their mother and begun to run towards her. 'Mummy, Mummy, we saw a jellyfish and a—' Jilly fell silent, her father's anger cutting the greeting short.

'I'm sorry, Paul. I had to come! Alec here is a policeman. This is his wife. They've come to help us.'

'Help us! Help us! Are you insane, woman? You could have helped us by keeping the hell away. You saw what they did to me. You *saw*! You brought this down on our heads, you and Neil. I've been keeping our kids safe, and now you bring them here? Who else knows you've come? *Who else*?'

Alec stepped forward. 'She was scared, Paul. Just scared. This place isn't safe now, you've got to leave.'

'Leave? No, no, I don't think so. We've been fine here, me and the kids. You're the ones that have to go.'

This could go on for some time, Naomi thought. 'Look,' she said. 'How about the three of you work it out and the girls take Napoleon and I for a walk on the beach?'

'Is that your dog?' Jilly asked.

'Can't you see?' Kay wanted to know.

'Can we, Daddy, please?'

'What harm can I possibly do them? I can't exactly run off with them, can I?' Naomi said quietly. 'It would be better than watching you and Clara, er, talk this over, wouldn't it?'

Paul gave in. She heard him sigh, could almost visualize him deflating. *'OK,'* he said. 'Girls, make sure you've got your drinks and snacks and take—'

'Naomi,' she reminded him.

'Take Naomi to the beach. You'd better come inside,' he said to Clara and Alec. 'And what you've got to say, it had better be good.'

'Will you be all right?' Alec sounded concerned. 'Napoleon doesn't know this place. He's not going to be a lot of use to you.'

'I'll be fine. He'll stop me heading out to sea, and Jilly and Kay know all about the beach, don't you?'

A few moments while the girls got drinks and stowed them in their packs, and then Jilly, suddenly very grown up, took Naomi by the hand. 'I'll look after you,' she said. 'Can I pet your dog? What's he called?'

'Napoleon, and yes, you can stroke him, but while he's got his harness on he knows he's working, so just give him a little stroke, *OK*?'

'Napolinon,' Kay tried. 'That's a funny name.' Not to be outdone by her sister, she slipped her hand beside Naomi's on Napoleon's harness. And the four of them, woman, children and dog, chattering and laughing, slowly walked away.

Gregory had planned to approach Paul and the children and either convince or force them to leave with him, aboard the inflatable in which he'd come ashore, an old Zodiac with a powerful outboard. What he had not expected was to see Naomi Friedman, a large black dog and the two little girls coming towards him, but he had no time to change or modify his plan. Already there were signs that he had made his move almost too late. Twice now, in the distance, he had glimpsed a helicopter casting along the shoreline, buzzing back inland and then turning back out to sea. It was still distant, and for the moment seemed to be moving away, but it would only be a matter of time before the pilot found his bearings and identified their position. Eddison would have instigated a search for the *Jeannie*, and there she was, moored out in open water.

He left his place in the dunes and began to walk towards the little group, Taking out his phone, he called Patrick. 'Where are you?'

'Um, is this Gregory? I mean, how did you get my phone number?'

'Munroe,' he said. 'He told me you and your dad are stubborn bastards. That you were heading this way. Now listen. I have a job for you.'

The girls had noticed him now, and so had the dog. The dog halted; sensing that this man was somehow 'wrong', he started to turn his mistress back.

'What is it?' Naomi asked.

'There's a man,' Jilly said.

'A man? What kind of man?'

'My name is Gregory,' he said. 'You need to leave with me now.'

Two children, one man, one dog all piled into a boat made for two or three, but the engine started first pull and the Zodiac powered away and Naomi talked to Patrick on the phone, shouting over the noise of the outboard. He could hear she was scared, and Kay was crying and asking for her daddy, saying she didn't want to go away.

The helicopter had changed direction, casting slowly back along the coast, what had once been a speck on the horizon now horribly visible. He tucked in close to the cliffs, which were rising suddenly as the landscape changed, and then headed for a small inlet he had spotted when he had first moored the *Jeannie*. They were now completely out of sight of the beach and the farm and the helicopter, though he could hear the sound of it as he cut the engine.

'I'm scared, Naomi. I want Mummy. I want Daddy!'

'Do we have to hide again?' Jilly said.

'I'm afraid so, sweetheart. I'm afraid we do.'

Gregory took back his phone and called Munroe. Explained what he was trying to do.

'The parents are still at the farm, and so is Alec Friedman. I'm going back.' He paused to listen. 'She can manage, don't underestimate her.'

Thanks for the vote of confidence, Naomi thought. She wasn't so sure it was accurate.

'Do you have a phone with you?' Gregory asked her.

'No, I left mine behind.'

'OK. You can keep this one. I have a spare. Jilly, let me show you. Come on, I won't bite. Now, see this is what you do.'

He had her repeat the instructions, wrote Patrick's number on a slip of paper and made sure she had stowed both in her pack. Wide eyed and scared, she was also amazingly calm. Her mother's daughter, Gregory thought. He wondered how much she actually understood about what was going on. Figured it was probably more than her father would have believed.

'Listen,' he said. 'Follow the stream back inland. Then follow your nose, *OK*?'

'Follow my nose?' Kay was distracted for a moment.

'He means keep going straight,' Jilly said importantly.

'Cross the fields and you'll reach the road.

Patrick and Harry will find you.'

'Have you ever seen Harry Jones read a map?' Naomi asked tartly. 'And what are *you* going to do?'

'Go back,' he said.

'And what the hell good will that do?'

'Go,' he said. 'Stay under cover as much as you can, close to the hedgerow, under trees. Harry will find you.'

'Wait,' she said as he began to move away.

'I need to hurry.'

'I know, I just have one thing to ask. Did you kill Jamie Dale?'

He hesitated, not sure she should be talking about such things in front of the two little girls. 'No,' he said. 'I didn't kill her. I'd have made it clean, not like...'

Naomi swallowed nervously. 'Someone called me,' she said. 'Someone played a recording of—'

'That was me and I'm sorry, but I had to know.'

'You! Know what? I don't understand.'

'What you'd do. If you were the woman Jamie thought you were. If you and Alec could be trusted.'

'I'm assuming we passed your test,' Naomi said heavily.

'Jamie said you were good people, that you believed in right and wrong.' He laughed. 'I always told her that was a rare commodity. I heard Alec and Travers had been brought on board the investigation, so I suppose I needed to know whose side you'd be on. How much she meant to you. What you'd do.'

'But the tape. I don't understand. Where did you get it? Why did she call me Naomi Blake?'

'I have to go. This is not the time.'

'And it might be the only time we have,' she reminded him. 'None of us knows how this will play out, not now.'

Gregory sighed. The sound of the helicopter was louder now. Closer still. 'Eddison likes to collect souvenirs,' he said. 'I know he ... interrogated her before she died. I know he let her think she almost escaped. She got to a phone, she made a call. But it went nowhere.'

'She tried to call me?'

'She thought she was calling you. Eddison laughed about it. He sent the recordings to me – that phone call that never was and the one made when Jamie died. And I don't know why she called you by your maiden name. Maybe she was so scared she just forgot. Maybe she was in such a state she thought it would throw Eddison off the scent. I just don't know. I just know she died and when she was at her most desperate she reached out to you. So I had to know.'

'To know?'

'If you were worthy of that,' Gregory said.

He left them then. She heard him walk away across the shingle and the outboard motor start and for a moment or two was utterly overcome by fear. She didn't know where she was, she didn't know how to get to the road. She was supposed to be the adult here, looking after the little girls. And she didn't know what was happening to Alec back at the farm. And she was terribly afraid for all of them.

'Helicopter,' Kay said. 'I can hear a helicopter.'

'We'd better go,' Jilly said. She took Naomi's hand. 'Follow your nose,' she said.

THIRTY-ONE

'Alec, get yourself out of there. Now!'

'Munroe? What the hell?'

'Naomi and the kids are safe, now you get yourselves away.'

'What do you mean? They're on the beach. They—'

'No, they're not. Look, trust me, Alec. I'll give you a phone number you can reach her on, but you need to move, *now*. Eddison's on the way, and he's bringing armed police with him.'

'What? What are you saying?'

'Alec, he's saying you're all in on it with Gregory. That you played a part in the attack on Travers and the motorway explosion. He's got helicopter surveillance and armed officers moving in. Alec, it might already be too late, but try and get out now.'

'I can talk to him,' Alec said. 'Munroe, this is ridiculous.'

'Forget talking, Alec. He's not about to listen, he doesn't want to know. And, Alec, I'm worried he's not going to want to leave live witnesses.'

Alec felt himself grow cold. He could hear the sound of the helicopter rotors overhead.

'What's happening?' Clara looked up as though she could see through the roof of the caravan.

'This is not good,' Paul whispered. 'This is not good. I'm going to get the kids.'

Alec grabbed his arm.

The sound of the rotors was joined by another. 'Armed police! Come out slowly and with your hands raised!'

'I think it's a bit too late,' Alec told Munroe.

Munroe swore roundly. 'Hang in there, Alec. I'll do what I can.'

'What do we do?' Clara demanded.

'What about the kids?'

'We do as the man says,' Alec told them. 'Move slowly, keep your hands where they can be seen, and don't do anything that might provoke anyone.'

'The *kids*,' Paul said again.

'They're with Naomi. Munroe promises me they're safe. That's all I know.'

'Come out with your hands up! No one will get hurt, come out with your hands up!'

Alec took a deep breath and hoped Munroe knew what he was doing. Then he opened the caravan door and slowly, carefully, stepped outside.

THIRTY-TWO

The sun was hot, the ground rough beneath their feet. Napoleon panted and whined, not understanding why they were in this strange place and why there was so much tension in the way Naomi held on to him. They had been climbing steadily since they left the shore, but now the ground had levelled out and the grass felt thicker.

'What can you see?' she asked Jilly.

'There's, like, this big field with grass in it and some cows and there's a big hedge all round it. That's all.'

'Look for a gate. Can you see a gate?'

She could feel the effort the child was putting into this. Naomi clasped her hand tightly. 'It will be all right,' she said.

'What about Mum and Dad?'

'They will be all right. I promise.'

'*You* can't make it all right. You shouldn't make promises you can't keep.'

Fair point, Naomi thought.

'I'm tired,' Kay said.

'I know,' Naomi sympathized. 'Do you want a drink?'

'I can see a gate!' Jilly said.

'Good, then let's get over to it, but Jilly, if we stay close to the hedge, then it will be easier to walk.'

'You mean it will be harder for the helicopter to see us.'

Naomi hesitated. 'That too,' she agreed.

'We take the next left,' Patrick said. They had abandoned the satnav. To use a satnav you really need to know where you were going, and this was three-quarters guesswork. Gregory had given them a map reference and told them that Naomi and the kids would be heading towards the little side road a couple of miles from the inlet where he had set them down. Or so he hoped. That did rather depend on one person who couldn't see being guided in the right direction by a dog who didn't know the way and two young children.

'Next left and then a right. Then we should be close to where they'll come out. There's the turn.'

Harry turned and almost immediately slowed. A police car was parked across the road, two uniformed officers standing close by.

Harry wound his window down.

'Sorry, sir, there's been an accident. You can't come this way.' He noticed the map in Patrick's hands. 'Where are you headed?'

'Um, here.' Patrick jabbed at the map, indicating a little village a few miles down the road.

'Right you are. Well, you'll have to go back

the way you came and take the first left and...'

Patrick seemed to listen, then thanked them, and Harry reversed back into a farm gate and drove slowly away.

'Now what?'

'Be glad there's a bend and they can't see we're going right instead of left,' Patrick said.

It was obvious to Gregory that it was all too late. Thankful that the noise of the helicopter rotors drowned out the noise of the boat, he cut the engine and drifted into shore at the far end of the beach. He slipped back into the dunes and made his way carefully back inland.

Did they have dogs? That was a complication he didn't want.

Keeping low, he circled the back field and watched from the cover of the trees as men moved back and forth from caravan to cars and scientific support moved up, the small van disgorging three figures in white coveralls. He moved on, towards the road, straining for a glimpse of Alec and the others, finally seeing them, handcuffed and between armed officers, being led towards a van. And then he saw Eddison, standing beside a car behind the van, watching as though detached from the process.

Gregory saw Alec try and turn to speak to him and Eddison look away. Then the van doors were closed and the van was driven away, a car in front and Eddison in the car behind.

What now, he thought. Now what should I do? He had given Naomi his main phone and now used the backup to call Munroe. He needed to get a car, Gregory thought. Follow the van, see what Eddison planned to do.

On the radio, breaking news that: '*—suspects from the motorway bombing have been identified in a remote part of Wales. Armed police are believed to be surrounding the farm—*'

'What now?' Patrick said.

'We find Naomi and the children, and we put as much distance between here and us as we possibly can. Then we stop and think what to do after that.'

'Right,' Patrick said. 'I suppose that's almost a plan. Look, pull in there, on to that verge, and tuck in under the trees. We can walk from there across the fields.' He peered closely at the map, running his finger down the road they should have taken. 'Look, there's a footpath. If we take that, we should get somewhere near where we ought to be.'

Harry cut the engine and studied the map. 'Let's just hope they don't go wrong and come out behind enemy lines,' he said. He tried to laugh, but it sounded hollow. He wished he knew what was happening to Alec and that he knew for sure which way Naomi and the little girls were likely to go.

Through the cow field, open the gate, into another field, cross that, then where? Still no sign of the road. No sound of the helicopter now either. Was that a good thing or bad?

Naomi had rarely felt so disorientated. The ground felt different now. 'What's this place like, Jilly?'

Jilly sighed. She was tired and scared and finding it hard to be Naomi's eyes. 'There's, like, a little path bit that we're on now, and there's a ... a stile? Is that right?'

Naomi breathed a sigh of relief. 'A stile, yes. That means we're on a proper footpath. Keep an eye open for a sign; sometimes the footpaths have little signs. Jilly, is there a gap by the stile that Napoleon can get through?'

'Yes, I think so. Oh.' She sounded suddenly anxious. 'There's a man there.'

Who, Naomi thought, and then she heard someone calling her name. A moment later Patrick had thundered down the path and was hugging her. She could have cried, she was so relieved and so overwhelmed. Harry arrived, breathless but exuberant.

'We found you!' he said.

Kay did begin to cry again. 'I'm hungry and I'm tired and I want my mum.'

'We all want our mums,' Jilly said. 'But we've just got to be brave, now, don't we Naomi?'

Naomi clasped her hand. 'You *are* being very brave,' she said.

THIRTY-THREE

Travers watched the news. Munroe had called and given him an update – it was not looking good. Alec had been implicated, and Eddison was triumphant.

'What can I do?' Travers wanted to know. 'He can't get away with this! It's all a nonsense, Munroe.'

'I'm doing all I can. Nick, you'll be getting a visit from my boss. My actual boss. Tell him all you can. What I'm hoping is that Eddison is just causing chaos so he can get clean away.'

'And what you're not hoping?'

'Is that he's just lost it big time and doesn't care who or what he takes down with him.'

In the back of the car Naomi sat between the sleeping children. In the rear of the hatchback Napoleon snored contentedly. The adults listened to the news.

'There are reports coming through that arrests have been made, but conflicting reports that the armed units have now been stood down and withdrawn from the scene.'

'What does that mean?' Patrick wondered.

'I don't know,' Naomi said. 'It's really unusual for the news to have broken so quickly, anyway. It isn't the norm. I mean, yes, if something happens in the centre of town, then you expect the media to be all over it in no time, but out here? Eddison has to have tipped them off.'

'What's he hoping to gain from that?' Harry mused. 'Just the glory, do you think?'

Naomi shook her head, nagging worry almost overwhelming. She wanted to go to Alec, but knew that was impossible, and anyway they had to make sure Jilly and Kay were safe. If safe was a possibility now.

So what did Eddison want? What effect were his actions having? 'Confusion,' she said. 'I think he wants to create as much chaos as he can. My guess is he'll then cut and run. I've no doubt he has plans in place. I think maybe he didn't want them to be implemented quite as soon as they have.'

'So what triggered all this?'

'My guess is Jamie Dale. What she knew, what she was about to tell. Those photographs, perhaps, if Eddison knew they existed, and the implications of them – that might have been enough for him to turn on her, and what better cover than to use someone like Gregory as the fall guy? Who would care?'

'Why didn't Jamie try and expose him before?' Harry questioned. 'Why send the pictures to you at Christmas and then do nothing about them?'

'I'm not sure,' Naomi admitted. 'Maybe she viewed them as an insurance policy. Maybe he didn't know about them until recently. Maybe she told him just before she died.'

They came to a junction. 'Left or right?'

Patrick looked at the map. 'Right,' he said, 'and then left, then second left.'

'You're making this up as you go along,' Harry grumbled.

'Well, yes. Actually, I'm trying to get us back to Bristol.'

'Why Bristol?'

'Big city, easier to disappear. Things to do to amuse the kids. I don't know. I just think that we're a pretty distinctive group, and it might be best if Uncle Harry and Auntie Naomi and Cousin Patrick find a place to go where there are other uncles and cousins and kids and we don't stick out like quite such a major sore thumb.'

He had a point, Naomi thought.

'And we've got to go *somewhere*,' Patrick added. 'We can't just go on driving forever.'

Gregory had obtained a car. He had gone beyond the area of investigation, crossing the road and cutting back across the fields to where uniformed and white-clad and plain-clothes personnel milled and roiled and tried to look purposeful. Something had changed in the minutes since he had lost sight of the farm, he thought. He could see two men gesticulating, a woman listening to her phone; another woman, standing close by, paused uncertainly mid action.

Something was not right.

He did not have time to consider what it was that had effected the change of mood; instead he moved on, looking for a vehicle. Finally, at the back of the farm, he found what he was looking for. An old hatchback, faded red and mud splattered. He guessed it must belong to one of the workers on Tilly's Farm or the one next door. It wasn't clear now, just where the boundaries were. Moments later he was off in pursuit of Eddison, knowing the police vehicles had a massive head start.

Munroe arrived at the farm about thirty minutes after Gregory had left, almost an hour after Eddison had taken Alec and the others away and forty minutes after the contradictory orders had started to arrive.

'What the hell is going on?' *DI* Southam, de facto commander of operations now that Eddison had gone, was fielding queries from officers, command centres and now from the media, who seemed oddly au fait with the incident at Northbeach Farm. And taking considerable flack from the owner, Mathilda Morgan, currently confined to her kitchen but making an almighty racket about it.

Eddison had ordered her arrest on conspiracy charges, but now Southam was not so sure.

Munroe showed his credentials.

'Counter intelligence? I'm not sure I get this.'

'You've been ordered to stand down?'

'Well, yes, but I'm sure you realize, you don't

just suddenly discontinue an operation this size, not without some proper authorization.'

'Consider your arse covered,' Munroe told him. 'Stand your people down, and I want you and two more to come with me.'

'On whose authority?'

Munroe told him to call his boss to verify the instructions, and then he went inside to confront Tilly Morgan. She regarded him with narrowed eyes. 'Who the 'ell are youm? You get this load o' rakes out my kitchin.'

'Go,' Munroe instructed. 'Now. All right if I sit down, Mrs Morgan?'

The eyes narrowed even further, but she nodded curtly. Behind him, Southam entered the kitchen.

'An 'e can bugger off too!'

'Two minutes,' Munroe told Southam, and he and his people retreated outside.

'Now, Mrs Morgan, you've been very kind to some friends of mine, letting them stay here.'

'Where have the kids gone?' she demanded. 'I see them bring the feyther and that woman, but not the kiddies.'

'Safe, I promise you. I arranged for them to get out before the police arrived.'

'How?'

'Boat. They were taken off the beach by boat.'

She didn't look convinced. 'You going to get 'im then?' she said. 'Youm goin' to take those daft buggers away?'

'I'm going to leave a few of those daft buggers here,' he told her. 'Mrs Morgan, the newspapers and the television, they're going to be interested in you, so I think it's best if there's someone here to keep them off your land.'

'Newspapers, eh?' she said, and he could see the wheels turning in her head.

'Until you're ready to talk to them, of course.' He stood up again, and then leaned close to the old woman. She smelt of lemon thyme and toast. 'Don't tell anyone I said, but you make sure the papers pay you for your story, eh? How your little farm was raided by all these daft buggers. Oh, and ask about some compensation, too, *OK*?'

She smiled at him then, though the eyes were still narrow slits in the wrinkled face.

You're not such a daft bugger, are you, Munroe thought as he left her. Satisfied, he noted that Southam was organizing an orderly retreat and that two men in full defensive gear stood close by, waiting for Munroe to emerge.

'Get a vest on,' Southam instructed, and Munroe complied, shedding his jacket and fastening the bullet-proof garment over his shirt. Not that it would make a damn microbe of difference, he thought. Both Eddison and Gregory had been trained to go for the head shot, and he was under no illusions. Gregory might have temporarily have joined forces with him, but that was only for so long as their interest coincided. Gregory was now after Eddison, and Munroe knew full well that he would shoot anyone who got between him and his prey.

THIRTY-FOUR

'What are you doing?' Eddison demanded. The front escort car had stopped, and so had the van, forcing Eddison's car to brake too.

His driver shrugged. 'Don't know, guv. Want me to take a look?'

The driver of the lead car was walking back towards them, speaking to someone on his radio. He looked concerned.

Eddison got out. 'What's the hold-up?'

'Well, we've just had a change of orders, sir. We're to go back to the farm.'

'For what reason?'

'I don't know, sir, but the orders come from the Chief Constable himself, sir. We've got to find somewhere to turn this lot around.'

'There'll be a farm gate a half mile on,' said Eddison's driver, a local man who knew the lanes.

'We're not going back,' Eddison said. 'We're going on.'

'Sir, the orders come from the Chief Constable. With respect, guv, he's a bit higher up the chain than any of us, including you.'

'And *I* say we go on.'

Looks of puzzlement became looks of shock

and then of fear. Eddison was armed. Two shots, and two dead officers lay on the narrow road.

'What the hell was that?' Paul said.

'That was a gun,' Clara told him coldly.

Paul looked to Alec for verification.

'Two shots,' Alec said. This is it then, he thought. He got up and banged on the partition between them and the cab. 'What's going on out there?'

A third shot told him he wasn't going to find out that way. He looked desperately for a means of escape, knowing there was none. They sat on benches in an inner cage.

'OK,' Clara said. 'We get one chance at this. When he opens the door, we charge him.'

'I like your spirit,' Alec said, 'But Clara, he'll just shoot us through the wire, he won't bother to even open the inner door.'

He heard a shout outside and another shot, something heavy stumbled against the van, and then the sound of running feet. Desperately, Alec tried to interpret the sounds. Three shots, he thought – three men down. Dead, or at the very least out of the equation. There would have been two officers in the lead car, maybe two in the van? And they would be armed on a detail like this. Had the second man in the lead car had time to get to his weapon?

Alec prayed that had been the case and that backup would arrive before Eddison got another shot at him.

Buy some time, he thought fervently. Just buy us some time. That, he figured, was the best they could hope for; the smart money, he knew, would be on Eddison.

THIRTY-FIVE

Gregory took the bends at speed; the police cordon meant he had no worries about anything coming the other way. The little hatchback roared and then screamed as he over-revved the engine. He slammed it into fifth and then retreated back to fourth as the road began to rise; old and tired, the engine couldn't make the hill. He changed down again, cursing the car and Eddison's head start, taking comfort only in the knowledge that the convoy up ahead would not be driving at such reckless speed. Even so, they still had half an hour on him, and anything could have happened in that time. It was a shock, then, when he veered round a particularly nasty bend in the road and came upon them.

The doors to the rear car were open, and Gregory could see the bodies of two officers, lying in the road. The van doors were closed. He swore as he caught sight of the bullet holes shot straight through the back panels.

Cautiously, he got out of the car and moved forward, not certain if, as his first instinct suggested, Eddison had already gone, or whether he should at any second expect it all to be over.

Not that he'd know, Gregory thought. Eddison was too good a shot for that.

Another body slumped in the front of the van. The second car was gone. A fourth beside the front vehicle opened his eyes as Gregory approached. Gregory assessed his wounds with a professional eye. Bullet wound to the shoulder, and one to the gut. He gave him a small chance, if help got there fast.

So, Eddison had run.

'I shot him. Leg.'

Gregory crouched down beside the fallen man. 'You hit him?'

'Yes. In the leg. Upper thigh.'

'Good on you,' Gregory told him. 'Lie still. Don't talk any more, *OK*?'

Gregory's first instinct was to get back in his car in pursuit. There was nothing he could do for the three dead officers, and hanging round would not improve the chances of the fourth. What about those inside the van? Irritated with himself for even pausing for that long, he went back round to the rear of the van and shot off the lock, then opened the doors.

Three slumped figures on the vehicle floor. Gregory watched as one slowly raised his head.

'You're still alive, then,' Gregory said to Alec.

'Just about. Paul is hit, in the calf, but it's a through and through. He'll live.'

He flinched back as Gregory dealt with the inner door and then began to walk away.

'You can't leave us!' Clara shouted after him.

'Watch me.' He gestured at the remaining

police car. 'First-aid kit in there I imagine, and here—' He picked up a mobile phone from where it had fallen beside one of the bodies. Checked it was still working. 'Best call for an ambulance. There's a man round the front of the van, gut shot. Don't move him.'

Alec scrambled down. 'You're going after Eddison?'

Gregory nodded. 'It's what we do,' he said. 'It's all I've ever been good at.' He paused for a moment. 'Oh, I should watch the news over the next week or two, if I were you,' he said. 'Jamie's story, it'll get out there by then. I've kind of made sure of that.'

Alec nodded. Clara had already picked up the phone. Behind them, Paul was groaning softly. Alec fetched the first-aid kit and went first to the fallen officer. This was way beyond plasters and bandages, he thought as he opened the green pack and assessed what was inside. He could hear Clara talking on the phone.

Sitting down in the middle of the road and deciding that Clara could patch her husband up without his help, he took the hand of the fallen man and held on tight.

THIRTY-SIX

The news that Eddison had been wounded was the best he'd had in a long time. How bad, he wondered. How far would he be able to drive?

He remembered that night so long ago when Travers had been shot, high up on the thigh, so close to the femoral artery that Gregory had been sure he would bleed out before help could arrive. Travers had been lucky, a finger's width away from not being here any more, and even then it was only that they had kept him immobile, kept the pressure on. Known what to do. On his own and he would have had, what ten minutes? Fifteen? And now, from the sound of it, he'd cheated death again.

Good luck to you, Gregory thought. Make the most of it, Nick.

Another bend, another rise and—

A police vehicle slewed across the road, the driver's door half open.

Gregory stopped the car and watched for signs of life.

No movement from the car. Had Eddison got out? Was he lying wait in the fields next to the road? He cut the engine and freewheeled down to the back of the other car, listening for any sound that might betray Eddison's presence.

There was none.

Slowly, cautiously, Gregory got out of the car and walked round to the passenger side of Eddison's vehicle. The man lay slumped in the driver's seat, and it was obvious to Gregory that he was dead. He had lost his kill.

For a while Gregory squatted beside the car, looking, just looking at Charlie Eddison. They had history, he thought, and once upon a time that history had been a good one. But that was far too long ago to matter now.

He rose, glanced back in the direction of where he had left Alec with the wounded man. He wished him well. Ironically, Gregory thought, he could have no idea just what kudos he had won in certain circles. Then Gregory got into the battered little car and drove away.

EPILOGUE

Patrick had called them from the airport. They would make their flight, he said. See them when he and Harry got back.

'Good,' Alec said.

They had taken up residence in Harry's home for the time being, and Naomi doubted she would ever want to set foot in their own house again. She wasn't really sure what she wanted now.

Napoleon harrumphed, as though that was his opinion of all this broken routine.

'Totally agree, old man,' Alec said.

Alec had spent twelve hours being debriefed – or interrogated, as he continued to think of it. Harry, Patrick and Naomi had also spent a good few hours trying to explain what they had done, though Naomi knew that Munroe had protected them from the worst of it. Jilly and Kay were with their mother, and Paul would be fine, as would the policeman who had shot Eddison. He had come through surgery, and all was cautiously optimistic. Naomi didn't think Paul and Clara's marriage had such a good prognosis though.

'Where do you think he went to?' Naomi

asked.

'I don't know, and I don't want to know. So long as it's far away from me and thee I don't think I care.'

Naomi agreed. 'I've been scared,' she said.

Alec laughed. 'Well, yes.'

'No, I don't mean because of this. I mean, because of what happened last year. I've lived scared. For no good reason. I mean, it's not as if ... I mean, the reason for me being scared had gone away, but the fear was still there, you know.'

'I think it's called post-traumatic stress,' Alec said. 'I think it's fairly normal.'

'Oh, I know. I'm not going to be all uptight about it. It's just that I'm not now, not scared any more.'

'*OK*. And what changed?'

'It was when Gregory dumped us on the beach. Me, dog, and two little kids and told me and Munroe that I'd be *OK*. Alec, I was terrified. I was just so out of my depth. But it *was* *OK*. I managed. And somewhere along the line I forgot to be afraid. Not afraid for me, anyway. I realized he was right, I'd be *OK*.'

She waited, expecting some glib response or some Alec platitude, the sort he resorted to when he didn't know what to say, but knew he had to try. Instead, he took her by surprise.

'I handed in my resignation today,' he said. 'And no, I'm not going to withdraw it. I'm going to go in tomorrow and clean out my desk, as you do, and then I'm coming back here and we're going to decide what we both want to happen next.'

It was clear from his tone that he expected an argument. She could hear the defensiveness in his voice. He had said this sort of thing before, when life had grown too complicated or the job too much. But she could hear that he meant it now.

'OK,' she said. 'I think that's the right thing to do.'

'You do?'

'Yeah. Time to let go. Time for change. We've got options, we've got money – we're in a really good place, as they say. Let's just take it a day at a time for a while. I'll come with you tomorrow, help you pack your box.'

She settled close to him on the settee, Napoleon's head resting on her knees and let the peace and contentment of the moment wash over her.

Miles away, aboard the *Jeannie*, Gregory stood quietly. Thinking of Jamie Dale and looking at the stars.